Where Death Speaks

Ronnie Stich

All characters and events in this book are fictitious.
References to events, locations, organizations,
incidents, and people are done so in a fictitious nature.
Any resemblance to actual events or real persons, living
or dead, is entirely coincidental.

Thanks

Thank you to the many supportive friends and readers of my works. This one was certainly intense for me, and a little guidance and technical advice here and there was always appreciated.

Thank you to all of those who serve in law enforcement, and as first responders, who took the time to answer my questions when needed; Fred Knoll Jr., Bill Rattay, Aurora Love, Officer Alejandro, Heather Latta, and fire fighter James Denney.

Thanks to friends Sylvia Galan, and Diana Carta for taking the time to read the draft manuscript before release. And thanks, Mom, for guiding me along the way.

I would also like to thank Adrian Jesus Falcon, talented artist and friend, for so many words of encouragement and support throughout the writing of this book. Also, I must thank my friend Johnrobert Salazar for his continued support in promotions, and Steven Juliano, lead singer of Requiem, for his amazing cover designs and artwork.

.

"But the worst enemy you can meet will always be yourself; you lie in wait for yourself in caverns and forests." – Friedrich Nietzsche

1

Let me explain something first about Simon before I tell you what happened to us in San Antonio. Simon didn't know he was psychic until he was driving back from New York after the Christmas holiday—and that was a few years before I'd met him. But even after he knew, he ignored it for a while because he wanted it to go away. Like a cold or something. At least, that's how he explained it to me.

When he told me the story, the first thing he said was that he'd been driving non-stop for hours. It was late December, just a few days after Christmas. He'd been driving for so long that his vision was blurry, and his legs and butt were numb. It didn't matter to him at the time because he was in a hurry to get back home. He couldn't tell me how fast he was going or anything like that, just that it was dark out and that there were lots of deer. He also remembered bright stars in the sky, highway cops, and local sheriff's department-types scattered along the shoulders of the road—but he was careful. He was glad they were there. All of those things along the way kept him awake and alert—including those twinkling stars.

At first, he said he didn't know where he was when all the strange things started happening to him, just closer to Texas. So I questioned him further.

"What were you doing in New York?" I asked, with a pen in hand. He wouldn't let me do an audio recording of the interview. It was too invasive or something.

"I have a brother there," he answered nervously.

"Did you stay with him?"

"Yeah."

"For how long?" I asked.

Simon's eyes shifted toward the ceiling as he thought about it. "A week, I guess. I wasn't keepin' track or anything."

"Okay, so you were, what ... in Oklahoma when it happened?"

He swallowed in discomfort and looked away from me. "Yeah."

"What made you want to get off the highway?"

And he said simply, "I had to piss."

Simon then explained how picky he was about restrooms. He'd tried holding it as long as possible, and when he couldn't any longer, he was forced to look for a place to go. A sign for a gas station flew past with an exit number he couldn't remember. So he prepared to exit.

He told me that, unexpectedly, the sharp swerve of a car up ahead distracted him just at the moment he was about to get off the highway. He missed his exit. The car had nearly slammed into his—it startled him, but he did his best to focus, and pushed on. It wasn't much longer until he saw the yellowish glow of a sign above some trees further ahead—not a gas station chain he was familiar with, but it would have to do. He took the exit.

As he slowed to approach the gas station, its aged appearance and faded-looking signage made him cringe inside—dirty bathrooms, he thought. There were only two cars parked there.

Admittedly, it wasn't just the restroom he was concerned about. He was worried that someone might attack him. Simon was a large man. I want to guess that he was 240 pounds and about 6 feet tall. Despite this, he envisioned himself being attacked as he pulled into the gas station. It was like a flash—just an image of something violent that went through his head, something random maybe. It didn't make any sense to him at the time, and he blamed it on a horror movie he'd seen with his brother. He was kind of embarrassed about that part of the story and didn't want to talk about it any further, so we didn't.

Then there was a sudden headache.

He was thinking, *oh my God*, over and over. The pain was strong. Simon hit the brakes hard, and as a result, he nearly slammed his head against the steering wheel. The pain in his head was so strong that he couldn't pull the car into a regular parking space, so he parked it, very crookedly, near a gas pump. He grabbed for the door handle and closed his eyes tight, hoping not to pass out before he could get out of the car. He inhaled a deep breath and then had some doubt in his ability to walk … to get inside the store.

Simon told me that when he opened the door, he practically fell out of his car. He described how the rocks slid beneath his feet as he struggled to gain his footing. He was hunched over in pain, pushing his hands against the sides of his head—he just needed enough strength to get inside and forced himself to toughen up.

The fluorescent lights inside the store were overwhelming. It poured out through the glass walls and into the small parking lot, bringing a sting to his eyes as he struggled toward the front doors. He had to force himself to look down as he pulled the door handle to enter. He recalled turning to speak to the clerk at the register, but there was no one there. "Hello?" he called out anyway.

When no one answered, Simon stumbled toward the back, hardly able to keep his balance, squinting his eyes, the searing pain in his head increasing. He was light-headed. He grabbed onto a large refrigerator door handle, unintentionally opening it. The cold air hit him … he saw rows of sodas inside. He slid his hand along the glass, and tried using the door to keep his balance. It swung, and he lost his footing as his legs shook and gave out. Simon was on the floor. He groaned and brushed the hair from his face.

The details of his story were interesting to me. As a writer, I craved every detail. I needed every piece of the story. The details would tell me things—everything … sometimes even things the storyteller might not realize were important. But during the interview, Simon was finding it difficult to go back to that place—or didn't want to. But I needed him to. I needed him to dig up the details for me. I needed to know everything about the first time he had experienced it—this psychic gift.

I saw something in his eyes and asked if he needed a break from the interview, but he waved it off.

"I'm fine," he insisted.

"Are you sure?"

"Yeah. I've got a headache, that's all."

So he took a sip from his water and we went straight back into it.

He told me that while he was in the convenience store, on the floor, he had difficulty focusing his eyes, yet he could see how filthy the place was. In fact, he could almost feel it on him. I found that interesting—remembering the filth while caught up in all that pain.

"Hello?" he called out to anyone that might hear him.

There was a muted sound someplace to the right of him. It was like a thud against the floor. Simon struggled to pull himself up using the handle on the refrigerator again. "Excuse me? Is anyone there?"

As Simon stood, and he was able to balance himself,

the pain in his head seemed to fade away. He flinched as another noise startled him—some sort of clanging. There was a muffled voice, but it was quickly gone, and something slammed against a wall. He couldn't tell where the sounds were coming from because he was too disoriented.

The clerk is in the back of the store, he thought to himself.

Simon's heart jumped in surprise as he realized that the pain in his head was suddenly gone. He straightened himself out, looked around, and then hesitantly walked toward the restroom. And as he got closer to it, there were now two muffled voices, and he was certain that they were coming from inside one of the restrooms he was headed toward.

He stopped to listen. The voices stopped. He glanced to his side to look out through the front windows. There were still only the two cars parked in front of the store, and his—the crooked one near the pump. There was nothing else out there, just lots of trees, and he couldn't see the highway from where he stood.

Something isn't right.

Another muted thud, a deep voice that spoke for only seconds, and then silence.

Simon went into a panic, and the pain in his head instantly returned. He turned toward the front doors, wanting to leave the building as quickly as possible. When he pulled the door open, it creaked. A wave of fresh air hit him as he stepped outside and collapsed onto the cold sidewalk below.

Simon doubled over in pain and felt around inside his jacket for his phone. His fingers shook as he dialed.

"*911*," someone answered.

"Please help me," he pleaded with all the strength he could gather.

"*What's the matter, sir?*" the female dispatcher asked in what Simon described as a disinterested tone.

Simon winced in pain and clutched at his phone, afraid it would slip from his hands if he lost consciousness. "I'm at a gas station. There's something wrong. Something's wrong ... inside—"

"*You need to speak up, sir. I don't understand what you're—*"

"PLEASE LISTEN!" A throbbing sensation inside his brain took over again, causing his eyes to water.

The dispatcher let out a sigh. "*Where are you?*"

"I think something is wrong inside the gas station!" Simon's breathing quickened.

"*What's going on inside the gas station? Are there any weapons?*"

Simon's head was beginning to tingle and his vision was now blurred. He explained to me that when this happened, when his head started to go numb, that it felt like he was starting to choke. But in the way he'd described it, it was like someone was strangling him. "It's a tall yellow sign ... it's old. All it says is 'gas.' I'm off the Interstate ... south. There's a car here ... that doesn't feel right. Oh my God. I'm ... something is happening to my throat!"

"*Sir?!*"

He could hardly see at this point. He felt something pulling him toward the trees near a row of dumpsters. There was something menacing about it. But Simon refused to move toward the place that the pulling wanted him to go. His eyes twitched and he allowed himself to look into the darkness, to force his eyes to see the car that felt wrong to him, near the trees. "It's a brown Chevy Impala. It's older. From the 80s."

"*Sir! I need you to tell me what's going on inside the store!*" The dispatcher's voice had changed. "*Are you inside the* store?"

"There's a man that drives that car," Simon continued slowly and robotically, the unseen hold on his throat intensifying. He pressed even harder onto the side of his head, hoping to ease the intense pressure that was coming from within. "He's got a burning inside. It's death."

The dispatcher gasped. *"Did you say a brown Impala?!"*

"X … J … P … 4—"

"Sir! Stay on the line! Every unit available to the southbound access road off the 35. It's the old gas station just off the exit when you're leaving town. There's a brown Impala that meets the description of Jack Lewis's. I repeat, a brown 1980s Chevy Impala that matches the description of the one that belongs to Jack Lewis! Sir?! Are you still there?!"

Simon had lost consciousness.

2

I'd only known Simon for about an hour when he told me that story. And it turned out that the Impala did, in fact, belong to an escaped convict by the name of Jack H. Lewis. Inside the convenience store, Lewis had one of the clerks at gunpoint in the bathroom. The other clerk had been left for dead in the back. The cops got their man, and then afterward, they treated Simon like "a freak." I explained to Simon that I'd heard stories like this before and that he didn't need to feel ashamed or different because of it. Then he told me that he'd lost his job afterward and that he didn't want to talk about it anymore.

That first meeting with Simon went well, I thought, and I was glad that I'd made the trip out to San Antonio. Dr. Miller Anson, a man known for his controversial experiments in the field of parapsychology, had contacted me only weeks earlier and invited me to tour his research facility. He offered to pay for the flight and hotel and explained that he was a fan of my work. In fact, a lot of his students were, as well. He hoped that I might like to speak to them about my novels. It was flattering, and I jumped at the chance to learn more about his research and his teachings.

I flew into San Antonio on a brisk Thursday afternoon—mid January—and was given a quick tour of the research facility that evening. That was how I met Simon, Dr. Anson's protégé.

I think, at first, Simon felt uncomfortable around me.

He was quiet and slumped over a table, struggling with a headache. After Dr. Anson introduced us, we sat together so I could ask him a few questions, sort of like an interview, and learn more about his psychic abilities. I asked him if he knew what kinds of books I wrote. He only nodded yes, then looked away from me. So I decided to tell him a little about myself to ease the tension between us.

Growing up, I was that kid that hung around the occult section of the library, digging through volumes of forbidden books. I remember the librarian peeking her head around the tall shelves to spy on me. Afraid to check out any of the books I really wanted, I carefully and quietly tore the pages out that I would need for later. I needed them because they intrigued and entranced me away from the reality of being a boy trapped inside a world of right angles, piano lessons, and structures created by grownups. I collected those pages, hid them under my pillow, and treasured every mysterious word, symbol, and drawing on them until adulthood—when my interest in peculiar things had developed into a steady writing career. At 34 years of age, the reviewers went crazy for a horror thriller I'd published. By that time, my research into the abnormal, paranormal, and arcane was not only justified—it was expected of me. I didn't have to hide it any longer. It was a justifiable part of my existence—and, admittedly, it wasn't as fun as it used to be back when I was a kid.

All the while, I had suffered from dreams that disturbed me.

I explained to Simon that as an adult, you learn that there are things that belong only in your head—that is, if you are unfortunate enough to know or experience them in the first place. And those things belong there—and only there—no matter how much it makes you suffer to keep it that way. And until you meet the right people, or discover the right outlet, it can consume you if you let it. I could relate to him.

As a child, some of my dreams would come true. Nightmares, actually.

They did stop for a while. But two weeks after my 42nd birthday, the nightmares returned. Here is where people might be tempted to blame those nightmares on childhood summers spent reading about witches and ancient, legendary ghouls, but these were not normal dreams. The worst part was that they had started up again in the weeks before I flew out to San Antonio. I didn't want to fall sleep because if I did, I was afraid that something from my dreams would destroy me. I was a 42-year-old man, afraid to sleep. The things in my dreams were like ghosts. And they weren't normal ghosts, whatever that means. When I say "normal," maybe I mean that they weren't like what I was used to reading about in parapsychology books. They were nothing like the kinds of ghosts I would see on the Internet or on TV. Like leeches, they craved something primal. Normal ghosts didn't seem to want or need anything from the living, I thought. But the ones in my nightmares did. That was the difference.

Simon seemed to connect with this confession of mine. He told me that he'd recently turned 37 and that he was pretty sure that without Dr. Anson, he wouldn't have. He told me that he wanted to know more about my dreams, so I continued.

I told him how the dreams I'd been having were real in ways that I couldn't fully explain. I could be the people inside the dreams, feel their feelings, and experience their fears. Each dream was different, and I was sure that in the next one, those things—the ghosts that kept showing up in my dreams—were going to kill people … in real life. I thought this because the people—people I didn't know or recognize in any way—would sometimes chase those horrible, moaning ghost-creatures no matter how much I wished that they wouldn't. These ghosts were desperate things, barely clinging on to some form of existence, and they wanted the innocent to die. They had been summoned by a man—a man that wanted them to hurt the people in my dreams. I had no idea who he was, but in my nightmares, he conjured up these ghosts, or perhaps demons, to destroy people in an attempt to steal something from them. Their bodies, their souls … I didn't know what.

That was how I met Simon. He seemed genuinely interested in the things I had to say. And after I explained my interest in all things paranormal, and how many of my novels had been influenced by this serious interest, I asked him how he learned he was psychic. I wanted him to trust me. And when he did, he told me the story about his trip back from New York.

I went back to my hotel that night feeling comforted, glad that I'd made the trip. Simon seemed like a great guy. Dr. Anson was enthusiastic about having me around and had promised to let me observe some psychic experiments with Simon in the days to come. I thought it would be a great research experience, maybe for one of my next books—but then things never turn out the way you plan them to. And I can tell you now, that what happened instead, was not at all what I had expected.

3

The next night.

"Have another drink," Simon said. It was only my second night in San Antonio and Simon had changed. Dramatically. On the phone that morning, Dr. Anson warned me about this. He asked that I meet up with Simon to observe some of his unconventional ways of picking up on things, but first, he wanted me to understand that Simon was at his best, psychically, while inebriated. And while inebriated, he also enjoyed barking orders at people. I had barely taken my seat at the bar when Simon started joking about how, since his name was Simon, I was simply supposed to obey everything he said—Simon says. It was an annoying joke that wasn't very funny no matter how many times he told it. "And don't give me any shit about how the beer tastes."

"Why didn't you just let me order a glass of wine?"

"Yeah right," he replied with a sarcastic grin. "I'm not sitting next to a wine drinker."

I looked at him blankly and wanted to go back to the hotel. I didn't care how talented Simon was. In my eyes, he was now terribly ugly and in need of a personality overhaul. I met up with him after he'd already downed several drinks, and his true personality was coming through. *This* Simon was obnoxious, crass, and he didn't care very much for me in his drunken state. When Dr. Anson introduced me to him, I'd thought he seemed like an all right guy. But at that moment, I wanted to be back home in Los Angeles. As soon as I'd walked into the bar, Simon had given me a disapproving once-over, complete with an eye-roll. I wasn't used to people doing that to me—judging me for actually having some taste in clothing.

I tried some conversation. "I had a strange dream last night. I might write about it. It's this one about these soldiers. Like, Revolutionary War soldiers, but then, the dream shifts and I'm in a castle. Anyway, they get attacked by these … creatures that some other people kind of conjure up, I guess. Like, a ritual or something. It was really strange. I mean, it might be something to write about some day. I don't know." I looked at Simon and wondered if he even cared. I was just trying to make small talk. I was pretty sure that he'd never read any of my books, and in a way, I was glad.

"Nice suit," Simon replied with a snicker, dismissing my dream entirely. And unlike the day before, I was beginning to pick up on many of his annoying habits. Changing the subject about everything I brought up was probably going to be one of them. He started going on and on about himself, the things he'd done that day, the food he'd eaten. Then he began to lean in close to my ear to give me his personal opinions about the people around us. There was something cruel about the way he stared at and picked at the details of every innocent person in the bar, but on the upside, his Texas accent entertained me. I liked listening to him talk—even when he was cutting me off or making fun of me or someone else nearby. "By the way, you look like the Prince of Darkness with your black suit and that red hanky-thing stickin' out of your pocket."

"This suit is a tailored Gucci," I replied flatly. "We obviously don't shop at the same place."

I looked at Simon for a reaction, but something in his

eyes had changed. I studied him as his attention shifted. I didn't want to ask him what was going on. Knowing Simon (which of course, I didn't at the time), he would be sure to lean in and tell me what was bothering him when he was ready. He had that kind of personality. So I carried on with my bitter beer, the one he had recommended— no, pushed on me—as I scanned the bar and its patrons.

"Hmm," Simon then began while staring over my shoulder, "That guy over there ... he's a bit off."

"Which—?"

"Don't turn around!" Simon hissed. He grabbed my arm, gripping it tightly.

"Okay! Shit. Let go of me. This is what we skipped the lab for today?"

Dr. Anson had wanted Simon to get some rest that morning. So I spent my day seeing the sights and checking out an art museum with the promise of a research-worthy evening instead.

Simon relaxed his posture and straightened himself up in his seat. "He's by the front window. In a black leather jacket. He's waiting for someone, but he's ..." He swallowed back some anxiety and closed his eyes. His eyelids fluttered and I had to look away. I didn't want to draw any attention to whatever was happening to him. Dr. Anson had already warned me about this, so I knew what was coming next—he was tuning in. "He's a traitor. That's what he's thinking about right now."

This was what Dr. Anson was talking about. This was what he wanted me to see.

I downed the rest of my drink while my mind raced. And I didn't notice the way Simon's hands trembled until I could hear the clicks of his fingernails on the bar top. He was locked into the thoughts of the man by the window in exactly the way Dr. Anson had described it would happen. I noticed a large, decorative mirror hanging on the wall behind Simon. I looked into it, doing my best to get a glimpse of the man he was describing to me.

"I'm goin' over there." Simon twitched a few times while doing his best to stay cool about it.

"No, Simon." I didn't know what to say or do.

"Yes, *Rich!* I *have* to!" he said these words with his sharp, beady eyes as much as he did with his drunken voice. He was five beers in against my one.

"Then what?" I pressed.

"Then you follow me and we drag him outside," Simon instructed. He brushed his light brown hair aside with rough, stubby fingers.

"*Drag him outside?* What about our tab?"

"Who cares about the damn tab?!" he hissed back. "Didn't Dr. Anson tell you to do what I say?! Because if you don't, I'm leavin' your ass here!"

Simon then stood abruptly and reached into his back pocket. He opened a mess of nasty-looking, cracked and beaten leather and glared at me in disgust. "Shall I get your drink, too, Your Dark Lordship?"

"What the hell is wrong with you?!" I asked. "I'm going back to my hotel! There's nothing going on here, and now you want me to help you drag some guy out of a bar just because you say so?!"

I could see in the mirror that the man in the leather jacket was now staring at Simon. A lot of people were. Simon was making an exaggerated scene with his wallet, huffing and puffing over it to make a point about having to pay the bill.

The man in the mirror looked extremely worried about something and his eyes didn't look right.

"Hurry," I warned.

"You come out here from L.A. and you think you own the place … with your Italian suit and your fancy rental car. You should be the one paying the tab, not me, Mr. Best-Seller."

"You drank a lot more than I did, and Dr. Anson told me he gave you a credit card that we're supposed to use … because this is a part of the research thing or whatever. 'Do not use your own debit or credit cards … only cash or the card I gave to Simon.' That's what he said, so don't give me any shit about the *one* drink I had."

The man in the jacket saw my reflection in the mirror and froze.

Simon noticed, and gasped. "Oh no."

Simon shoved his wallet back into his coat pocket and rushed toward the door, pushing past tables and chairs with enough force to cause people to jump out of their seats. I could hear a few of them agree with each other that Simon was a jerk. And as the bartender approached me, I reached into my pocket and backed away while stammering something about having a few twenties someplace. But as Simon exploded through the front door, I quickly turned and headed for it also.

"Hey!" the bartender yelled.

"I'll come back and pay you!" I yelled back as the bartender dialed the police.

Outside, I could see Simon's shadow and a part of his brown jacket slipping into the side alley next to the bar and, of course, I followed him.

"Why are you running?" Simon barked at the man. He caught up to him and grabbed him by the sleeve and a part of his collar.

"Let go! You'll regret it!" the man screeched in return with a distinct English accent.

"Why'd you run?!" Simon yelled into the man's face.

The man looked back at me and his eyes widened. "Because you're chasing me!"

"Did you run because of him?" Simon nodded back at me and smiled. But it wasn't a nice sort of smile. It was one of those rude, mocking sort of things. Simon pointed at me. "You recognize this guy?"

I took a few steps closer to them. I wanted a better look at the man's face. There had to be a reason why Simon was chasing him like this. The man sank into his leather jacket as I approached. He was terrified.

I asked Simon nervously, "What are you doing? Just let him go."

"Please," the man proceeded in a whimper. His face was chalky and pale. "Take whatever you want! Just don't hurt me!"

"I think your suit is scaring him." Simon turned back and shot a sarcastic smile at me.

"Please let me go! You want my credit cards?" the English man asked with tears welling up in his eyes.

I was thoroughly confused and had no idea what to do. "Just let him go, Simon! What the hell are you doing?"

"*This* is what Dr. Anson wanted you to see," Simon said to me as he tightened his grip on the man. "I can pick them out every time."

"See what? What the hell is wrong with you?"

"You wanna see something fucked up?" Simon asked me with a sick smile across his face.

"No. Who says *yes* to something like that?!"

"This guy's not what you think he is, Rich," Simon said.

I quickly reached for Simon's arm, wanting to pull the two of them apart. But then, Simon started to shake the man vigorously by the collar. The man's pale face started to go transparent. It flickered back and forth from see-through to solid as his jacket started slipping from Simon's grip.

The man screeched, "What do you want?! Let go of me!"

"Which kind are you?" Simon asked the man angrily. "You got some weird kind of smell and your accent is … just like the last one. How'd you make yourself solid enough to blend in with people? How'd you get here?"

"Tell this man to let go of me!" the man begged me, ignoring Simon completely. There was desperation in his eyes. Then he flickered again.

"Did you see that, Richard?" Simon asked proudly.

"Yes," I breathed out in disbelief.

"Let go of me!" the man begged again.

Something about the man's voice and the pale gray of his eyes struck me. It was unnatural.

Fear got the best of me. "Just let him go!" I yelled, panicking.

Simon threw the man to the ground, causing him to slip out of his jacket. The jacket hung in Simon's hands as the man spun around on the ground to face us.

Simon looked back at me with a snarl on his face. "What the fuck is wrong with you? Didn't you see the guy change? He's not real!"

"What the hell does that mean? What do you mean he's not *real?*"

Simon pointed back at the man and started yelling even louder. "This guy is—" He turned to look, but there was no one there.

There was nothing. No wispy smoke or anything else. He just wasn't there any longer, and I didn't see how he could have escaped. The end of the alley was blocked off with a high fence that would have been too difficult to climb.

I took a step back and checked behind myself. "Forget it, he's gone," I told him.

"Where'd he go?"

"I don't know."

"Did you see him get up and leave?" he growled.

"No."

Simon didn't react the way I expected him to. He just stood there, still pumped and riled up, playing the tough-guy without losing a single step in the process. I didn't get it. I wasn't used to seeing things like that. I was light-headed and was doing everything I could to pretend I was okay. I had to take another step backward … I had to concentrate on keeping my balance. I kept checking behind me … for what, I didn't know. The man had *vanished*. I think I knew that, it just hadn't clicked yet.

"This is your fault," Simon barked.

"What?!"

Simon turned to me, the leather jacket still hanging in his hands. "You got somethin' to write about now? You happy?"

"No, I don't … I don't know what the hell just happened. We need to leave. What if the cops are coming?"

"Don't fuckin' tell me what to do. I don't give a shit what kind of a writer you are. Stay out of my way." Simon threw the jacket at my chest and used his shoulder to push past me. "I'm dropping out of the project. I don't care what Dr. Anson says. I don't need some guy followin' me around, fuckin' things up … sittin' next to me in public, drinkin' wine."

Simon stalked out of the alley.

"Hey!" I called out. I spun back around to make sure the see-through guy wasn't coming back.

"Leave me alone," he slurred. "I'm going home. I have better things to do."

"I don't know what's going on here!" I said angrily. "I got this email from Dr. Anson and he asked me to come to San Antonio to meet you! He said there was something in one of my books that was really interesting, and he said something about showing me some stuff he was working on, and having me speak to one of his classes. Then he said something about meeting you. He said you were one of the most gifted men on the planet. And when I met you yesterday, I'll admit, I was impressed. But then tonight, I'm, like ... *seriously?!* I mean, I respect Anson's research ... I've even read some of his books ... but this *sucks!*"

Simon applauded slowly. "Watch some more movies, Richard. That speech wasn't dramatic enough. Nice try. I have to admit though, it was really nice of you to pay for our drinks."

"I didn't *pay* for anything! Dr. Anson said *not* to pay for things! I ran out the door to follow you while you chased some ... *thing!* I don't know what's going on! They're probably going to scan the security video at the bar and come looking for me! I'm going back to the hotel and I'm calling Dr. Anson!"

Simon sneered at me before stumbling away and leaving me alone in the alley. He was off to look for his car. I was sure that he would drive home drunk. I hated him at that moment, but felt sorry for him at the same time. He was a fractured man being shadowed by a writer he didn't know. It was true that after seeing that man disappear in the alley, something didn't register inside my head. I wanted to book the first flight back to Los Angeles as soon as possible. A guy had just turned on and off like a light bulb and then disappeared into a bunch of invisible floaty nothingness right in front of my face. But a large part of paranormal research is also learning to be a skeptic about things. Something didn't sit right with me about this guy Simon. Magic tricks to impress me? Most likely.

4

The next morning at the university lab.

"This whole thing is a mess," Simon was already complaining. He looked tired and his clothes were wrinkled and sloppy. There was a variety of half-eaten foods in front of him on a table. A piece of lettuce was stuck to his shirt. I had come to the conclusion that there were probably always pieces of food to be found somewhere on Simon—he was a disgusting slob.

"What can we do to help you feel more comfortable, Simon?" Dr. Anson asked. He was seated across from him at a large rectangular table in the middle of an otherwise empty room.

"I'm just not in the mood," Simon explained without even bothering to lift his head. "You know I have to be in the mood to do this."

"What can we get you? A soda?"

Simon shook his head. "No. I just wanna go to sleep. Maybe a nap."

"Now, Simon," Dr. Anson began like he was coaching a child. "We have been preparing for this experiment for weeks. Months, actually. And you know how difficult it is to get funding and to explain the validity of our work to the Board. Please try to understand how much we need you today. And Richard has come all the way from California to see what you're capable of. He researches these sorts of things for his books."

I sighed. And I did this in a way that was intended to

be just as harsh and rude-sounding as it came off. I was sick of Simon and the stupid faces he made, especially now as I watched him trying to get out of something that he had committed himself to do. It was like dealing with a child. Dr. Anson obviously depended on him and put an enormous amount of faith into his "talent." It sickened me to see Simon taking advantage of this kind-hearted man.

"Maybe a beer?" Simon suggested with wide, hopeful eyes.

Dr. Anson leaned forward in his seat and frowned. "Simon, that's not a part of the conditions we have in place for the test."

Simon leaned forward. "I know, but … I really think it would help. Honestly."

Dr. Anson pressed his lips together nervously and crinkled his face.

"You remember that guy? The one that could do those psychic photos? I learned about him in that class you taught last semester."

"Yes, Simon. I remember," Dr. Anson replied apprehensively.

"Remember how he had to have a few drinks before he could put the images from his mind onto the film?"

Dr. Anson's face softened and he crossed his arms. "Simon, I know it helps you—how you *think* it helps you. But the test conditions are already set in place. I can't alter them."

"He does this before *every* experiment?" I asked impatiently. I was sitting on a chair against the wall. It was supposed to be just far enough out of the way, but close enough to still observe what was going on.

"Why's *he* here?" Simon asked angrily. "*Him* being here doesn't help either, you know? This whole thing is supposed to be about concentration. I can't concentrate with him around."

I detested the way he grumbled like some over-privileged teen. Even from where I sat in the stale, empty room, I could smell the alcohol escaping from Simon's skin and clothing. His unwashed hair and the breadcrumbs scattered all around him bothered me. And as he was sitting there—sorry—slumped there … smiling that sickening smile at me like it was a weapon, I tried to see some point to his existence.

Simon sighed. "If I'm the most gifted viewer in the entire world, shouldn't I be allowed to concentrate better?" he asked with his horrible head tilted to the side. "And can we get this guy out of here, please?"

"He's here to observe the process," Dr. Anson explained to him. "He's our special guest."

"Well, he won't be observin' anything because I'm distracted and unable to concentrate."

I couldn't take it anymore. "Oh, come on, Simon," I blurted out. "You're *gifted*, remember?"

"This is verbal abuse. Is this part of the study?" Simon looked at Dr. Anson, waiting for an answer.

Dr. Anson cleared his throat. "Richard should see how this is done. Experiments with psychic abilities are conducted in a very controlled manner, and I would really like him to see how carefully we prepare and document things … even if we aren't following the rules as closely as other researchers might."

I stared at Simon and wondered, for no reason, how long the piece of lettuce had been on his shirt and why Dr. Anson had said nothing to him about it. I wanted to leave. When I arrived that morning at 8 a.m., as requested, I was prepared to give Dr. Anson some speech about my presence being needed elsewhere for some research on another book I wanted to write. Not that I didn't appreciate being there or anything, I just didn't understand why I needed to see or be around anything else that involved Simon. I just wanted to give a quick speech to Dr. Anson's students and leave.

"Richard," Dr. Anson said in a more scientific tone. "What Simon will attempt to see has been determined according to the guidelines we discussed earlier. I'm sure you had a chance to go through the scientific journals I gave you. All Simon has to do is describe the person or object that he sees accurately enough for it to be considered a success."

I nodded in agreement, wondering what was keeping me from telling him that I was going back to Los Angeles. Perhaps it was the guilt I felt for accepting the free airfare and hotel.

"It's like that submarine game," Simon interjected. "You probably played it as a kid. I can't see what's going on someplace, but I have to describe it or know where somethin' is. I have to tune into it like it's a target."

Dr. Anson looked at me to see if I understood.

"I read through the journals," I let them both know. "I understand how it works."

"And you've written about this sort of thing in a few of your novels." Dr. Anson smiled. "Very cleverly, too."

"Yes." I nodded shyly. "Thank you."

"One more thing that I wanted to mention," Dr. Anson said while purposely avoiding eye contact with us. "Last night, whatever happened at that bar, please, let's keep that negativity out of this room. Agreed?"

I tried to explain, "I don't really know what happened last night—" but then Simon got defensive.

"What happened was that I tracked down that defector I told you about, Dr. Anson, and when I tried to confront him, Richard ruined the whole thing."

"What's a defector?" I asked. "That's part of the problem here, Dr. Anson. I have no idea what's going on. I wanted to talk to you after this experiment if that's alright with you, sir. I'm not really sure how much longer I can stay in San Antonio. I really appreciate it, but maybe I should just speak to your class soon and—"

Dr. Anson raised a hand into the air. "Let's begin the experiment. I'll explain what's going on as soon as we're finished."

"Thank you, sir," I said. Sitting through an experiment seemed a little boring. I could have been exploring the city and finding something touristy to do instead. But if I had to sit there and watch Simon do his thing, I guess I could put up with it. I wasn't even sure what I had seen him do last night, and the more I thought about it, the more I was beginning to believe that Simon was actually a very talented magician. That whole disappearing-guy thing was probably some set up. Whatever I was about to see him do now was probably going to be more of the same.

"Okay then," Dr. Anson replied with an uneasy smile. He turned back to face Simon. "As you know, Richard, I do not know anything about what Simon will attempt to locate. No one involved with the study, working inside this facility, knows what has been selected for Simon to see or contact. I hope you read up on the whole mental cross-contamination theory?"

I nodded in return.

"Good. I like to think of it as a mental pollution. If I knew what his selections were—which are determined, documented, and sealed inside envelopes at another location—I could provide the answers to Simon without intending to do so … just by thinking about them. You get the idea."

"Yes, sir," I said politely.

"I need to use the bathroom," Simon mumbled.

Dr. Anson did his best to contain any frustration.

"And I'm getting a headache. Can I please take something for my head—?"

"Simon," the professor began, "you can take something after the test—"

"It takes hours sometimes to get through it the way you guys do it!" Simon complained. "I don't feel well and I want to go home—"

I couldn't sit through it. "Can I speak with you, Dr. Anson?" I asked, tired of the whole thing.

And apparently, Simon was tired of it also. "The first one is a satellite that was launched … by some fucking corporation in August of last year." Simon's eyes were blinking rapidly. "The next one is … no, the third one is a lake… no … somethin' in the lake. A boat … shit, maybe it's a body … oh man … yup. There's a body in that lake. Okay, and the fourth one is a—"

"Simon!" Dr. Anson was shaking.

I rose from my seat and the professor held out his hand for me to stay where I was. His eyes were frozen on Simon. "Please wait, Richard," was all he could manage to say. He looked like he could hardly breathe.

Simon's eyes were shut tight and his hands were shaking. "Richard is botherin' me." His voice was strained and cracking. "I can't see the second one because of Richard, but the fourth one is a person on a chair. The person is at a table in a café … in France. The café is … the table is outside. There is a coffee on the table. It has that frothy stuff on top that I hate."

I stared at Simon and thought of a million questions to ask. I looked at the professor and waited for his reaction to the things Simon was saying—the things that he was describing to us from inside his head. These things were supposed to be unknown to him; people or actual things happening someplace, things that Simon shouldn't have been able to see or know about.

Simon relaxed his shoulders and took in a long breath. "Dr. Anson, I need something for my head. It feels like a migraine."

The experiment was over. Simon had raced through it in anger, maybe to prove something. Maybe because he sensed that I wasn't interested or that I didn't believe. It didn't matter either way—what Simon had done was impossible. Effortless to him.

"Alright, Simon," the professor said calmly. He quickly walked toward the door behind Simon and exited the room.

In the silence, I didn't know what to say. Simon placed his head into his hands and slumped over. His elbows slid across the table in front of him as he pressed his palms against the sides of his head.

"Are you okay?" I managed to ask.

"Fuck off," he groaned.

"Simon?"

"Leave."

"Maybe I should just wait here until Dr. Anson gets back—"

"No, I mean leave for California. It's all you've been thinking about." Simon struggled to look up, his head still in his hands. "You gave me this migraine."

"What are you talking about? How could I ... *give* you a migraine?"

Simon squeezed his eyes together tightly and let his head rest on the edge of the table. "You started thinkin' about that guy we chased last night and about how you wanted to go back to L.A., so I just told Anson what the targets were so you could have your talk with him and leave."

"Did you make up the answers?" I had to know.

"Are you serious?"

"Yes. Did you make them up?"

"No, asshole."

I couldn't take it seriously. Even the migraine seemed fake to me. I was trying to remember that he was just an over-blown magician.

"They're checking the envelopes and making their phone calls right now to the other team," he told me. "Go ahead and leave."

"What was going on with that guy last night?"

"What the hell does it matter?"

He was right. I didn't know why I wanted to know. "Because he disappeared. That's why."

Simon covered his eyes with his hands and grimaced. "He was inter-dimensional."

"What does that mean?"

"When Dr. Anson asked you to follow me last night, it was so you could see how I find them. I can find things. Especially things that are out of place."

"What are they?" I asked.

"They're like ghosts. I think they're solid in their own dimension, but I don't know. They might be ghosting-out for travel. That's what Dr. Anson is tryin' to find out. He wants to figure out why they keep showin' up here. There's a lot of them."

When he stopped speaking, I listened to the silence for a moment, hoping I would hear the professor coming back so I could talk to him, but then I remembered that the door was soundproof. "Didn't you think it was strange that Anson contacted me? I write fiction. I mean, yeah, I write about ghosts and stuff like that, but it's still fiction. No offense, Simon, but all of this sounds nuts to me. I don't belong here."

"*I* asked him to contact you."

I definitely hadn't expected to hear that. "What for?"

"Because a few of them ... the defectors I found ... they had you in their thoughts," Simon struggled to say. "They wanted to find you."

Dr. Anson opened the door and walked in with a bottled water and a bottle of pills. "It's a muscle relaxer, Simon. Here. Looks like it's hitting you pretty hard."

"Did you call the guys with the envelopes?" Simon asked him with his palm pressed against his head.

"Yes, Simon. Here. Take your pills."

I looked into Dr. Anson's eyes, unable to steady the racing thoughts in my head.

"They were exact, Simon," the professor told him. "Except for the café in France."

"What are you talkin' about?" Simon snapped.

"It was more like an apartment patio area. Not a café. She did have a cappuccino, though."

Simon threw back his head after placing two pills into his mouth. He took a long drink of his water while his eyes moved between me and the professor. "Rich wants to talk to you about goin' back to L.A."

Anson's eyes widened.

"No," I said. "I think I can stay a few more days. Maybe a week ... maybe."

Simon made an effort to smirk at me through his pain. "I think you'll be stayin' longer than that."

5

That evening.

What happened at Simon's favorite burger place isn't worth writing about in any detail, so I'll do my best not to. Basically, I agreed to meet him there before following him to some guy's apartment. The guy had something to do with Dr. Anson's research and his name was Frans Brunstrom. He was some award-winning researcher from Sweden. That was all I was told. I was pretty sure that Dr. Anson had asked Simon to introduce me to this researcher to keep me interested in the work they were doing. I wasn't sure if he was a part of their current project or anything, though, because when I asked, they wouldn't tell me. Brunstrom was an expert in physics and had a great interest in parapsychology—*that* part, I had to look up on the Internet. Either way, I didn't mind meeting with him, but I didn't appreciate all the secrecy behind it.

It was around four in the afternoon when Simon started texting me about getting together for dinner before heading over to Brunstrom's apartment. He wanted to meet at a burger place on the way. It sounded fine to me. I'd given up on vegetarianism months ago … again. But then everything went wrong. The burger place forgot to put an extra piece of processed cheese on Simon's double deluxe and he flipped out.

I didn't understand why at first, because he was so

caught up in the moment, but apparently, forgetting that extra piece of cheese in Simon's burger had become this on-going thing that Simon believed was an intentional act. It was some form of burger revenge since one of the cooks was out to get him. I didn't really have a chance to get into that part of it with Simon, not that I was very interested in the background story on it anyway. All Simon had a chance to explain to me, before he started throwing his french fries into the kitchen, was that every time he requested the extra piece of cheese, the cook in the back would purposely leave it out. The deluxe already had two pieces of cheese on it when ordered. That didn't matter to Simon because he was a very difficult person. In his mind, they owed him an extra piece of cheese for being a loyal customer. So basically, just because he said so.

I didn't get to eat my onion rings because the manager called the cops and Simon ran out the door. He left me standing there with my mouth hanging open. Since they hadn't set my onion rings on the tray yet, I grabbed my burger and hurried to follow him out the door and into the alleyway he ducked into.

From a safe enough distance, in the shadows, we ate our burgers and watched what was going on at the restaurant. Simon was perfectly fine sitting on the street and eating with his mouth open, while I stood and leaned against a brick wall instead.

"You're not a celebrity," I thought I should remind him. We were a block away from the burger place. There were two cop cars parked out front, and the manager was waving his hands around as he spoke to them.

"What? 'Cause I don't write books? You don't know how many years I've been goin' to that place. I sent a lot of business their way. They owe me."

"They owe you *cheese?*"

"Yeah."

There were creatures rummaging around inside the dumpster right beside us. This didn't seem to bother Simon as much as it bothered me. I wondered how often Simon hung around in alleys since he'd led me into a few already. As I looked him over, I went ahead and assumed that it was fairly often.

Simon wadded up his wrapper and then started to search inside his pockets for something in extreme frustration. I just wanted to get the night over with. I wasn't really given any details about what was going on anyway. Anson made the whole thing sound like it would be a great way for me to learn about how Simon tracked down these ghost-beings. It also sounded like the Swedish researcher had some pertinent information for me. And after the psychic viewing demonstration, Anson had danced around a lot of my questions. I had a feeling that he was worried about scaring me off and that if he could just get me to go meet this one Swedish guy, maybe it would seal the deal and make me want to stay longer.

I looked up at the building behind us. It was dilapidated and couldn't have been up to code. I was beginning to wonder if Simon was messing with me. "Is this really where he lives?" I asked.

"Yup."

"So this researcher you want me to meet lives here, huh?" I asked. It didn't seem right. I couldn't picture an award-winning researcher living in a place like that. It was run-down and falling apart.

"Yeah. Since he left the project he was workin' on, he's a little down and out. I know he's here, though. I can feel it."

"And we're here to talk to him because you want me

to interview him?"

"Yeah, yeah … ask him whatever you want. He hasn't been feeling well lately, but you can try. He ended up in this place because he was on drugs or something … left his wife. He's not the same guy he used to be. He's probably into some weird kinky shit that he doesn't want her to know about or something. You know?" Simon unwrapped a stick of gum and shoved it into his mouth. "He was workin' at a lab downtown. Part-time. But he hasn't shown up there for a while now."

"But you're sure he's here?"

"Yeah."

I gave Simon a look that told him I wasn't buying into the story he was telling me.

"Dr. Anson sent some guys out here yesterday to do some snooping around," he tried to assure me. "They asked some people questions, did some energy readings …"

"Okay wait … why are we dealing with this? Has his wife reported him missing, or are you guys working with him on a project or what? I don't get it. Why are we here?"

"He's one of those defectors I was trying to tell you about," Simon answered. He looked up toward the second floor and studied the building we were about to enter.

"And you call him a defector *because* … he's one of those ghost-people?"

He scrunched up his face when he looked at me. "If I say yes, you probably won't want to go up there with me."

I couldn't believe it. But then again, I could. "Oh. Okay. That sounds bad."

"Come on. Let's just get up there and look around."

He unfolded a piece of paper. "It's apartment 201. I'm going to do an energy read first before we go in. It'll be fun."

The hallway leading up to the apartment seemed normal enough ... for it being a complete dump. It smelled a lot like old cigarette smoke and there was some mildew on the upper sections of the walls. The ceiling sagged in some brownish color. It was definitely not the type of place I would expect to find one of the world's most respected researchers. His doctorate was in physics, I think. If he really was staying there, I guessed that he'd chosen the place in an attempt to exist off the radar. That part of it was obvious.

Simon reached into his jacket and pulled out a small black electromagnetic energy reader. He stopped in front of apartment 201 and switched on the device. It lit up in a series of green, yellow, and red lights that faded as Simon held it up to the door. "He's not here."

"Simon, let me see that thing," I said. "That's not how it works."

He turned to me and handed over the reader without any hesitation. I held it up in front of me, expecting the green lights to change, but they didn't. I placed it against Simon's arm, and still no change. I smiled at him. "You're human. Sort of."

"Give it back," he hissed. "Do you even know what this is?"

"Yes, actually, I do."

"Well, this one was developed by Dr. Anson. It's *very* sensitive. And I'm not reading that he's here. It's got a good range for detecting energy. These defectors emit a very strong amount of energy."

"But if this thing is anything like the ones you can buy

online, it can also detect power lines, microwave ovens, and refrigerators," I reminded him. "So even if it did pick something up, it could be wrong or catching some interference from something else."

"Yeah, okay. Let's just get inside."

"Aren't you going to knock?"

"No."

"How are we going to get in?" I asked.

"Screwdriver."

"Oh."

If Simon hadn't crossed paths with Dr. Miller Anson, I was certain that he'd be in prison by now. Of course, the screwdriver he used to break the lock with was completely unnecessary. Simon could have probably unlocked the door with his mind—but he lacked in disciplined training and confidence ... patience, also. I had read a great deal about telekinetic energy while doing research for my first novel. It seemed that Simon's talent was raw. And it wasn't my place to bring that to his attention, either. Dr. Anson had already explained to me privately that Simon's gift was more spontaneous in nature. That meant that he didn't know how to control much of it. And I was only following him around to observe at this point, not to give pointers.

Once we got inside the apartment, we saw that it was almost bare. There was an ornate-looking rug, a stack of books, and that was about it. Simon handed me the screwdriver and headed straight for the kitchen. He held the reader out in front of him.

"Fridge is off."

"No microwave either," I added.

"This guy isn't here very often. It looks like he hasn't been here for a while."

"You said your guys were over here yesterday—"

"Oh yeah ... I did say that. Huh."

I studied the floor and ceiling, feeling bad for anyone that lived in the building. "We should check the rooms and closets," I suggested before thinking it through. "Wait. This guy isn't *dangerous* or anything, is he?"

"He's not here."

"Why did we come up here then? And we just broke in, didn't we?"

Simon glared at me. He walked up to me with his head tilted and his eyebrows raised. "Give me the screwdriver."

I did as he asked and he disappeared into a room in the back. I could hear the opening and closing of doors. And it didn't take long before he called out to me in panic.

"Richard! Get back here!"

I ran toward the bedroom and stopped to look inside before entering. The room was empty, the walls filthy and stained. There were black bed sheets nailed above the windows.

"Richard!" Simon called out again from inside the bathroom. "Get in here!"

I hurried toward the dim light that came from the tiny bathroom to see that Simon had found Brunstrom. The man was pale, thin, and weak. His eyes were almost completely lifeless and lacked color. I'd seen eyes like that before in those strange dreams I was having. Brunstrom was hardly clothed and he was crumpled into a tiny bathtub, shaking and holding a gun to his head with a boney, malnourished hand.

Simon half-turned to look back at me as I walked in. "It's him." The man in the bathtub began to tremble harder.

I knew he was right, but this didn't look anything like the photo I'd seen of Brunstrom online. "You're certain?"

I asked. As I took a step closer to Simon, it was hard for me to believe that this man was the genius I had read about. He had to have some sort of a disease ... maybe it was the drugs.

"Back away," the man warned in a frail voice.

"Are you Dr. Brunstrom? From Sweden?" I asked.

The man attempted to smile, but in doing so, revealed that he hardly had enough strength to curl his lips. "Not any longer," he growled.

"Put down your weapon," Simon commanded sternly, holding the screwdriver out in front of him.

"Don't come any closer," Brunstrom replied. His voice was raspy and his accent heavy. "I do not wish to turn the gun on you, but I will if you force me to."

Simon's breathing intensified. He shifted his eyes to me frantically. "Man ... it's strong in here, like a fog. He's bleeding out his emotions all over the place ... the reader didn't pick it up."

I was lost again, not knowing what to say or do. I didn't know what Simon was talking about. He was starting to look light-headed. I cleared my throat so Simon would look back at me. When our eyes met, I did everything I could to read his face ... to try and make sense of what he'd just said.

"You're bleeding out, too," Simon added. He looked at me with his eyes wide. "You have to stop, Richard. Stop thinking."

"You came here to stop me," Brunstrom said. He steadied the gun at his temple and closed his eyes. "You can't stop me from being free."

"Listen to me, sir," I spoke quickly, thinking Simon wasn't going to step in—the room's energy was affecting him. But I wasn't prepared and didn't know what to say. "I don't know why you're doing this to yourself, but maybe we can help you. This isn't the answer. You have a wife and you have a home."

"Your research is all fucked up and wrong," Simon struggled to say.

"How dare you question the validity of my findings! I have proven them to be true! *And soon, I will be that proof!*"

"Please, Dr. Brunstrom," I tried desperately. "What are you trying to do? What findings are you talking about?"

Simon said to him, "If you take this path, you will become nothing but an empty … *thing*. You won't survive the cross over."

"Mr. Richard Ravestone," Brunstrom said while turning the aim of his weapon onto Simon. "I respect your work. Many of us do … you are ahead of your time, so to speak. But I belong with the chosen ones. And nothing will stop me."

"What are you talking about?" I asked as I stepped in closer. I reached out for Simon's arm—he was frozen in fear at the sight of the gun aimed at his chest. "Please, Dr. Brunstrom, don't do this. Let's talk for a few minutes, okay? Just for a few minutes so we can try and work this out. I think if we can get you some help, then maybe we can figure out what's going on here, all right?" I just wanted him to put the gun down.

"You want it all for yourself," Brunstrom said to me in such a raspy voice that it petrified me.

"I'm just a writer," I said to him. "Please, put the gun down. I really don't know what you're talking about."

"You lie," Brunstrom said, aiming the handgun more steadily at Simon's chest. "Once I have changed over completely, you can never kill me and I will know the real Heaven."

I couldn't stop him. He shot Simon. I lunged toward

Brunstrom, landing on top of him, trying to pull the gun away before he could fire it again, but as quickly as I had a hold of him, he was gone. He had aimed the weapon at himself and taken his own life.

6

Another dream.

They medicated me at the hospital while I waited for word on Simon's condition.

And after the meds put me to sleep, I had another one of those terrible dreams—this one, a repeat of the ones that I'd had before, but with details so vibrant that it only felt more real, more disturbing.

In the dream, I had somehow traveled to an old village, but the whole time, I knew I wasn't supposed to be there. It was bleak and empty. I stood alone in a field, looking at the small homes from another time, medieval maybe, scattered in the distance ahead of me. This place looked deserted. There were no signs of people. I just stood there trying to understand what had happened to the village.

I wasn't me. I was another man, a hunter, and this was his home.

When I tried walking, it was like moving through water. I focused and pushed myself through it, forcing myself to move through whatever was trying to hold me back. The whole time, a single thought kept repeating inside my head, asking me where the people from the village had gone. All I wanted to know was where the rest of the people were.

Being this man confused me. I was thinking his thoughts *and* mine. It was like being trapped inside a movie or a memory.

I walked through a field of rich green grass to approach some cottages, still hoping to see people. My mind and my body felt heavy, my reactions slowed. I couldn't seem to find the right way to connect my thoughts with the dream world around me as I moved. The light of the Earth's sun burned my eyes in a way that was torturous to me.

With great effort and concentration, I studied the insides of the cottages. I looked through opened wooden doors and windows. I worked as hard as I could to will this man's body to walk into one of those homes, but he was petrified, refusing to go in.

There was an ungodly smell.

That quiet stillness, I will never forget. Walking from home to home in that silence, with that lingering smell surrounding me …

Some powerful force didn't want me or the hunter there any longer, and I was pulled away. It was the Black Death. It still remained there, and it whispered into my ear, "Leave this place."

We caught a glimpse of an entire family through an opened door.

The man, the one I was inside of, collapsed to the ground. Horrible things flashed through his mind. He knew what had taken his people while he'd been away on his long journey … he wanted to die and willed it to happen as I was pulled back into my own reality. I couldn't get the images of those ravaged bodies out of my head. The children … the mother clutching onto them. Why?

The hospital … a nurse said my name and I thought I saw her.

But then, I was pulled back in.

Another place, a different time. Another dream.

I was alone, pacing back and forth on horseback as I stared into the trees. Occasionally, I would look back and see other men nearby, stumbling around in uniform. Their laughs echoed in the night. Behind them blazed a fire. These men depended on me to keep watch while they drank and slept, but I was freezing cold and jealous. Still, it was what was expected of me, and I had given my word to follow orders. There was an expectation of praise and glory in these men—underneath the layers of drunkenness and fear. I knew this feeling because I'd had this dream before. This exact one. But I hated being one of the Red Coats. At least in this man, I had better control and more fluid movement.

At this point in the dream, I would venture out a bit further to get away from the drinking and the men's exaggerated stories. In the quiet, when I could hear the sound of my horse's hooves again in the dirt, it became hypnotic. But I was so tired. I had to get down and walk to keep myself awake and focused. Even with the harsh chill of winter blowing through the air and into my face, I fought to keep my eyes steady. I would look back periodically toward the camp to see if anyone else was awake. Their voices had quieted. I leaned against a tree, just to close my eyes for seconds ... and heard something in the darkness. Something wrong. There was a breathing sound coming from the trees—something dark and cruel. I stood straight and at full attention, listening for it again. I scanned through the trees but couldn't catch it with my eyes, as much as I tried, but I knew that something else was there, watching.

I backed up to my horse and reached for my knife. I grabbed her reins and pulled, guiding her toward the camp while keeping my eyes on the trees.

As soon as I was close enough, I called out, "Someone

is here! In the trees!"

But it was not my voice. It was his, that soldier with the British accent.

A man in tall boots rushed up to me. "What are you saying?"

"I heard someone in the trees!" I was panicked.

The man squinted and scanned the trees with a heavy crease in his brow. "Where?"

"I don't know, sir. I couldn't see."

"Get back to the camp and wake the—"

It grabbed him mid-sentence and snatched him into nothingness. Something had placed a ghostly hand over his face and pulled his body away without making a single sound.

The air changed. I stood in shock, holding my breath, my eyes quickly searching everything around me, trying to focus. I gasped and ran toward the camp, screaming. I felt its thoughts pulling at me. Behind me, in the steps I had just taken, leaves moved in ways I couldn't explain—it was a movement against the wind and against nature's intentions. Branches snapped behind me, beside me, closer … closing in. These things were dropping from the trees.

I called out to anyone who could hear. "Help! Wake up!"

Wake yourself, Richard! Fight it!

It was grabbing at my coat, the scraping of its fingers on my shoulder forcing me to run faster. I was screaming until I had no voice left. Helpless and running, the horse had already left me.

I couldn't be in that nightmare again. I had lived through it already, hopelessly trying each time for a different outcome. Desperately trying and failing.

As I approached the camp, sudden images of corpses

flooded my mind, flesh defiled and ravaged with illness and filth … putrid, horrors—the darkness of many years. The impossible horrors of a world that wanted nothing more than to be rid of us, had returned. God had saved us from this before—death chasing man through the ages. I, or the man I was then, knew this. Somehow, he knew.

Then I could hear the voices, human voices that I couldn't see, chanting inside my head, making me crazy again. It was *them*. The ones dressed in black, the ones that bring the demons. They controlled everything.

We are protected by the pentagram and by the light of the candle.

Their voices terrified me.

I screamed and reached for a soldier who stood in shock with his rifle aimed loosely into the air behind me. Those voices … they were the bringers of the demons—*they* had done this to these men. I pulled the soldier by his collar, the chanting in my head growing louder. One of the hellish creatures grabbed at him, its ghostly hands around the man's neck. I pulled the man closer to me as he screamed, but the creature fought against me, pulling the soldier away from me to bring its face up to his, using its pale gray eyes to stare into him … it wanted to live again. It wanted to know life the way the soldiers did—these men of the Revolution. It turned to me and screeched, the demon's jaw opening so wide—I wasn't going to let it win this time. The thing then turned back to the soldier and pushed its transparent, ruined face through him. It pushed itself into his face … into his skin …

The bell sounded and the black candle was lighted.

Wake up, Richard. The demon has won.

As I woke up, the fluorescent lights above stinging my

eyes, I remembered Simon being shot in the shoulder and sighed. He wasn't my friend, and I didn't have to care about what happened to him. I just wanted to get out of San Antonio, I wanted to stop having these dreams ... that was it, too—Texas. The dreams hadn't started up again until I arrived in San Antonio.

After dealing with the police at the scene and answering tons of questions with lies, I wanted nothing more to do with the ensuing drama that this so-called "project" had created. I had stayed with Simon—this callous, selfish man that I hardly knew—until they loaded him into the ambulance. I had listened to him complain and whimper as they began to treat his wound ... I felt sorry for him, but I still wanted to leave. Simon had told the emergency technicians that he didn't have any relatives to contact and went on and on like that as I stepped away and hyperventilated as inconspicuously as possible. Nobody noticed.

I decided to let Dr. Anson know that I had plans to book a flight back home in the morning. I would wish him well but let him know that this was just too much for me. They had the wrong guy for this, obviously. And now those disturbing dreams were back in my head ...

7

Awake.

"We don't have much of a program without Simon," Dr. Anson admitted to me. His voice was hoarse. He was extremely worried. "I know it's hard to understand that. He's not very good around people."

The hospital was busy that night. We sat across from each other in the emergency waiting area, Dr. Anson looking a lot like he could use a good drink. My medication was wearing off, just a little something to relax, something for the anxiety, but they told me that I'd slept for almost an hour after they gave it to me. I woke up around the time Dr. Anson arrived at the hospital and I was offered a coffee to help wake me up. Anson was stressed out. He'd been at the police station answering questions for a while.

I nodded, still coming out of my haze.

Anson looked me over and frowned. "And I'm sorry you're dealing with this. Definitely not what I expected when I invited you ... when *we* invited you here."

I didn't know what to say.

Dr. Anson's eyes dropped to the floor. "When Simon volunteered for his first study with us, I could tell ... I knew he was only doing it for the money. I don't think he realized how talented he was."

Dr. Anson's face had gone pale. His fingers traced nervously along the armrest of the chair he was in. Inside my head, a quick image of that weak, shriveled man taking a shot at Simon. Then I remembered how hard it had been to stop the bleeding until police arrived. And after convincing them to listen, I immediately called Dr. Anson.

"I'm sorry," I said to him. It felt generic, but it was honestly all I could come up with to say.

"Did he tell you how many times he tried hiding from me?" Anson asked.

"No, sir," I answered. "What do you mean?"

"Simon. He hid from me—wouldn't return my calls." Anson smiled, his eyes distant as he remembered. "After we realized what a strong gift he had, he wanted nothing to do with it. I think it frightened him. Severely. Naturally, the drinking calms it down some."

I wasn't sure how rude it would be to ask, but there was a question on my mind. I just didn't know how to ask it with just the right amount of sensitivity. "Dr. Anson?"

"Yes, Richard?"

"If Simon's ability is so strong, why didn't he know about it until he made that trip back from New York? The one where he ended up at the gas station?"

Dr. Anson looked at me and smiled. "His ability was sudden. He may have always had it in some dormant form, but since he'd never tried using it before, it simply didn't exist to him yet."

I glanced down the hallway where nurses rushed back and forth. "Is that when he started drinking, also?"

"No, but that's certainly when it intensified. After his first day in the study, he went home to his apartment and strange things started happening to him almost immediately." The professor edged up even closer in his seat. "It began with the voices. He described them to me as moans and ... deep labored gasps. Unearthly voices. Sometimes they were commanding. They were on a frequency that only he could hear, but I believed him. He was frightened out of his mind, but I believed him because he could talk to them. He could ask them questions that he received answers to. Impossible answers.

"So you have to understand, Richard. Simon is doing everything he can to calm those voices down. But once they know they can be heard, they have a lot to say ... and they speak to him quite a bit. That's part of the reason I also have to make sure he doesn't talk to a lot of people about what he's going through. Not yet, at least. He still has a lot to learn about it, and about himself. I've asked him to keep the use of his talents to a minimum— only at the lab unless I give him permission otherwise. I know that sounds a little strict, but it's for his own safety."

I let some of it sink in. My first thought was that Simon needed a doctor, a psychiatrist, but not one connected with parapsychology. He needed some sort of an evaluation. But then I let myself look back into Dr. Anson's eyes again and saw the sincerity in them. Dr. Anson believed that Simon was hearing voices, and he was convinced that they were not the voices of insanity.

Dr. Anson was studying my face. "Of course, I did give him permission to tell *you* things."

An honor I wasn't too sure I wanted. "He never told me about the voices."

Dr. Anson looked at me with worry in his face. "There's a reason for that. It's difficult to sound sane when you speak about hearing voices. Especially voices like that."

I was too skeptical for this. And deep inside, I wanted to believe that Dr. Anson was as well. All of that research he was a part of at the university was actually started by him to *disprove* all things paranormal and replace them with "logical explanations." That's how he put it to me when we met. Just ten minutes off the plane and he was telling me about his research and how it all began. "Have you ever recorded them?"

"The voices? Yes," he answered.

I had to be careful with the next question. I didn't want to sound condescending. "Are they ghosts?"

"Some are. But many of them are much different."

"So ... were they once human?"

Dr. Anson tilted his head to think on that last question. "Yes and no. They are much harder to analyze than the more common recordings we've studied. Those common ones—ghosts—do creep in from time to time. But these voices are distinctly different from those."

"How?"

"Well, more recently, Simon has heard a lot of voices that seem to be purposely reaching out to him. They keep asking for his help." A serious look crept onto his face. "I know he told you ... about how he asked me to contact you. There was a reason for that. I meant it when I said I was a fan of yours, but it was the voices ... the things they were saying to him. Simon told me that you had to be here."

I tried not to look as disturbed as I felt. "Be here for what?"

"He couldn't tell me that part. He said he doesn't know why. All he said was that *they* wanted you here. They were harassing him, trying to force him to make it happen."

"They *who?*"

He looked away from me briefly to glance around the room before leaning in closer. "They are like angels, some force watching over us." His voice was now a whisper.

"And that is all I can tell you, Richard."

Angels. Not angels … *like* angels. Not freaky at all. Totally normal.

I risked it. "Voices told Simon to contact me?"

Dr. Anson hesitated, and then replied quietly, "Yes."

"And you think they were … angels?"

He twisted his lips. "I couldn't tell you for sure, but that's how Simon described them."

I was baffled.

"Please don't mention anything about this conversation to Simon. It's been very troubling to him, emotionally."

I watched as a family suddenly rushed in from outside and crowded around in front of the admissions desk. The woman was in tears and her small children looked up at her in their night clothes, confused. The woman was demanding to see her father … shrieking at the hospital staff.

"Excuse me, sir?" a woman's voice startled me. "Are you Richard?"

I had to catch my breath. "Yes, sorry."

"Mr. Wallace would like to see you, sir," the woman informed me. She wore medical scrubs with a cartoon animal pattern repeated all over them.

I looked at Dr. Anson, realizing that I never really knew Simon's last name. He only smiled.

"Is he all right? I mean, is he okay enough for visitors?" I asked as I stood, ready to follow her.

"Yes. Well, no." She stopped herself mid-sentence and looked at me with a heavily creased frown. "He's going to be fine. He's stable. But he's extremely irritable and demanding."

Dr. Anson threw his head back in laughter.

"Can I bring my friend with me to see him?" I asked

while motioning toward Dr. Anson.

"Yes, but only if Mr. Wallace *wants* to see him. We don't want him around anyone that will set him off. The doctors are starting to joke about strapping him to the bed."

Once inside the room, I took a seat next to Simon and waited for him to acknowledge me. Dr. Anson walked over to the machines Simon was hooked up to and studied them intensely. There was an awkward silence, and Simon's eyes were on me, waiting for me to speak. And since Dr. Anson was too busy with medical screens and gadgets, I decided to go first.

"Hey, Simon. The nurse says you're doing pretty good—"

"Richard, listen to me. Close the door," Simon struggled to say. "I'm serious. Do it."

I looked at Dr. Anson, thinking it was a bad idea to listen to Simon. I didn't know what to do.

But Dr. Anson didn't react the way I expected him to. Instead, he made his way over to the door and peeked into the busy hallway like some sort of a spy. "Go ahead, Simon. I'll stand watch."

"Fine," Simon began. "Richard, I had this … thing happen to me after I was shot."

"It was a graze, Simon," Dr. Anson reminded him.

A graze? I thought. I didn't know if I was relieved or angry about it. In a way, I kind of felt ripped off. I knew how bad it had looked when it happened—I'd been there. But I'd sworn it was worse than that.

"Okay." I said, still interested in hearing whatever he had to say. I was practically holding my breath at that point, waiting for him to tell me.

"It was all black and I heard these voices. They said to

look for you."

"I was there the whole time, though, Simon. I stayed next to you. I was putting pressure on your arm."

"I know," Simon reached over for me but stopped midway as pain struck.

"Simon, relax." I hesitated to touch his arm, but knew that there was something oddly different about him. His body was tense with anxiety.

"Okay, listen." He gritted his teeth, still in pain. "The voices told me to show you. They told me to … bring you to them."

"Bring me to *who?*"

"To the ghosts. The bad ones … the demons."

I turned in my seat just enough to catch a side glimpse of Dr. Anson. He was staring intently.

I had to keep my promise. I pretended not to know about the voices Simon could hear.

"What ghosts, Simon?" Dr. Anson asked. "And what do you mean 'demons?' You never said anything about stuff like that before."

"I never had anything communicate with me like that before. I've heard voices—I know that's weird—but these ones … they're not like the other ones I've heard." Simon closed his eyes. I could see the frustration in him. He was struggling to make me understand. "The ghosts, they said they watched you lookin' for the villagers. That's what they told me. Then, the bad ones jumped down from the trees … in some forest with the soldiers. I don't know what they are. I think they have somethin' to do with the defectors."

This threw me back in my seat. "When did you see all this?"

"In the ambulance. I think."

I couldn't believe it. "I've had dreams like that. I just

dreamed that again … here at the hospital. *After* they checked you in."

"So I saw it before you dreamed it?"

"Yeah, but I've had that dream so many times …"

"Simon, stop," Dr. Anson warned sternly. "You're scaring him."

"I want out of here, Anson!" Simon yelled. "I have to leave! There's too much electricity in here … it's hurting my head!"

"You're not going to get out acting like this!" Dr. Anson snapped back. "Richard, let's go. He's getting too worked up. It's not good for him."

I stood slowly in disbelief. How could he have said that? How could he have known what happened inside my dreams? I looked into Simon's bloodshot eyes, unsure of what to say. He was trying to relax. His breathing slowed as he studied my reaction—he knew I understood, and he began to smile at me, relieved. "I just dreamed about them again … those things, exactly like you said," I told him.

"The ghosts from the trees, too?" he asked.

"Yes," I agreed. But it was impossible for him to know. I felt sick to my stomach. They were horrible things …

"We're going to find them."

I was shaking my head. "Simon, I—"

"You can't say no, Richard," Simon said, his face almost absent of color and his eyes glassy. "They said you had to … the good ones, I think. I think there's good ones and bad ones. It felt like both of them were talkin' to me. Pulling on me. Some of them want revenge. They had the plague … the Black Death. They say they were abandoned. They're ready to come back because they've found a way. They want to live again."

I wanted to run out of the room in denial. There was something horrible about the two of us sharing this nightmare. "Simon, you have to try to calm down so you can heal. We'll talk about all of this later."

"… with spells, Richard." The desperation in his eyes said everything. He had seen something more than I had—he could tap into the details that I couldn't. "There are scientists that know what's going on … they *think* they know what's going on. There's, like, a group of them using witchcraft to communicate with the other side. They don't even know what they're doing. They don't know what they're doing to us! They're *bringing* these things over!"

"Simon, stop," Anson warned. The medication had to be messing with Simon's mind.

"Richard," he said while grabbing a stronger hold of my arm. He pulled me in closer to his face. "That's what Brunstrom was doing! That's why he tried to kill me! He knew I was going to find out! Others are trying to bring them over, too!"

"Simon!" Dr. Anson tried to stop him.

"Dammit, Anson!" Simon began to hyperventilate. "I have to tell him this stuff! He has to know! The voices told me to tell him!"

Dr. Anson peeked outside the room again.

Simon lowered his voice. "I saw them—the bad ones—watching you in the village, and then I saw them in the forest."

I nodded.

"Then when I got to the hospital, after the nurse checked on me, they whispered in my ear. They kept sayin' your name. It scared the hell out of me. They're demons, Richard. They're tryin' to come back here. They're making deals with people … but these things are evil. I feel things like black magic and sorcery. Then, there's these men, like, secret people. They're the ones controlling it. I know it sounds crazy … a lot of it doesn't make sense, but it's why we brought you out here."

Dr. Anson touched my shoulder. "Richard, we should leave. He's been through enough tonight." His voice was commanding.

Simon hesitated, then released my arm—his glassy stare still on me.

I nodded in appreciation, just to let Simon know that I'd heard him, and that I was interested in finding out more. "Dr. Anson's right. You need rest. We'll talk once you get out of here."

Satisfied, Simon broke his steady eye contact with me to glare at Anson. "Get me the fuck out of here, Miller. Please."

"You'll be released when the doctors think you're ready, Simon," Dr. Anson replied coldly. He looked extremely upset and I could tell he was shaken.

As Dr. Anson headed toward the door, I slowly got up to follow him. Every word that Simon said to me was now swirling inside my head. Simon looked angry, confused, and worst of all—trapped.

"Get some sleep, Simon," Dr. Anson added. "And watch what you talk about. These walls, and all others outside the lab, have ears. Don't forget that, and don't make me warn you again."

8

At the hotel room.

There was someone knocking at my door.

I stared at the wall in front of me, wondering who it was. Forty minutes ago, I'd been at the hospital visiting Simon. I couldn't make sense of the things he'd said to me—how he knew the details of my dreams. What he'd seen was incredible, more detailed than what I could see. It was terrifying to think that something inside my head could be shared like that, seen by anyone else. And I was certain that the trauma of being shot had triggered it.

And with everything that Simon had said, I didn't even have a chance to tell Dr. Anson that I was ready to go back to L.A. But of course, I had some doubts about that again.

Wait ... what if it's him at the door?

No. Dr. Anson would have called or texted before coming over. And since I wasn't getting to the door fast enough, whoever it was decided to impatiently knock again.

I pushed myself away from my laptop and walked toward the door. I leaned forward to look through the peephole. I hadn't expected to see a woman standing there and was certain she had the wrong hotel room.

I opened the door. "Yes?"

She was plain-looking, possibly in her mid-thirties, and her light blonde hair could have used some anti-frizz serum. I couldn't help noticing things like that. Red carpet events and award ceremonies had tainted me in some ways, I guess. Regardless, I also noticed that she probably could have used a little makeup.

"Sorry to bother you like this, sir," she began, "My name is Claire. I was one of the police officers that responded when your friend was shot."

Since that whole part of the night felt like an endless blur, I had no idea if she'd really been there or not. And with everything that was going on, I couldn't help being suspicious. "Oh. Okay. How can I help you?"

She wasn't in uniform, which didn't mean that she hadn't been there, but it didn't ease my mind any. A uniform just seemed more official. Instead, she wore a plain blue shirt and a pair of boot cut jeans. I thought maybe her shift had just ended. She couldn't have come to the hotel to conduct any case-related questioning.

"I know you're a writer. I read one of your books," she said shyly and smiled.

"Thank you. I think."

She giggled. "No, I liked it."

The way she said it wasn't convincing enough to me.

"I'm sorry about your friend. I called the hospital to check on him." She fidgeted nervously with the strap of her handbag. "Sounds like he'll be all right soon."

"Since it hit him in the shoulder, I think he'll be fine. Really, it was just a graze. Kind of a deep one, but he'll be fine."

She took a quick glance inside the room. "Can I come in and talk to you about something?"

I stood in silence for a moment before answering, "Sure." Even though I was unsure, I didn't see any harm in it. As odd as it may sound, I was used to meeting with strangers and interviewing people I didn't know. Hotel rooms, restaurants, park benches … it didn't matter to me. The tables may have been turned this time, but that part didn't worry me. The potential questions she might have, on the other hand, did.

I stepped aside and motioned for her to take the chair next to the desk as I sat on the end of the bed. She didn't seem too uncomfortable with the fact that she was walking into some guy's hotel room—but I credited that to the nature of her job, and mine. I looked at her, giving her permission to take the conversational lead, but her eyes were too busy wandering around the room. They stopped when they hit the window. The awesome view of the San Antonio skyline was, admittedly, distracting and had interfered with my TV-watching late into the night.

"So you responded to the shooting?" I decided to remind her.

"Yes," she answered. Her eyes remained on the city lights. "And I was called out there a week earlier, too."

"To the same apartment?"

She looked at me with large blue eyes. Her face was expressionless, but worry was creeping through. "Are you … writing something about that place?" she asked me.

"No. I mean, I don't think so," I answered honestly. "Why?"

"Why would you hang around a place like that?"

I had to think fast. "I just went there with my friend."

"So he knew the man who shot him?"

"Is this a part of the investigation? Are you a detective or—?"

"No, sorry … I'm not good at explaining things sometimes." She let out a long, nervous breath and moved her mouth a few times as if she was about to say something, but wasn't able to get the words out.

"You wanted to talk about writing?" I asked.

"No. Well … a little," she replied. "I was wondering if you were doing research for your next book."

I didn't exactly know how to answer that without giving away too much. Dr. Anson had asked that I keep things quiet for the time being—and I didn't know what I was doing as far as research went anyway. I did my best to put on a neutral expression as I answered her. "I don't think so."

She smiled, not buying any of it. "Oh."

"Why do you ask?"

"I'm asking because I'm a fan, and also because of that call I responded to a week ago. The lady in the apartment across the hall called about an intruder in her apartment. A man."

"Interesting," I lied. I just wanted her out of my hotel room. I'd been around enough cops for the night. "I hope she was all right."

"She was pretty shaken up by it."

I only felt a little relieved at this point. She seemed to think that I was researching crime in the area … no big deal. So what if I was? Now, I just had to get her out of my room. I needed to get back to my research—the research on the laptop that I forgot to close before letting her in. The laptop she was sitting in front of. "No, I wasn't there because of that. I didn't know the area was so dangerous, actually. Um … Simon just wanted to check on something. *Someone*, I mean. Uh, I think he might have known that last guy that lived there. Not that other guy … not the one who shot him." I sounded like an idiot.

Claire's eyes traced where mine had glanced back to a few times as I spoke, and I could tell that she wasn't buying my story. She turned to look behind her and studied the screen of my laptop. After a few seconds, she turned back to me with a grin on her face. My search on ghosts and the most effective ways to record them was still on the screen. *Dammit.*

"You think the place was haunted?" she asked.

I answered, "Those apartments? No."

"The call I responded to at the apartment across the hall wasn't a typical call," she said. "I saw the lady from that apartment again tonight. She was standing in her doorway with a strange look on her face."

"I guess I didn't notice."

She quickly moved her eyes to the carpet. "Of course you didn't notice. You were concerned about your friend."

It was interesting to hear it put that way. There was no point in explaining anything about the status of mine and Simon's relationship, though. And if I had to, I wouldn't have known where to begin. "Yeah. I guess so."

"That lady was staring straight into the apartment … the one you two were in. 201."

"Maybe she was concerned. The gun shots were pretty loud."

"That's true. But you didn't see her face." Claire was looking through me now as she continued to speak. "She didn't seem very concerned about what was going on with you guys. Not in the way she should have been."

"What do you mean?"

She thought on it for a moment, then shrugged her shoulders. "I mean, she was emotionless. She looked like a statue. When they were carrying Simon out, she didn't even bother to look at him. She just kept staring over him, into the apartment. Like she was expecting something."

I watched the features on Claire's face change. She'd become more serious as she spoke. I could see in her eyes that something about the woman from the apartment building had gotten to her.

"I thought she was waiting for them to bring out Brunstrom's body," Claire said slowly. "But that wasn't it either."

After Brunstrom shot Simon, he turned the gun on himself. At the time, I did what I could to avoid looking at him afterward, but I had to make sure he was no longer a threat to us. I hated what I saw—the mess Brunstrom had made of himself, and I was angry that I'd been put in a position to witness it. While I tried to absorb the shock, Simon took to hissing obscenities while covering his wound with his hand. He slid down to the floor, blood oozing from his shoulder. But after about thirty seconds, he was arching his back and grabbing into the air in panic. I tried using my phone to call for help, but it was dead. I reached into Simon's pocket to grab for his, but it was dead also. I had to drag Simon out of that horrible, tiny bathroom. I couldn't be near Brunstrom's body any longer, and I needed to find a way to call for help. So I screamed and screamed ...

"I thought maybe you were researching the place," she said again, breaking me out of my thoughts.

"Uh ... no. I wasn't."

"So your friend knew the guy that lived there before Mr. Brunstrom?" she asked.

"I don't know. I don't really know how well Simon knew him. *If* he knew him. I was going where he told me to go," I explained uncomfortably. I knew she didn't believe me.

"Oh," she replied.

I was still curious about something. "What happened with the call? The one you responded to a week ago?" I decided to ask, hoping to find a few things out while I had her there. It was clear to me that she wasn't just some nosey fan. Something was bothering her. And as the conversation went on, I realized that there was something more to this than she might be willing to share with me.

"She called saying that Mr. Brunstrom was in her apartment."

"Doing what?"

She ran her fingers through her frizzy hair. "Walking."

"That's it?" I mean, a guy walking around inside a lady's apartment—uninvited—isn't good. I guess I just expected him to be doing more than that. Brunstrom was nuts. "I know that's weird. I would have called the cops, too. I'm sure the lady was scared out of her mind. I didn't mean for it to sound like that, but … that was it? Do you think he was on drugs or maybe trying to steal something?"

"He was walking through her walls."

Now I was the one staring blankly.

"That's why I thought you were hanging around there. I thought you were interviewing him or looking into the report about what happened."

"Oh," I said stupidly, wishing that Dr. Anson had told me a little more about this Brunstrom guy before Simon had taken us over there. "No, I didn't know about the wall thing."

"Do you believe it?" she asked me sincerely.

"I don't know," I answered honestly. "Did you believe it when she told you?"

She looked away. "No."

And here was where I had to play things with caution because I didn't need some cop getting into our business. "The woman probably has emotional issues. Does she live there alone?"

Claire hesitated. "Yes, she lives there alone. But I don't

see why that matters. A lot of women live alone. *I* live alone."

She was offended. In a way, I didn't care. I just wanted her out. So I kept on. "People walking through walls? Come on."

She got up slowly and smiled. "I should probably go."

I guess she believed the wall thing.

"Thanks for stopping by. Sorry I couldn't help you with ... whatever you needed." I was eager to get her out of there. I wanted to get back to my quasi-research. "Quasi" because it was Internet-based, and I couldn't order the books I really needed for research while staying in a hotel. And with books, I still preferred physical copies to digital ones so I could add them to my collection. I wanted to look into a connection between ghosts and dreams ... and if it was possible to record them somehow—while I was sleeping.

"I should have brought a book for you to sign for me. I know that sounds kind of selfish, but ..." As she walked toward the door, she looked back and smiled shyly.

"No, no. It doesn't sound selfish at all. Normally, I have a few books with me when I travel. I just didn't bring any on this trip." Normally, I would have felt compelled to take down her address so I could mail a book to her later. But that sort of public-relations kindness certainly wasn't on my mind. The closer she got to the door, the better I started to feel.

"Maybe I'll see you around," she suggested.

"I'm not going to be in town much longer, but you never know."

The door handle clicked as she opened the door and stepped out. "That's a true statement."

She's finally out.

"What is? 'You never know?'" I repeated back to her.

"Yes, because you think you know something but then most times it turns out that you don't really know anything about what you thought you knew … anything about."

"Hmm. That's pretty interesting." I put my hand on the door and smiled politely as I began to close it. "It was nice to meet you. Thanks for your help with Simon."

"Of course. Could you let him know that I'm thinking of him?"

I must have reacted with the strangest look on my face. She grinned slyly at me in response to it and waited for me to speak.

"Okay," I said slowly. "I will … let him know. That's very nice of you to be concerned about him like that."

"He's helped us solve some of our biggest cases. You know … with his psychic abilities. Of course, he doesn't like people to know about that stuff."

I wanted to punch Simon. Lightly, though, because I was pretty sure he could hurt me. Even with an injured arm.

"But you already knew that since you two are friends." She waved dismissively and turned to leave. "Bye!"

"Yeah, bye," I mumbled back as I closed the door. *So you're selling it to the PD, huh, Simon? Wait until Anson finds out.*

9

"He *what?*" Dr. Anson asked in disbelief.

"She said Simon's been helping the police department solve some cases," I repeated into the phone.

There was some silence mixed in with Dr. Anson's angry breathing. I assumed it was anger. After our little talk at the hospital, it was pretty clear to me how important the project was to Anson. And it made sense to me—keeping Simon's psychic abilities under wraps until he had a better handle on it. The experiments he was a part of were being funded by private investors. This project was important to Dr. Anson. Discovering Simon's talent had helped him acquire additional funding—and even then—the funding was provided largely by an anonymous investor that Dr. Anson felt obligated to impress. And here was Simon, recklessly risking it all.

"He's not supposed to be doing things like that," Dr. Anson whispered into the phone. "It's too dangerous and … we *pay* him."

"I'm sorry. That's what the officer said. I just wanted to let you know. I wasn't trying to get Simon in trouble."

"What trouble can he really get into?" Dr. Anson asked facetiously. "He knows how much we need him for the project … and funding."

"Do you know when he's being released from the hospital?"

"Sometime today. They're just worried about an infection or his blood pressure or something."

"Do you want me to talk to him about it?" I offered, not knowing why I had.

In the short silence that followed, I could tell he was actually considering it.

"No, that's alright, Richard. I'll take care of it myself. What he's doing is a violation of our agreement. I'll deal with it."

"Okay." I honestly felt bad for him—not Simon.

"Richard, I do have a question for you, though."

"Yes?"

"Would you stay another week?"

I closed my eyes and felt a sudden pain searing through my head. I was intrigued by what I'd seen so far, and I wanted to learn more—Simon knew something about the dreams I was having. But I didn't understand Dr. Anson's objective. I didn't know if he truly understood what I'd been through in that Brunstrom situation.

"You see that we're a part of some very important scientific discoveries here, Richard."

"Yes, I understand that," I began. "I mean, I sort of understand. I don't really get what's going on, but—"

"I haven't shared this information with any outsiders. Only you."

I picked up on what he was trying to do, whether he meant for me to or not. He was trying to send me on a first-class guilt trip.

"Dr. Anson, I appreciate your trust in me and that you've invited me to … experience some of what's going on with your research, but this is a world I don't really belong in. And actually, I have to admit something—I really have been having some seriously disturbing dreams since I've been here. It kind of freaked me out when Simon mentioned some of the details about them at the hospital. I think it might be best if I get back to L.A. soon. I think I need to see a therapist or a psychiatrist or something like that. Maybe some sleeping pills, or … I know a lady back in Los Angeles that I see sometimes when I have writer's block. Maybe she can help."

Dr. Anson let out a short burst of laughter. It didn't make a lot of sense to me, but at least he wasn't upset. I was doing my best to be as honest with him as possible, without offending him.

"I hope you understand, sir," I said. "What you and Simon are doing is valuable. Maybe I'm getting in the way. I'm sure you understand that tonight was kind of … not fun for me."

"Richard. There is no way in hell I'd expect you to stay if you aren't interested." Dr. Anson chuckled. "It sounds like these dreams are a big disruption in your life. It must be extremely difficult. Especially with the type of creative work you do."

I froze mentally. I felt a way out. "Yes, it is. Thank you for understanding."

"We invited you here, Richard. Simon had some interesting communications, your name came up, and he was curious about the connection. Trust me, you're not in the way."

"That's the other thing, Dr. Anson." I thought about the right way to say it. "In the hospital, Simon started talking about things that were in my dreams. *Specific* things."

"Yes. See? Now you know why we contacted you."

"Yeah, but—"

"I can help you with your dreams, Richard. I know they're troubling you."

I closed my eyes, as if doing so would help chase the memories away.

"Let's put the class lecture on hold. Why don't we focus on helping you for a little while instead."

"Like therapy?" Like, what I was using as an excuse to get away from there?

"No. Let's think of it as an experiment. Simon is an intense, powerful seer. Now, seeing into dreams—that would be something new and different for us. Why don't you let us try to delve a little deeper into that?"

I knew he could sense my hesitation through the phone.

"You'll learn more about what we do, have some time to see a little more of San Antonio ... and I have a great surprise for you. You're going to love it!"

All expenses paid, I kept thinking. "I really do feel like I'm in the way."

"Do you find the research interesting, Richard?" he asked with excitement.

"Yes, I do," I admitted in confusion.

"Don't you think Simon is a unique and fascinating person?"

I cringed. "Uh ... I guess you could put it like that. Sometimes. Maybe."

"Would you stay another week, Richard? I can help you with your dreams. I'm almost certain of it." He sounded so optimistic when he said it.

I shook my head in frustration. "Look, everything that's been happening here ... I'm just not sure that I ... I mean, I'm open-minded and all, but ..." It felt horrible, trying to think up excuses to break free. Part of me didn't know why I was doing it, and the other part of me just wanted to get as far away as possible. "I don't understand why you'd allow a writer to be around research like this. I mean, thanks for trusting me but, um, and ... I don't know. Maybe the shooting thing didn't help. That's not something I enjoyed or anything."

"Hmmm," Dr. Anson replied. And since we were on

the phone, I had no idea what type of *hmmm* it was.

"I'm sorry, sir."

"Well, it's all right. I understand. You've been through a lot. I will cancel the demonstration I had planned for tomorrow evening," he said with disappointment.

"Okay," I said quietly, my head filling with tension and guilt.

"It's a shame, too. When Simon told me about those entities, the ones that wanted to find you, I thought it would be a good idea to try and figure out what was going on—to help you. It *has* to be something important if beings from another world are interested in you, right?" He paused for a brief sigh. "Simon called me from the hospital after we left. Now, please understand that this will be difficult for me to say. He said the vision he had in the ambulance, after he was shot, was of you and some … ritual. Possibly Satanic, but how can we really know unless we look into it further? But since you're leaving, well … I do know an occult specialist who would be happy to help us decipher some of what Simon saw. I was hoping that you'd be meeting him tomorrow."

My heart jumped. "What?"

"I wanted to help you figure out what's been going on, Richard. I wanted to help you figure out your dreams. For some reason, Simon can see into them. He calls it a 'bleed.' Something so emotionally charged and powerful that he can pick up on it, even at a great distance. Of course, sometimes he picks up on those things because something terrible is about to happen. Like a premonition. Not that I'm trying to say you're in danger or anything, but—you never know. So when Simon crossed paths with one of those defectors a few months ago and it was thinking about *you*, that's when he knew it was something interesting. Simon recognized you from an interview they showed on television, and … well, you know the rest. And the fact that he can see into your dreams, well … I don't think it's a coincidence."

It was like I couldn't remember how to breathe. My lips quivered uncontrollably and my mind raced.

"Should I call off the demonstration with the occult specialist? He flew so far, all the way from Italy. I guess I can find something else for him to do … for a little while," Dr. Anson pressed on, knowing full well what my answer would be.

I was shaking. "No. I'll stay."

10

The next evening.

We sat inside a dimly-lit lecture hall. I had fond memories of rooms like this from when I was an eager college student. I used to drink tons of coffee back then because my stomach was made of steel. I loved school. I admired every professor I had. Well, except that calculus one in my freshman year. Most of them truly loved what they were doing and had been a great inspiration. I wouldn't have become a writer without them.

Simon, with a bandaged shoulder and his arm in a sling, leaned over my shoulder from the row behind me. "Who's this guy Anson brought here?"

I turned and looked back. Simon was kind of snarling at the man standing at the podium next to Dr. Anson. They were flipping through an old hardbound book together. "He's some occult expert."

"So he's a devil worshiper."

I rolled my eyes. "I seriously doubt it."

"He dresses like one," Simon scoffed before leaning back in his seat again.

The occult expert then noticed us watching him and smiled awkwardly—like he knew we were talking about him. He wore a simple light brown suit with a darker brown wool vest underneath, and he had a dark blue tie tucked into it. His hair was a thinning dark brown mixed with gray, and he had a goatee. He wore round thin-framed glasses. And as he looked away from us to return to his preparations alongside Dr. Anson, his glasses kept sliding toward the tip of his pointy nose. His olive-colored skin was turning red as he got into a conversation with Anson. They started flipping through the large book in front of them with greater resolve.

"Yeah. He's some kind of a freak," Simon added. "You two would get along, I bet."

The man seemed harmless. But something about him worried me. He was extremely nervous and fidgety. If he was an expert in something—in anything—I would have to assume that he'd done presentations before or given several lectures during his career. He'd have an assertive aura, poised maybe. But that sort of confidence just wasn't there. It seemed like he was flipping through this old book in a state of panic, totally unprepared.

I looked behind me, up toward the back of the lecture hall. Besides Simon and me, there were four researchers seated in the very back with clipboards, pens, and paperwork stuffed into manila folders. A little too cliché if you were to ask me. I stared until one of them looked down at me in return.

"Are those men a part of Anson's team?" I asked Simon.

"I wouldn't look at those guys," he warned. "I have no idea who they are. I don't trust them."

They were concealed in the shadows, waiting for the presentation to begin. I pretended to look at something on the seat next to Simon so I could spy on them a little longer with my cunning peripheral vision. Their stiff mannerisms and shadowy faces didn't feel right.

"Shouldn't we move back a few rows?" I realized out loud. We were only four rows from the stage. "Why are those researchers sitting so far back?"

Simon placed his hand on my shoulder and moved in

close to my ear. "Shut up, Richie."

I flinched and quickly brushed his hand away. "Fine, I'll move. You stay here."

As soon as I stood, Dr. Anson switched on the microphone attached to the podium and began to speak. "Um … good evening," he began in a more nervous voice than usual. "Thank you all for being patient with us as we set up the experiment."

He noticed that I was half-standing and quickly waved his hand up and down at me. "Please, Richard. Have a seat. We're about to begin."

I sat back down, still concerned for my safety. The word "experiment" didn't sound very safe to me.

Dr. Anson gripped the sides of the podium. "I would like to introduce Mr. Raul De Luca. He's an expert on all things related to witchcraft and the occult … in a historical sense, of course." He chuckled.

"Fuck," Simon mumbled. "This doesn't sound good."

"Mr. De Luca has been asked to help us test a theory that I, and my research team, have been working on for some time. In the papers I've handed out, you will see that the theories I have developed are heavily related to quantum mechanics, but that here, the main focus will be entanglement," Dr. Anson announced to the men seated in the back of the room.

I glanced back at Simon. "I didn't get any handout. Did you?"

"Nope."

Dr. Anson held his arm out and moved aside to make room for De Luca. "I'm going to allow Mr. De Luca to go ahead and begin with his introduction."

De Luca nodded and took his place at the podium. He adjusted the microphone to accommodate for the few extra inches in height he had over Dr. Anson, and squinted as he looked toward the back of the room. "Hello, gentlemen. Thank you for taking the time to attend this evening." His Italian accent wasn't as heavy as I'd expected, and it didn't have the ring of certainty in it that I was hoping for, either.

"I'm hungry," Simon grumbled.

De Luca then focused on the open book in front of him. He smiled wide. "It is an honor to be here. I say that because, at first, I didn't expect Dr. Anson to return my phone calls or emails. I was certain he would think I was crazy. But as soon as I discovered the transcripts, I knew he was the person to contact."

I tried to peek over my shoulder again at the men in the back—to gauge their reactions, but their faces were unnaturally blank and expressionless. I turned back to Dr. Anson and watched as he nervously swayed back and forth while hanging on De Luca's every word.

"Entanglement. Intention. Words both used to describe just a piece of what you are about to witness. And my standing here before you, trying to explain it like this, is nothing compared to what I can show you instead. So if we can go ahead and dim the lights a bit more in here …"

Dr. Anson responded by quickly making his way toward a light switch.

"As I have demonstrated to small groups like this one before, the intention that I will place into this … into my words and thoughts, has everything to do with the potential outcome. The only difference this time is that what I intend and will to happen, I will do with the help of the transcripts that Dr. Anson and I have studied."

"What is this guy talking about?" Simon asked into my ear.

"I don't know," I answered. I raised my hand. "Excuse

me?"

Simon put his hand over his mouth and started snickering.

"Yes, sir?" De Luca said.

"We, I mean Simon and I, didn't get any kind of a handout. So, basically, we have no idea what's going on. What transcripts are you referring to, and what's about to be demonstrated to us?"

"Yes, that's a good question," Dr. Anson replied for De Luca. "I didn't provide you or Simon with handouts due to the sensitivity of the information contained within them. You understand, don't you?"

"Um ... I don't know," I answered back.

"Is it secret military stuff or what?" Simon asked.

Dr. Anson's eyes widened. "Why don't we just continue?" He turned to De Luca and quickly pointed at the book.

"Yes," De Luca agreed. "I will begin with the first spell, a simple conjuring of what many people refer to as an orb. It will appear as a ball of light someplace in this room, and I will do my best to will it to appear bright enough for all of us to see. And with the lights dimmed like this, I don't think that will be very difficult to accomplish." He grinned.

"What the fuck did he just say? *A spell?*" Simon blurted out. "Hey, Dr. Luca?"

"*Mr.* De Luca. Sorry, still working on my thesis, actually."

"Okay," Simon replied. "You're going to do a spell? Like a magic trick?"

De Luca shook his head frantically. "No no no, not a magic trick. The transcript is very clear and precise. The wording within it, as we have interpreted it, reads more like ... an instruction manual. I refer to this part of it as a 'spell' for simplification purposes."

So he thought we were dumb. And I was fine with that, except now I urgently wanted to leave. "We should have moved back a few rows," I reminded Simon.

"Please begin, Raul," Dr. Anson instructed in a most serious tone.

It was then that Raul De Luca inhaled a deep breath. When he released it, his eyes blinked rapidly and his lips quivered. He stepped in closer to the podium and bowed his head. I couldn't tell if his eyes had then closed or not, but I knew he was in deep thought. The way his head hung over the mysterious book was unsettling to me. I didn't bother looking back for Simon's reaction—his stillness and lack of sarcastic input at that moment said enough.

"I will need total silence as I attempt to invite the orb to manifest before us," De Luca said in a monotone voice.

I watched Dr. Anson focus his attention at De Luca's hands like he was expecting them to do something. De Luca had a strong, claw-like grip on the sides of the podium. It was so intense that his boney knuckles were sticking out.

"*What was, is now, and always will be. Exist with us, share our energy, and be in our presence.*" De Luca's voice was rhythmic and dark. As he took a short break to look into the air before him, I noticed beads of sweat dripping from his forehead.

His eyes scanned the room before he continued. "*Come into our world. Be enough for our eyes to see. Allow a piece of you to exist here, if only for a short time. Any spirit near us is welcome to show themselves and communicate with us.*"

Then, De Luca just stood there.

That's it? I thought.

The silence that followed was unsettling. It was a silence that plays tricks on your ears as you wait for something to happen. I could hear Simon rustling around in his seat, but I couldn't turn to look at him—my eyes were on De Luca as he stared expectantly into the empty seats in front of us. And it didn't take long to figure out why.

A small ball of light, about the size of a golf ball, rose out of a seat just two rows ahead. It stopped mid-air and hovered, pulsating and glowing brightly in place.

I glanced at Dr. Anson for his reaction. He was smiling and nodding happily.

"Yes!" De Luca called out with delight. "Do you see it?! Can you see it from back there?!"

I quickly turned to see what the back row of researchers thought of this strange demonstration. They sat cold and emotionless. I then looked at Simon. His reaction surprised me—he had his hands over his ears and looked extremely upset.

"Well," De Luca continued excitedly. "Here we have summoned what paranormal researchers most commonly refer to as an orb," he said as the orb still hovered in place at the exact spot where some person's head might be if a person had been sitting there in that seat.

"I say *we* because all of us here in this room had some part in bringing this orb into our world. Our energy was donated, just a little from each of us—expectation, anticipation ... our desires to want something to happen. And from myself, an ancient meditation to help conjure the energy. You can see it from back there, right?" De Luca wiped the perspiration from his face.

One of the men in the back row slowly nodded yes, but his face remained expressionless.

"Good. Okay. Well, I will now release this energy—

the orb—so that it may go back to where it normally exists." De Luca flipped a few pages in his book and cleared his throat. *"We now release you to your world swiftly, and peacefully. As you return our world's energy to us and go, we become what we both were again."*

The orb faded and disappeared. Upon seeing this, De Luca sighed and took a few steps back from the podium. He looked exhausted.

Simon rose abruptly from his seat. "What the hell are you trying to do?!" he asked.

Dr. Anson quickly answered, "Simon, please take your seat so Mr. De Luca can continue the demonstration—"

"Continue?!" Simon said with more force.

I slumped down, embarrassed.

"That ... *thing* you brought here ... you didn't hear it?!" Simon's voice trembled horribly as he spoke. "It was screaming. It didn't want to be here ... it was trapped!"

Dr. Anson's eyes went wide and his mouth dropped open. "My God."

"You could *hear it*?" De Luca asked.

"YES!"

De Luca walked to the edge of the stage with concern on his face. "What did it say?"

When Simon hesitated to answer, I turned to look at him.

His shoulders were tense. His wild eyes stared at the empty seat two rows ahead. "It said, 'I ... I need help.'"

My eyes shifted back and forth from Simon's shaking body to the men in the back row. Two of them were now leaning forward with great interest. Simon's teeth clicked together rapidly.

Dr. Anson rushed down from the stage and made his way toward Simon. When he reached him, he stared and looked him over before speaking. "What happened? Are you all right?"

Simon's eyes went blank and his mouth hung open. But with Dr. Anson at his side, I could see him starting to relax. "I have a migraine," he answered softly.

"What did you hear?"

Simon looked to the floor. "It said, 'Tell her I'm sorry ... tell her I did my best ... tell her I'm sorry she's alone. Tell her. Tell my mother I'm so sorry. Tell her ... tell her.'"

"That's what it said?"

"Yes."

"Do you know who it was?" Dr. Anson asked.

"It was some kid. Some kid that used to come to this room for class. As soon as he popped into the room, he started delivering his message." Simon looked at me for only a second before looking away. "He died in a car accident on the way to school."

Dr. Anson frowned. "That orb ... was a college student?"

"Yes."

"There's an explanation for that," De Luca announced from the stage.

Simon sneered at him. "I don't care what your damn explanation is. I'm done with this shit. What you did was wrong."

"Mr. Wallace, sir? If you will please give me a chance to tell you—"

"No. I can't do this right now," Simon explained calmly. "I don't know what you're doing, and I don't care. I don't ever want to be put through something like that again."

There was panic in De Luca's eyes. "Sir, we're doing this to find a way to stop the defectors. To stop them from changing over. I contacted Dr. Anson because I need your help."

"*My help?* You just conjured up some innocent college kid and ... you didn't have to listen to it! I did! How's that helping anything?!"

"A defector shot you while attempting to cross over, isn't that right?" De Luca asked sternly.

Simon stared angrily at him in return.

"I summoned the orb ... any orb that was available and willing to show itself, to make a point, not to cause it any pain. It *wanted* to be here, maybe to deliver its message. That's why I was able to call upon it." De Luca relaxed his posture slightly and fixed his gaze more intently on Simon. "With the transcripts I've discovered, we can work together to summon people that have transitioned, intentionally, like Dr. Brunstrom did. Without your help, I can only do this with random, unpredictable results. This thing's sort of like a telephone book. Do you understand?"

"Why would I want to help you? That's sick."

"With your gift for viewing, we can catch defectors right as they cross over." De Luca looked at him with desperation in his eyes. "*Before* they cause an imbalance." He was pleading with Simon.

"What imbalance?" I asked.

Dr. Anson collapsed into the seat next to Simon's. "There's an imbalance that occurs when people attempt to pass into, what we refer to as, the 'in between.' It's not death. It's like this existence that makes a person feel powerful or god-like."

"That's what Brunstrom was doing," Simon added. "He was trying to become one of those defectors."

"So they're ghosts but not ghosts?" I asked.

"Yes, Richard," Anson replied. "They are people—highly educated most of them—that have learned to manipulate the quantum field for their own selfish purposes."

"It's messin' everything up." Simon took his seat again.

Dr. Anson sighed heavily. "True. They don't see it as selfish because they think that they've discovered a future state of existence—life without the maintenance of fragile human bodies. But they're wrong, Richard. They are creating, instead, a terrible, destructive imbalance that we don't know how to repair."

Simon pressed into the side of his head. "They're bringing bad shit here, basically."

De Luca chimed in with excitement, "And that's why I contacted Dr. Anson as soon as I discovered these transcripts. The transcripts explain the process of crossing over—*and* bringing things back. Well, from an ancient perspective. But it might help us understand *how* they're doing it. I think we can reverse the cross over. We might be able to stop them from defecting."

"Or we can at least bring them back if we can catch them soon enough," Anson explained.

I was confused beyond words. "I don't understand."

"We have to stop them, Richard. They are causing an imbalance that can affect our world and others." Anson's eyes were huge and urgent. "They exist on the fringe of things instead of within someplace."

Simon lifted an eyebrow at me. "It's like karma, man. Think of it like that. Everything has to stay even out there."

I asked, "So if a guy crosses over, he messes up things by existing in between worlds?"

Simon nodded. "If a guy crosses over using the quantum secret research crap, he becomes like a ghost," he explained in his layman's terms. "When he does this, he lets his body go, but he's not really dead, and he's not really a ghost either. I should say he *or* she … chicks can do it too, not just dudes. But they can exist in both worlds and in between them—our world and wherever ghosts go."

Dr. Anson jumped in. "They don't really die naturally. The death part is skipped all together." He waited for me to understand what he'd said. "So it's not the same as dying and moving on to the next stage. They aren't transforming into pure energy like they're supposed to."

I thought I was starting to understand. "So some group of scientists have discovered how to become ghost-like … without dying?"

"Yes, Richard. Personally, I don't prefer the term 'ghosts,' but you get the point," Anson replied.

"And it's messing up the universal structure because …?"

"Because everything in the universe must balance out. People cannot half-die and then half-exist. It affects things in multiple worlds."

"That's why we need your help, Simon," De Luca said. He glanced at the men at the back of the lecture hall before continuing, as if seeking permission to do so. "And you too, Richard. I think those dreams you've been having has something to do with this."

"Maybe if we can look into your dreams," Anson said to me. "We can stop them."

I watched Simon's face, my heart pounding against my chest.

"The dreams seem to be an important part of it somehow," Simon said in a quiet voice.

"What are you talking about?" I asked them.

De Luca answered, "Your dreams, Richard. They're like keys. They could help capture the defectors."

Dr. Anson frowned at me. "When Simon told me about the rituals in your dreams, I knew it had something to do with this."

Simon explained, "When this whole thing began, when these guys started their cult, I viewed where their secret meetings were being held. It's real, Richard." He looked down at his hands. "But I don't know what happened. After a while, I just couldn't see them anymore, like I was being blocked from things. Now they're in your dreams. In the ambulance, on the way to the hospital … I saw them again, like it was in your head."

"These people have become a threat to the balance of everything," Anson said. "So when Mr. De Luca contacted me about his interpretation of the transcripts, I knew he could help us."

"But we don't have a lot of time," De Luca added.

"He's right," Dr. Anson agreed. "I need to have a serious talk with you, Richard. I need you to stay in San Antonio until we can figure this whole thing out. You see," Dr. Anson said with his head down, "if you don't stay voluntarily, I might be forced to keep you here against your will. Please understand, Richard. It's almost out of my hands at this point. I'm sorry."

11

"I just want to know what's going on." I demanded. "Did you trick me into coming out here?" We were crammed into Dr. Anson's office: Simon, De Luca, Dr. Anson, and myself. I had no idea where the strange men from the back row of the lecture hall had gone, and I didn't care. My only concern at that moment was being brought up to speed on things. I wanted the truth.

Dr. Anson had offered his comfortable-looking office chair to De Luca as Simon threw himself onto a small greenish-colored sofa. I sat in some wobbly brown chair that had probably been dragged into his office for students to sit on while Anson discussed their grades or homework with them. On the small amount of floor space available, Dr. Anson took to pacing back and forth while his eyes darted from wall to wall.

"I'm going to do my best to explain things to you, Richard," Anson began. "But you need to understand that a lot of this is probably going to sound insane."

"Yeah," Simon agreed. He had removed his sling and jacket, and was messing with the bandage on his arm. "You're going to freak the fuck out."

"I am not."

An evil smile formed on Simon's face. "Yes you are. Wait and see."

"Simon, please," Anson hissed. "I still need Richard's help. Don't try to scare him off." Dr. Anson stopped pacing and sat on the edge of his desk. He placed his fingers under his chin and then ran them down to his Adam's apple in contemplation. Then he focused his eyes on me. "Richard, I really hope you'll want to stay and help us."

"I didn't think I had a choice anymore," I replied.

Anson sighed. "That's only partially true. You do have a choice. I just can't guarantee that it'll stay that way if you don't choose to help us voluntarily. And that's not the way I wanted it, but our situation has become dire. People, government people, are starting to take notice. I'm sure you can understand that they keep track of the things I do here." Dr. Anson looked away from me. "They have stepped in before and ... changed things around a little."

Simon leaned forward. "Remember those jerks in the back of the room?"

"Simon, please," Anson said to him.

I was tired, upset, and ready to leave. "No. I don't understand. That's why I'm kind of confused right now," I tried to remind him. "And, I might want a lawyer."

"I think you should start with the cult part." Simon grinned at Dr. Anson as he spoke. "Tell him how Carrol started recruiting his weirdo buddies and ghosting-out."

My eyes were probably bugged-out a little, but that didn't matter, because none of them seemed to notice. "Yes. Begin with that."

Dr. Anson studied me apprehensively. "All right then." He made himself more comfortable on the desk. "About four years ago, I taught a course on parapsychology topics ... it drew some attention from other universities, and the media. By my second semester, I was being contacted by all kinds of people. Some of them were total nuts, but one of them, a self-proclaimed psychic medium, stood out. She told me that she had some serious concerns about a man she'd met. His name was Dr. Peter Carrol. He's a Swiss researcher ... physics and psychology. Actually, she wanted to report him to the police, but wanted my opinion first. It's difficult to go to the police about something paranormal." Dr. Anson glanced over at Simon before continuing. "Her name was Marisol. And Dr. Carrol was the head researcher for the Institute of Alternative Mind Studies. The medium claimed that she had been contacted by Dr. Carrol through her website, by email, inquiring about medium services that he wanted to hire her for. He wanted her help with some séances. Carrol wanted the entire thing kept quiet and was willing to pay the medium good money for it. The medium agreed, at first."

"Until the séances began," Simon interjected.

I glanced at De Luca who was now leaning back comfortably in the nice rolling office chair. And even though it looked like he'd already heard the story before, and knew every detail of it, he was waiting very patiently for Anson to continue.

Dr. Anson smiled weakly. "Yes. The medium attended the séances, not knowing that she was actually participating in something much more serious. Carrol was ... *is* an eccentric quantum mechanics researcher. His views are not shared by many in the scientific community. He became interested in Marisol's services after she boasted on her website and in newspaper interviews about her ability to communicate with the dead. But what set her apart from other mediums was the claim that she could not only communicate with them in an auditory fashion, but also by seeing flashes of where these ghosts or spirits existed."

This piqued my interest. "Where they lived *before* they died?" I asked.

"No," Dr. Anson replied with the most serious look on his face. "Where they existed on the other side … *after* death."

Simon leaned forward, his face now close to mine. "She could see into their world. She could describe it in detail. At least, that's what she claimed. Dr. Carrol liked that."

"Yes, he did," De Luca jumped in. "Because that way, he could use her to scope things out for him before he and his associates attempted to cross over."

Dr. Anson rubbed at his chin. "Richard, Dr. Carrol was always very interested in the paranormal—obsessively interested. But he tended to drift more toward the darker side of things. He wrote a few articles on topics that incorporated his views on some alternative, and mostly unaccepted, theories that dealt with entanglement and its links to ghosts." Dr. Anson paused to read the reaction on my face before continuing. "He had hired the medium, Marisol, to participate in some experimental studies—séances to look into the other side. To collect the details that he needed for his future plans."

"To defect," Simon clarified.

De Luca smiled wide. "She said she could see the world that ghosts lived in, through their eyes."

I sat quietly, moving my eyes from face to face, waiting for one of them to begin speaking again.

"That Brunstrom guy was one of Carrol's associates," Simon added.

I turned to him. "Okay. I understand. But why? What's the point?"

Anson sighed. "They see it as a form of evolution. Carrol is convinced that future humans—purely evolved humans—will no longer need their bodies in order to exist."

"Because bodies are frail and require care and maintenance," De Luca said.

It frightened me. The thought of people intentionally becoming ghosts was difficult to understand. Questions were piling up in my head. "Why are you trying to stop them? I understand the imbalance thing, but shouldn't the government take care of this kind of thing?"

De Luca smiled at Dr. Anson.

"They are taking care of it," Anson said to me.

I nodded. "They asked for your help."

"Exactly," he answered. "Dr. Carrol is a dangerous man. He's been on the radar for years. The government believes that Carrol has convinced a small group of researchers and followers that his methods are revolutionary and that anyone associated with his research will live on as some sort of a ... scientific pioneer. He has a cult-like following." Dr. Anson took in a deep breath and his brow furrowed. "Carrol's methods are selfish and ill-conceived. He knows that by leaving the human body behind, without allowing it to die in some traditional manner, it will create a type of imbalance. But he doesn't care, Richard. He wants fame and fortune. He thinks that if he can pick and choose who crosses over, it will be all right ... that it will be under his control."

De Luca took over at this point. "Part of what they plan to do is to leave the body while the mind is in a meditative state. Similar to an out-of-body experience, but trained and perfectly disciplined exactly for the purpose of leaving the body permanently. The methods being used are ancient ... very secret. It is said that he acquired some transcripts, similar to the ones that I have, from a wealthy artifacts collector. The collector didn't understand what he had in his possession, and sold the documents for a hefty price to Carrol. The collector knew he had something unique, and extremely old, but that was about it. But Carrol knew *exactly* what he had purchased. The documents were rumored to have been stolen from somewhere in the Middle East—years ago." De Luca paused, giving me a chance to catch up a bit mentally. "They're dangerous. The whole point of keeping something hidden is so that man will not use it for the wrong purposes. But that's not what ends up happening. Man looks for things forbidden. He can't help himself. He digs and excavates … seeks relics on the black-market. Whatever Carrol's learned from those transcripts, he may be using to further his teachings."

"Like a cult," Simon reminded me in an eerie voice.

"Yes," Anson agreed. "An extremely dangerous cult due to the level of intellect involved."

Simon was nodding his head. "Brunstrom left Carrol's group months ago. You saw the state he was in. He was on his own. Probably going insane. For whatever reason, he was done waitin' on Carrol."

"Besides," De Luca said, "we think Carrol's group is planning to cross over simultaneously. Or at least in some patterned form—together. There's power in numbers. It creates more energy and a greater chance of success."

I was still a little lost, and was beginning to feel sort of stupid again. "So they're trying to become kind of like ghosts without dying. And they all want to cross over at the same time."

Anson replied, "Yes. To prove that they can, and because they believe that it will make them more powerful, immortal."

I asked, "But they'd be dead. How would that make them immortal?"

Simon nodded. "It's a different kind of dead. In between, remember?"

"Okay," I said. "I understand. It does sound crazy, but honestly, I still don't see what the big deal is. If some weirdos want to become … half-ghosts, or whatever … what does it matter?"

Anson replied, "Richard, we are not evolved enough mentally to handle something like this. If Carrol's group does this and then others discover how it can be done, it will be devastating."

Simon crossed his arms. "Imagine criminals never being caught again. They could commit a crime and then disappear. And what about terrorists?"

Anson frowned. "Also, the energy of our universe will be out of balance. We'd be able to feel it in our daily lives. The more people who cross over this way, the more unsettled the balance will become. The entire planet will be … haunted by these things."

I tried again not to look too confused. "So we would actually see a difference around us?"

"Yes," Dr. Anson replied.

"Brunstrom wasn't the first to defect, Richard," De Luca said. "The first that we know of, in modern times, was a researcher back in the 1950s named Winston. Winston was friends with the father of the man that sold Carrol the transcripts. It is said that the transcripts once belonged to Winston, and that he was able to train a few select people to become spectral beings. Witnesses, who were willing to speak to paranormal investigators at the time, said that Winston could bring ghosts into our world and also travel back and forth into theirs. Real ghosts. The ghosts of people who actually *died*."

Simon released a shaky, coffee-infused breath. "That's how Dr. Carrol got ahold of those papers?" he asked Anson.

"Wait," I wanted to clarify. "Dr. Carrol wants to do

the things this guy from the 1950s did. He purchased some ancient papers on how to do it, from the guy who was friends with the guy from the 1950s? Am I getting this right?"

"From the guy's son," Anson added.

"So what happened to Winston?" I asked.

"Good question," Anson said without making any eye contact.

De Luca smiled. "People like me have been searching for him for years. He disappeared in the 1970s."

"How did you find this stuff out? How did you know Carrol got the documents?" I was afraid to ask.

"Because the medium, Marisol, told me," Anson replied.

Simon jumped in again. "So that's why he wanted her to channel Winston." He looked almost as confused as I was.

Anson explained, "We think Dr. Carrol showed her the transcripts to convince her to help him. He wanted her to understand how historically important they were. He told her that he had to find the man that used them. So Carrol convinced Marisol to channel Winston. She said Winston spoke through her to Carrol. She said that after Carrol learned everything he needed to know from Winston, he didn't even care about the papers anymore. He got to speak to the man that had used them successfully. He learned how Winston had done it—how he had traveled to other dimensions and how he brought ghosts into ours. Dr. Carrol didn't want to make any mistakes, and whatever Winston had done, whatever methods he'd used, that's what he was going to do because all the rumors said it had worked."

"But the problem with that part is this—Winston was a Satanist," Simon said. "So how do you think he did all this shit? That's right. He did it evil-style."

Dr. Anson shook his head. "But Carrol isn't doing it exactly the same way. He can infuse his own methods into it."

It was unsettling. "So are the transcripts *evil?*"

De Luca jumped in. "The papers can be used by anyone, no matter what their beliefs are. Which is why they shouldn't be used at all. If Carrol is trying to copy Winston, he's only doing it to ensure success."

"Let's not get ahead of ourselves," Anson announced with his hands out in front of him. "This is a lot of information to give Richard at once."

"Now you know how I felt when I was told this stuff," Simon said to me with a yawn. "You get used to it, though, Richie. At least they keep things interesting around here."

Dr. Anson turned to Simon and smiled, his eyes crinkling.

Simon smiled back at him. "What?"

"We need to have a talk about your side job with the police department," Anson replied.

"Uh ... what?" Simon jolted up in his seat. "I don't really know what you're ... I thought we were talkin' to Richard about his dreams or somethin'."

Anson turned back to me. "We'll discuss more with Richard later. I think he needs a break. I'm sure he's started putting some things together on his own about what's going on ... and why we need his help."

I sat there, slowly shaking my head. It was beginning to sink in. My mind was connecting the dots, but it was still unbelievable to me. The ritual in my dreams—maybe it was this Peter Carrol guy. Everything these men were telling me seemed to fit, even if it didn't make complete sense to me. The things I'd seen—the beings, phantoms, or whatever—they were evil. There was no doubt about that. I didn't care how they got here, I just wanted them to stop. I wanted them out of my head.

"It's Peter Carrol that you're dreaming about, isn't it, Richard?" Anson asked me.

He must have read it on my face. "Yes, I'm pretty sure it is." It felt so uncomfortable admitting it. "And the ghosts ... or demons, in my dreams. They are from, like, different times and places. I don't know how to explain it."

"Do you know why you're seeing these things?" he asked. There was excitement in his voice. I knew he was doing what he could to mask it, to be more professional, but it was there.

"No."

Dr. Anson rubbed his hands together nervously. "Your dreams are a window into his madness. Please, Richard. We need your help."

12

The coffee place.

I didn't want to go straight back to the hotel. There was a bed there. A bed that I was supposed to fall asleep in at some point. That frightened me. Instead, I asked Simon if he wanted to get some coffee. At first, he looked at me like I was joking, but I wasn't. So from the university, he drove us to this coffee place a few blocks from my hotel. It looked nicer on the outside than it did on the inside.

I wanted a booth with some privacy, away from other customers. I needed a few more answers.

As I took my seat at the booth, I hesitated when I noticed the dead bugs underneath it.

"Not nice enough for you?" Simon asked when he saw the look on my face.

It was one of those situations in which you want to seem all right with things, things that you aren't actually all right with, so you wouldn't get criticized for it. Normally, I would've walked right out of the place. But Simon had some strange influence over me, some sadistic power. I didn't want him to think I was too high-class. I was a regular guy, too. I didn't know why I let him get to me like that, but I did.

"It's a dump, but the coffee's good," he said. He opened a filthy menu and strained his eyes to read it. "You orderin' anything?"

"Why are my dreams so important in all of this? I don't even know how to control them."

"Key lime pie," he answered.

I sighed in frustration, pushing my menu aside.

"Anson thinks your dreams are coming to you like a radio signal. He doesn't know why, though. Maybe it's another way nature tries to balance things out. You might be getting some type of an S.O.S. message on some universal level that we don't understand. Something we can use to help stop Carrol."

"How's that supposed to stop him? I can't even figure out what I'm dreaming about?"

Simon didn't look away from his menu as he turned to the next page. "You can see the ritual itself, right?"

"Yes. Well, I can remember bits of it and I hear some things …"

"I didn't get it at first either, but that has to be why Miller … Dr. Anson, brought in De Loco." Simon laughed at his own joke. He stopped when he noticed that it wasn't very funny to me. "If De Luca can decipher the rituals you're seeing, then maybe we can figure out a way to counteract them with those transcripts he has. Whatever details you can see … symbols, clothing … any of it. You know what I mean?"

It was actually the smartest thing I'd heard Simon say since I'd met him. The idea was sort of brilliant. "Wow. Yeah. That would make sense."

"So the things you can see, you can describe them in detail?"

"Yes."

Simon slammed his fist on the table. "Man! That's fuckin' cool!"

I looked around for a waitress. "Not really. It's pretty unsettling when it happens. I don't enjoy dreaming about demons and rituals."

"Well, yeah, but you're gifted, man! That's a very powerful skill."

"I don't know. I guess my dreams have always been intense. It's kind of helped me in my writing, the way I describe things. I think of writing as my actual skill ... not so much the dreaming thing."

"I flipped through one of your books," Simon scoffed. "Dreaming is your skill."

I tried not to show any sort of a reaction to what he'd said and ignored the insult, considering the source. "But I still don't understand why you can't just view the rituals without me."

"I told you. They blocked me or somethin'. Maybe they could feel an intruder there. I don't see things in detail like that anyway. It's more for finding stuff. When I see things, it looks kinda vague. I don't hear anything when I see things from a distance. I can hear things sometimes, things around us, like ghosts, but not when I'm trying to view things that aren't around me."

It was true that in these dreams, I could see vivid details. The dreams felt real and extra colorful. It was almost like I was awake inside them, experiencing something magical and surreal. But it was terrifying.

Simon thought on it for a moment with heavy creases on his forehead. "You didn't know the ritual you were seeing was Satanic? Goddamn, who's gonna take our order?"

"No, I just get confused in the dreams. There's a lot of other things that happens in them sometimes. It's hard to focus. Like, when I see the ghosts in them, they're really distracting. I stop focusing on the other things when I see those around me."

"You just need help learnin' to control it." Simon

looked out the window and into the busy street. Vehicles swished back and forth, their lights streaking past us in the darkness. He focused on a pedestrian in a trench coat and twisted his lips. His thoughts looked distant.

A lady approached our table.

"Oh, here's someone," Simon grumbled. "I guess this place *is* open."

"Hi. What can I get you?" the woman asked dryly. She was hunched over, holding a small notepad. She had it pushed up so close to her face that it looked like she was going to poke herself in the eye with the pen she was using.

We both ordered coffees. Simon's black and mine with creamer. Three of them because I always did it that way.

"I thought you wanted a piece of pie?" I reminded him.

"I do, but I can get it later. Maybe to go."

"Oh."

His eyes shifted to the window again and the distant look returned.

"What's up?" I asked.

"Well, Anson's pissed off at me. I don't know. I guess I feel kinda bad."

"For what?" I pretended not to know. But I knew it had something to do with his crime-solving gig.

Simon ran a finger across the table and into some sugar that had been left there.

"I did some work for the PD. Psychic work. I wasn't supposed to."

The woman then returned with our coffees.

"Oh."

She set them down and we waited for her to leave.

"Yeah. Anson's pissed 'cause he says if I do any kind of work like that it puts his project in jeopardy."

I shifted in my seat a bit. "I mean, I can kinda see why he said that. If you think about it from his perspective … all the money involved and—"

Simon crouched down slightly and leaned in across the table, lowering his voice before speaking. "Yeah, but I helped the cops find a few killers. That's serious shit, Richard. Like a good deed for society."

I stared into his bugged-out eyes, understanding instantly how important and accomplished it must have made Simon feel to use his talent for something more rewarding than sitting through monotonous experiments in a lab. But I doubted something about his intentions with it, even though I really wanted to believe in him at that moment. "And I bet it pays well, too."

Simon sat up a bit and his face hardened. "Fuck the pay."

I held my breath, feeling his anger. I could see the passion in his eyes—it was real. He really *was* trying to help people.

"It's the only thing I've ever done that's mattered."

"I'm sorry. I didn't mean to say it like that."

He studied my face and relaxed his shoulders. "It's okay. I don't care about things like money. How are you supposed to know that? You hardly know me."

"Shit," I said with a sigh.

"What?"

"Nothing." I just couldn't tell him. I couldn't admit that I'd sold him out. And maybe I'd done the right thing by doing so, but either way, I felt like a jerk, good intentions or not.

"I was kinda in the middle of a case, too," he said.

I was biting the sides of my tongue. I wasn't good at hiding things from people. "Oh man. That sucks. What kind of a case was it?"

Simon slammed his fist on the table. "WHY'D YOU TELL HIM?!"

The café went silent.

"I'm sorry! Some cop-lady came to my hotel room and started asking all these questions! What the hell was I supposed to do?!"

"You should have told *me*, not Anson!"

"You were still in the hospital!" I was pretty sure that everyone in the coffee house was staring, but my eyes stayed on Simon, too scared to check.

"Do you hate me that much?" Simon asked calmly. He tilted his head and looked me squarely in the eyes.

"No. I just ... how did you find out? Did Anson tell you that I told him?"

"Are you fuckin' serious?!"

"Uh ..."

"I'M PSYCHIC! I FUCKIN' KNOW YOU TOLD HIM! YOU'RE BLEEDIN' IT OUT ALL OVER THE PLACE!" Simon stood abruptly, his chest heaving. His eyes darted nervously around the room after realizing how loud his outburst had been. "Great. Now everyone is staring at me."

"At *us*."

"Sorry." His head and chest sank low. "Man, I can't believe you did that. You messed up a lot of shit for me."

"Let's just pay and get out of here," I suggested. I waved over the lady who'd taken our order and did what I could to ignore everyone's stares.

Simon sifted through the pockets of his trench coat, looking for his keys. "I thought once you realized that you were like me, you'd stop being so cold and judgmental."

The server hurried over and dropped the ticket on the table without looking at us.

"I'm not judging you. You're the one who's been cold and judgmental."

"You told Anson because you think I'm just some sideshow freak that doesn't deserve to be psychic."

"That's not true. People don't choose to be psychic. They just are. I don't judge you for that."

"Liar." He scowled at me as he snatched the ticket from the table. He clenched it in a tight fist. "You think I'm trash. You think I don't deserve to see the things I see."

I wanted out of there. I was thoroughly embarrassed. "That's not true."

"Yes it is."

Everyone was now pretending not to stare, but they were. One guy was even using a crinkled up magazine to help shield his face while he did it.

"I do deserve it, Richard. I was meant to do this. I wouldn't wish it on anyone, either. How could I wish for anyone to see the things I see? Would you wish your dreams—your nightmares—on anyone else? They couldn't handle it, could they? And you know it, too."

I slid out of the booth and held my hand out to him. "Here, give me the ticket. I'll pay—"

"You *can't* pay. I have to pay with Anson's card, *remember?*" he snarled. "They own me. They own *us.*"

13

The ride back to the hotel in Simon's car would have been too awkward, so I decided to walk. I tried waiting for him outside while he paid for our coffee, but he took forever. I paced around in the cold, wishing he would hurry. And when I looked through the front window to check on him, he wasn't there. I figured he was probably in the restroom, and it didn't matter to me anyway—I was ready to leave him there and head back to the hotel on foot. It was my fault anyway. I shouldn't have rode with him that day.

About an hour after I got to my room, my cell phone rang. Of course, it was a pissed-off Simon.

"Yeah?"

"How long did it take you to get back?" he asked without any emotion.

"Five minutes?"

"Oh."

I was tired and in bed, ready to get some sleep. "What's up?"

"Anson wants us to investigate somethin' tomorrow morning. Forgot to tell you at the coffee shop."

"Well," I said as I propped myself up with my elbow, "I don't have a choice. I have to go where you tell me to, right? So when and where?"

"You don't have to do anything you don't want to. It's your life. You're the one that has to suffer the nightmares, and you can keep on havin' them if that's what you want.

I just know that being involved with Anson's studies helped me. And if you take off back to L.A., it's not Anson that will be after you. It's bigger than him now. So you might as well stay and help us straighten some shit out."

I was gritting my teeth. "What time?"

"Tomorrow morning, 9 a.m., at the lab."

"Okay, fine. I'll be there. And I'm driving myself. Don't pick me up."

"'Night, sweetie," he said sarcastically before ending the call.

The next morning.

"What are we doing?" I asked after about five minutes of silence. My stomach was rumbling. I pulled a chair away from the table Simon was at and set it against the wall furthest away from him. I guess I was trying to make a point about something, about not wanting to be there. But it wasn't working. Simon had fallen half-asleep, his head flat on the table.

"Simon?"

"What?" he answered groggily.

"What are we waiting around for?"

"Anson," he moaned.

"What are we doing when he gets here?" I was completely irritated. Every single thing about being there annoyed me; the blank walls, the "hidden" camera in the corner near the ceiling, the fluorescent lighting that didn't seem appropriate.

"I don't know. Let me sleep."

"Oh my God." I stood and headed toward the door.

"*Please have a seat, Mr. Ravestone,*" an unfamiliar voice said over the speaker system.

I stopped and smiled at the camera. "Great."

"Yeah. Sit down," Simon grumbled. "You're not goin' anywhere. They won't let you."

Reluctantly, and because I was slightly freaked out by the voice I'd just heard, I walked back to my seat. "I'm only staying five more minutes."

"And then what?"

"Then I'm leaving."

"I used to think that, too." Simon yawned. "Just get used to it. You need them and they need you. What's going on back home? You got a chick there?"

I didn't know why I bothered to answer. "Women don't like being called 'chicks.' And, no, I don't right now. Women tend to get in the way of my writing."

"And they get in the way of seeing other women," Simon chuckled.

Dr. Anson walked in and nodded at me. "Hello, Richard. Good to see you." He kicked a leg on Simon's chair, jolting him upright.

Dr. Anson was in a simple pair of gray slacks and a white button up shirt, his sleeves rolled up a bit. He looked tired. He rubbed his hands together and took in a long breath. "All right. We're going to begin."

"Rich doesn't know why he's here," Simon said as if complaining about it.

Dr. Anson had a guilty look on his face. "That's because I didn't really have a plan for what we were going to do until about five minutes ago," he answered nervously.

Simon rubbed his face with his hands. "He was tryin' to escape. I stopped him."

"Escape?" Dr. Anson repeated with concern.

"What? Come on, Simon!" I snapped nervously.

Simon looked at Anson and said, "I was going to tell

him about how you guys make sure to lock the doors and stuff, but the guy on the speaker told him to sit down, so …"

Dr. Anson laughed in return. "Simon, please. Escape … very funny. Richard, the door wasn't locked. I'm sorry it took so long for me to get down here. I had a meeting in my office and … I'm behind on a few things. I have to juggle this project with students and lectures … I'm a mess right now."

"It's all right," I replied. But I was ready to get to the point. "What are we about to do here?"

Anson shifted his eyes between mine and the back of Simon's head. He looked like he was about to cringe, but then stopped himself. "We are going to have you describe your dream, the one with Dr. Carrol in it, to Simon."

"But I've already seen it," Simon replied. "Sort of."

"You've seen flashes of it … while you were medicated at the hospital. He needs to tell you about it in detail." Anson took a few steps closer to Simon and crouched down to get a better look at his face, and, I think, to show some authority. "Specific details."

"What for?" Simon huffed in return.

"So you can retro-view what's happening in his dreams."

"Oh. Okay."

Dr. Anson turned to me and smiled. "I would like you to lead him through the dream step by step."

Simon sat up with excitement. "Cool. I've never done anything like that."

"Which dream?" I asked. "I've had a few that are kind of similar?"

"Whichever one is the most vivid in your memory," Anson requested.

Simon leaned back in his seat and yawned. "As long as

you describe it to me as it happened, I should be able to see into it—like it's really happening again."

Anson nodded. "He should be able to follow along and try to grab onto that moment, to see it like you do. Our goal here is to see if he can pick up on some things that you might have missed while you were dreaming. A different perspective. Simon does more of an undisciplined version of seeing things, which can really help us in situations like this. Just try to use as much detail as possible so he can travel mentally into your dream. And as you think about it, try to *feel* it. All right?"

I nodded in agreement since I really didn't know how else to respond.

Anson shrugged his shoulders. "And that's it. Making plans around here doesn't really work. Guidelines, rules … we get better results without them. This isn't a strict program like others you've probably read about. And we'll be keeping this below radar, anyway. If you know what I mean."

"All right," I said. "How do I begin?"

"You'll just describe your dream and lead him through what you've seen. In order."

I respectfully, and robotically, nodded again in agreement. Unorthodox methods were okay with me, as long as it was being done off the record. Even though the parapsychological community seemed to be at odds with itself most of the time, I still didn't want my name attached to any experiments that might be considered dangerous or controversial. That's what *not* following the rules meant in this business—danger.

"What about De Luca?" Simon asked Anson. "You trust him?"

Anson paused to think. "I have to take his word that he'll be discreet about what he's involved with here."

I asked, "What if he's in it to make a name for himself?" I wasn't sure if De Luca was watching through a camera in another room. "No offense to him, but you'd be risking a lot if he was."

"Yes, I would be. But we've got a serious problem to deal with, and I need his help. Almost as much as I need yours, Richard."

It would have been stupid of me not to admit that I'd become emotionally entwined in the project at this point. My thoughts of booking a flight back home had ended the night before—even after the embarrassing coffee house incident. The nightmares that had plagued me for weeks were about to be … analyzed, I guess. And even if they weren't being sifted through by a psychiatric professional in some clinical setting, at least someone was interested in them. This group wanted to hear about my dreams because they took them seriously. It couldn't possibly make them any worse, could it? And then a sudden concern struck me. What if Simon couldn't handle what he was about to see in my head?

"Are you ready to begin, Richard?" Anson asked.

"Yes," I replied hesitantly. "I guess I'll describe a dream with a lot of ritual stuff in it. Some have more than others." I looked at Simon and wondered if he'd ever even tried to see inside another person's dreams before. There was a part of me that feared it to be awkwardly intrusive on so many levels.

"Don't worry, Richard," Simon said to me with a wicked grin. "You'll be okay."

14

The séance.

"Everyone is quiet," I said to Simon. He sat across from me at the rectangular table. The top of the table was made to look like wood, but it was something else. Something cheap that reminded me of the 1980s. When I used to visit my dad at work as a kid, I would see tables like that. "The lights are off. There's a candle."

Minutes earlier, Dr. Anson had left the room and assured us that he'd be watching through the camera. He'd be listening closely, as well. Simon lowered his head when he was ready and started sinking into himself—going into his own mind so that he could travel outside it.

"Do I just keep going?" I whispered nervously.

Simon remained still, breathing shallow and slow. I glanced up into the camera in the corner. I wanted the scary voice to break in and give me instructions, but there was only silence.

So I turned back to face Simon and continued. "Okay. Uh … there are … six of them. They're all dressed in black. There's a man standing in front of them, like he's in charge of things, with a book in his hands. He's facing the rest of them. There's a large window behind him. I can see the city through the window. It's night."

"Think about how the city looks," Simon murmured softly.

"Okay." I sat there, watching Simon's eyes flickering

and his hands shaking, and focused on the memory of the unfamiliar city skyline in my mind. I remembered the shapes, the tops of buildings, the large antennas sticking out of them, and even watched an airplane float across the sky.

"Okay," Simon said in a shaky breath.

"Okay. Can you see it?"

"Yes. Just keep going."

"They're on the floor—the others. One is a woman, she's at the opposite end of the leader, farthest away. There are four men facing each other, two on each side … I don't know how to describe it. It's like they're sitting at a large table, but there's no table and they're on the floor."

"What are they wearing?" Simon asked.

I thought I'd already told him. "Black. They're all wearing black."

"Black what?"

The question caught me off guard. "Um … black pants and shirts. Dress shirts. The men are wearing suits and the woman—"

"The woman wears a dress," he interrupted softly. "Describe the leader."

Yes. He could see them, and he was right. She *was* wearing a dress. And there was something different about the leader. The man at the head of this group, holding the book, was a person that I would divert my eyes from while dreaming about him. I had a deep fear of him, almost as if my eyes were being pushed away from his direction—not allowing me to see something. This was the man I suspected to be Dr. Carrol. "It's difficult."

"I know."

I did what I could to focus. I could see the man's shining eyes behind an intense darkness that surrounded his face—but I couldn't see his hair, only a blur instead.

"Richard, you have to describe him to me."

"I know. I'm sorry."

"We have to be sure it's Carrol." Simon's voice was soft but raspy, and his words drawn out slowly.

I shut my eyes. He was there, standing with his back to the large window. Outside, the electric lights of endless buildings twinkled.

He was gripping a closed book with both hands as the rest of them waited for him to speak. They feared him. I could see the face of one of the men that was kneeling on the floor, watching with fearful anticipation, waiting for the man with the book to speak to them. They were as afraid to look at him as I was.

"Then there's a bell," I told Simon.

"Like a doorbell?"

"No. Like a chime. *Ding.*"

He frowned. "Look at the man."

"I'm trying to remember him."

"No, look at the man. Now. In your head. Stop trying to remember, just look."

I closed my eyes and did what he told me. I felt myself push through a murky fog to turn my head and face the man, the man surrounded by darkness. I felt my jaw tighten and the tingling spikes of numbness shooting through my face.

"What color is his hair?" Simon asked.

"I can't see it. It's covered with—" I gasped, "a hood." I'd never seen that part before.

"Yes."

I opened my eyes to see Simon nodding. "He is like a dark priest," he whispered. "I see him in your head. It's Carrol."

A sharp chill went through me. Simon was validating

something, something I had never wished to possess— my dreams contained pieces of reality. A real person, a person I didn't know, was inside my dreams. Someone horrible.

Simon continued. "The people on the floor … are afraid." His breaths were heavy.

"Yes," I agreed.

"The white candle … is in the center of them."

"Yes."

"Tell me what happens next," he instructed.

"Okay. The man starts speaking, but I don't understand what he says because in the dream, I'm afraid, and I tune it out. The people then close their eyes, except for the lady—"

"Describe her."

"Well, she's pretty. I think she's in her 30s. I can't tell … I'm not very good at guessing people's age—"

"*Fuck*, Richard. Just describe her."

"She's not wearing black."

Simon smiled, but kept his eyes closed. "You see that now. But you didn't see it before, did you?"

He was right. "No, I didn't. But I can now. It's red. It's a flowy dress … kind of soft-looking. Her makeup is dark around the eyes. Red lipstick."

"Carrol is attracted to her," Simon added.

"Yes. But she's afraid."

Simon's head tilted and his forehead started to crease. "Because she's noticed … the inverted pentagram on the floor … in the middle of where they sit."

"Oh my God." I let out a shallow breath. "It's a satanic ritual."

I knew that pentagrams weren't evil. I knew about their true origin—but I also knew how they had been misused and misrepresented by people.

"I don't know for sure. Keep going." His voice remained calm and monotone.

I shut my eyes tight. I could see the pentagram on the floor and wondered why I hadn't seen it before. "She's more frightened than the others. It's because she thinks they might hurt her. And it's about now in the dream that I start to think she can sense my presence. It feels like I'm actually there and I think she can sort of see me. So I back away from them, and her eyes follow me."

Simon opened his eyes and locked them onto mine. "Yes. She *can* see you."

I could feel my throat begin to tighten. Simon's ability to feel and be inside a dream that I was describing, to see what I saw, with such accuracy, without fear, was incredible. "And then, there's a noise. And Carrol starts speaking louder."

"He's reading from the book. He's excited. He's reading ... with strong emotion ... he's ... like he's conducting something." Simon's shoulders tensed, his robotic, intrusive stare on me, stronger than before.

"Something else is in the room now."

"Where?" Simon asked in an intense whisper. "I don't see it."

"It's in a corner. Way back. Behind them. This room is so large ..." A chill shook me. The massive size of the room was helping hide things within it. "It looks like a ghost, but ... gray. Dark gray. Almost black."

"Like a misty, thick shadow."

"Yeah!" I agreed.

"I can almost see it ... not clearly," Simon said. "But I can feel it. It feels dark and cold."

I didn't want to disappoint them, but the dream's description was about to end. I knew that I could go back and be a little more detailed in my walk-through, but as

Dr. Anson had said to us before leaving the room—this was just a test run. I would get better at it with time, if I wanted to.

Simon closed his eyes again. "Do you think Carrol knows about the ghost in the room?"

"I think he does."

"What happens next?"

I hesitated. "Well, then the woman stands up to leave, but one of the men next to her … to her right, grabs her arm." It was hard to replay these things in my head. I was afraid for the woman. This was the worst part of the dream for me. She was trapped, like I was, but I was certain that they could actually hurt her, and I wasn't too sure about what they could do to me or if they even knew I was there watching them. "She yells at Carrol. She says, 'Let me go!' and starts crying and trying to pull her arm away. The man holding her arm stays perfectly in place. He's still kneeling and bowing his head down, not even looking at her as she fights him. He has a strong grip on her arm … she's like a rag doll."

"She fears for her life," Simon added.

My mouth was dry and my throat felt like it was closing. "Yes. And she's looking at me. She starts yelling … for me to help her."

"Carrol?" Simon wanted to know what he was doing.

"I try not to look at him, but I can feel him. He's trying to see me. Because of the woman. He knows the woman can see me because she's turning back to beg me for help. Carrol's still chanting. He's louder than before because the woman is yelling."

Simon frowned. "There's a lot of activity in this room. A lot of emotion."

"Then I force myself to wake up." I felt terrible for saying it. "Sorry."

Simon flinched and kind of shook himself awake before looking at me with raised eyebrows. "What?"

"That's where it ends."

"No it isn't."

"Yes. It is."

"No, that's where you *choose* for it to end. The next time you have that dream, you need to pay more attention and stay in it longer so we can figure some more things out," Simon demanded.

"Why can't you guys just ask the woman from the dream? Dr. Anson said she went to him after—"

"That was over a year ago. This dream is all we have."

"Then how do you know it's the same woman?"

The door suddenly flew open. "Simon, you did very well. You too, Richard. I am very impressed."

I had to ask, "Dr. Anson, why can't you just ask the woman—the medium—about some of the details? I know she's probably afraid, but maybe you could convince her to—"

"She's dead." Simon's voice was cold and flat.

I was stunned. A form of guilt that I can't explain, the kind that tingles through your veins like ice, rushed through me and numbed my face. "*What?*"

"Simon," Dr. Anson said with disappointment and a heavy sigh. "Why didn't you let me tell him? You heard the way he described the dream. He feels like he knows her. You must be more sensitive in matters like this."

Simon diverted his eyes from me and brought them down to the table between us. "That's the case I was working on with the PD."

It was like a dagger, and it stung hard.

I looked at Anson, who was now staring at the back of Simon's head. "We'll talk about this later."

Simon looked at me again. "Fine."

"We'll go over this session and the—" Dr. Anson stopped and his face lit up. He walked up to Simon and touched the back of his shoulder. "Could you see the skyline that Richard was telling you about through the window?"

"Yes," he answered flatly.

"Could you draw the buildings? Their shapes? So we can try to locate where this ritual took place?"

"I don't have to draw the skyline. I know exactly where it took place," Simon answered confidently. "I was just there."

"Perfect!" Anson cried out.

Simon sank further into his seat. "I have a migraine."

"Yes, of course. We'll get your muscle relaxer." Anson turned to the camera in the corner and made some hand gestures into it that could have somehow made sense to someone watching on the other side of it, then spun back around to face me. "See, Richard? Isn't this exciting? Your dream is helping us!"

"Yes," I replied while watching Simon massage the sides of his head. "I feel a lot better now," I lied.

She's dead.

15

Later that night.

My cell phone rang at about 8 p.m. I was either in the bathroom, or I just didn't hear it for some reason. But at about 8:32, it rang again.

"Hello?"

"Hi," a woman's voice said. "I'm sorry to bother you, but I really need to talk to you about Simon."

I had to think for a few seconds. "Who is this?"

"It's Claire Sandoval. I was at your hotel the other day after Simon was shot."

"Oh. Yes, okay."

"I don't want you to think of me as a pest or anything, but ... he wouldn't answer my calls." Her speech was rapid and flustered.

"I don't know anything about the work he was doing with you and the PD, so ..."

"Please, Mr. Ravestone," her voice cracked as she spoke. "I already sent one of our guys to his house. He's not answering. And I'm worried."

I couldn't help but sigh into the phone. "Look, I saw him this morning. He's fine."

"Yes, I know you did. I followed you. I saw you guys walking out of the university together and get into your cars."

I was kind of angry upon hearing this. Other people seemed to have more control over my life than I did.

"What?"

"You think we just fuck around over here at the police department and drink coffee, don't you? Simon and I were in the middle of a really important case, and now he's not answering my calls. When people working on a case start avoiding you, you go looking for them and try to figure out what happened to them."

I was stunned. *Now* she sounded like a cop.

"Could you please give Simon a message?" she whined.

"I don't know if I should."

"Are you being serious?" Now her tone was angry.

"The reason he's avoiding you is because he's not supposed to be helping you." I was explaining what I thought was obvious at that point.

"Listen," she proceeded to say, more calmly. "I'm a rookie. I'm the one that talked Simon into helping our detectives. I was trying to score some points with the department. I'm not going to lie about it. You know what I mean?"

It was starting to make more sense. The persistence, the aggressiveness … "Yeah."

"I met him at a burger place and we started talking."

"The burger place near those apartments where he was shot?"

"Yes! Exactly!"

I laughed.

"Anyway, he was a little flirty. I don't think he expected me to keep talking to him after I turned him down a few times, but I did. He seemed interesting … a little pathetic. Plus, I thought it was a little ballsy that he was hitting on me while I was in uniform … most guys tend to back away from that pretty quick. And he said something that really struck me." She paused.

"What did he say?"

"He was talking about the way I was pulling the edges off my hamburger bun. He didn't ask me why I was doing it, he just said that I didn't need to worry about my figure … and that my grandmother only said that stuff because she loves me."

"I don't understand."

"My grandmother used to tell me to pull the extra bread off the hamburger buns. She said it would make me fat. So I was sitting there in front of Simon piling little pieces of bread on top of the wrapper."

"Okay."

"I asked him, 'How did you know that?' and I started tearing up a little because my grandmother's gone now. And he said, 'I don't know, I was just saying that,' like he was embarrassed and trying to brush it off or take it back, but I knew that he'd read my mind, because I was thinking about her. I was thinking about her smile while I was pulling off the edges of the bun." She was talking so fast that the words ran together. "Please, Richard. Please tell him to call me or meet with me. You don't understand how important this is."

I sat there silently, tuning out the annoying commercial that blared from the television in front of me. I could hear her trying to slow her breathing. There was guilt still inside me—the guilt that came from telling Anson about Simon's connection with the police.

"Richard?" she said softly.

"Yeah, I'm here."

"I'm not crazy. I know I sound crazy, but I'm not."

"I know," I said, even though I really didn't know. I had to hope that she was sane since she carried a gun to work and had my phone number. "I'll call him."

"Thank you!"

"Maybe we can all meet up someplace." I was definitely curious about what was going on.

"Maybe tonight?" she asked sweetly.

"Oh. That might be a little too soon ..."

"Can you at least try? It's really important."

I answered without thinking it through. "Okay, I'll call him now."

"Great! You can call or text me back at this number. Try to get him to meet with us in about an hour. There's lots of bars near your hotel."

I closed my eyes, regretting my offer to help. "Okay."

She ended the call. I sat on the edge of the not-so-comfortable-anymore bed and stared through whatever was happening on the television. It was almost 8:40. If Simon wasn't already drunk by now, I figured it would be a fucking miracle. So I dialed his number.

"What's up?" he answered after only one ring.

"Wanna meet up for a drink?"

"I don't know. Why?" He was onto me.

"Can you tell me exactly why Anson doesn't want you helping the cops?" I asked.

"I guess because it's a security risk to the program?"

"It's not because it's dangerous, right?"

"Dangerous?" Simon asked. "What do you mean?"

"I mean, like, if you tell people what you see, is there some information that could ... harm someone, because they know something that they shouldn't? Like, then it ends up destroying them or the universe...?"

"I don't know," Simon laughed. "That all sounds a little too science fiction to me."

Again, I had to try to believe that someone I thought might be crazy, wasn't. "Claire called me."

"Shit. She's been callin' me all day."

"Let's meet her for a drink and talk."

"Are you settin' me up? To get me in trouble with Anson again?"

"No. I want you to help the police. I'm not going to tell Anson."

I reached across the bed to grab the remote control for the television. It was folded into the sheets, but I saw that telltale bump. I pressed the mute button. In the silence, I waited for Simon's answer. The distrust he had in me was expected and deserved.

"Okay, man. But you gotta keep your word," he warned. "Because that lady, Marisol, when they called me to help, they *told me* she was shredded, man. But you know what, Rich? She wasn't. They were fuckin' with me to test me out, you know? It was worse than that. She was done worse than that. All right? So can I trust you? You'll keep your word?"

All I wanted to do was not hear what Simon had just said to me, because now it echoed in my head. *Shredded.* What could be worse than that? "Yes, I promise."

16

Our meeting with Claire.

Simon and I drove to the bar together. He insisted on picking me up in his truck instead of meeting me there. It was an obvious sign of nervousness, that he didn't want to drive alone, but I didn't dare mention that to him. Then again, maybe he wanted to read my mind on the way over. Either way, I agreed to let him pick me up.

When we walked in, I recognized the song that was playing in the bar. Of course, I couldn't remember the name of the song or the band, and that kind of bothered me. Once inside, Simon's nervousness seemed to subside a little. He was comfortable enough to take the lead, actually pushing past me as we moved in between tightly packed tables and chairs, scanning the place to see if Claire had already taken a seat somewhere. It was crammed. Most everyone was involved in a conversation or staring at one of the televisions on the walls.

"What time is it?" Simon asked me.

I looked at my phone to check. "9:36. She said 9:45ish."

"*Ish?*"

"Yeah … oh, there she is, I think."

A woman was waving at us from a booth in the back.

"Yeah, that's her," Simon confirmed.

We made our way to the booth and Simon motioned for a waitress to meet us there.

"Hi," Claire said enthusiastically. "I'm glad you were both able to make it. How's your arm, Simon?"

His cheeks flushed a little. "I'm fine. Just a bandage on it. No big deal."

I slid into the booth on the opposite side of Claire, thinking that Simon would do the same, but he was already cramming himself into Claire's side. I shook my head at him.

Simon gazed into Claire's beer and said to it, "I'm sorry I didn't call you back, Claire." He was using a nice voice that I hadn't heard him use before. "It's just that … I'm not supposed to be helping you guys. I want to, but I can't."

"We're so close to solving it. I just know it." Her voice was strained.

Our waitress approached.

Simon raised a finger into the air. "I'll take a bourbon on ice," then he pointed at me, "and this guy wants a glass of wine."

"Do you have a cabernet?" I asked, trying not to be too specific and hoping for the best.

"Red or white?"

I smiled. "Red, please." *Finally.*

Claire ran a finger along the rim of her glass. She was drinking a honey-colored beer, and this time, she had makeup on. Her hair was pulled back. And she looked much softer than before. "Detective Trevino is really pissed off at me."

"Why?" Simon asked her.

"Because I'm the one that brought you into all of this!" she said.

"It's not my fault, Claire. Dr. Anson won't let me help because I'm supposed to be, like, a secret." He looked across the table and shrugged his shoulders at me. "I don't know how to explain it. I want to help, but I'm not supposed to."

"That doesn't make any sense," Claire replied. "You've helped us before. And other departments, too, right?"

Simon looked at me, waiting for my reaction. "What, Rich?" he asked. "Just say it."

So I did. "You've helped *other* departments?"

"Yeah," he answered defensively. "Only a few. Like that situation in Oklahoma … stuff just happens sometimes."

"What situation in Oklahoma?" Claire asked.

"Don't worry about it," Simon answered.

She sat back in her seat with concern on her face. "I'm dead."

"Wait," I said, "the case you're working on … Anson knew it had to do with that medium, right?"

Simon twisted his lips. "Yeah."

"How much does he know about this?" Claire asked Simon while pointing at me. "You didn't tell him everything, did you?"

"He knows because he saw her when she was alive."

"*He did?!*" She leaned in across the table and stared wide-eyed at me. "When?"

"I don't want to get involved with the case, Simon," I tried to explain.

Simon leaned over the table. "Then why are we here?" he asked bluntly.

"Because Claire called me and asked me to bring you here."

"And you brought me here because you want me to help find out what happened to Marisol," Simon replied.

In Claire's eyes, I could see hope. "Did you really see her?"

I didn't want to answer. It felt too intrusive and I

hadn't expected Simon to bring me into it like that. "I don't think I'm allowed to talk about it."

"Fuck," Simon sighed.

I was irritated. "What, Simon?"

His mood instantly soured. "I don't know. Never mind. Where's my fucking drink?" He turned to search for the waitress for a few seconds before giving up. "You can't talk about it, I can't talk about it, everything is off-limits … what the hell are we doing here?"

In Claire's face, I could see her trying to contain her emotions. She looked at me with glassy eyes. "If you know *anything* about the case, please help us. We have to find out who did this to her."

Simon pointed at me. "He's the one that told on me," he mentioned dryly. Then he smirked at me. "That's why I can't help you guys anymore. Richie ratted me out."

"*What?*" Claire snapped.

"I didn't know he was helping with *this* case," I quickly explained. "He wasn't supposed to be helping with *any* cases. I was just trying to help Anson protect his project. How was I supposed to know what was going on?"

Simon practically lunged across the table at me. "You shoulda asked me!"

Claire pulled Simon back by his coat. "Stop! Don't make a scene. Let's just figure something out. All right?"

Simon's eyes met mine. They were vicious. "Yeah," he began, "I'm gonna help. And this time, Rich is gonna stay out of it, aren't you?"

He was waiting for me to agree to something that I knew I shouldn't agree to. It sounded more like a threat. "What do you want me to say, huh? You want me to look the other way while you help them?" I asked.

"Yeah," he answered with a nod.

"What if … now listen to me … what if Dr. Anson

doesn't want you to help because it's dangerous?"

Simon blinked sarcastically at me. "What the fuck are you talkin' about?"

"I've researched some of the strangest stuff in the world. I can promise you that. You think Anson was the first government-connected type to ever contact me?"

Simon shrugged.

"No, he wasn't," I answered. "I get strange emails and weird phone calls all the time. Anything I've written about related to anything paranormal becomes really popular, you know? Even though it's fiction."

"No, I don't."

"I do," Claire said. "I follow your work."

"Okay." I smiled. "So you know I try to develop my stories so that they have an accurate feel to them."

"Yes."

"So, to get them that way, I take my time to research whatever it is I'm writing about—usually something pretty weird—and sometimes it's the kind of stuff I'm not supposed to look into."

I paused as the waitress returned with our drinks and set them on the table. Simon actually tried to snatch his from her tray, but she beat him to it and quickly set it down on top of a white beverage napkin with a sly grin on her face.

Simon took a long drink from his glass. "Get to the point."

"Okay … what I'm trying to say is that, what if by helping to solve this case, you—*we*—end up doing more damage than good?"

Claire frowned.

"You're nuts," Simon chuckled. "We're not going back in time and messing up peoples' futures or anything! There's nothin' to damage!"

"That's not what I mean. I'm talking about energy. I'm not a scientist, but if we're concentrating on a case for the police, what if the killer can pick up on it? You're psychic. Which means that you don't just read things, you send things out, too—things you're thinking about. In psychic experiments and tests, it's been shown that thoughts can be projected by a person with psychic ability … much more than an average person's thoughts. It's like that bleed thing you talk about."

"I don't get it," Simon mumbled.

"The victim was a medium," Claire said with realization in her eyes.

"Yes!" I leaned in closer to the both of them. "And her killer could be into that sort of thing also. Especially if it's a person connected with Dr. Carrol. You know, if Carrol did this, or anyone connected to him … he was into some weird stuff. He researches things like this, right? Telekinesis, psychic ability … isn't all this stuff in his field of research? Maybe Anson doesn't want you doing case work because it's too dangerous for you—especially in a case like this."

Simon thought on it while taking another swig of his drink. "You think they killed her because she went to Anson for help?"

"I think they killed her because she was a threat to their group. Going to Anson could have been a part of it. Maybe he sensed her fear and figured it out. Maybe he always intended to get rid of her. Who knows?"

Simon asked me, "You're pretty sure Carrol did it?"

Claire interrupted. "The Peter Carrol we talked about before?" she asked Simon carefully.

He nodded.

How could I be sure? "I don't know. It looks like he did it. Either way, it may have had something to do with her psychic abilities. I mean, Carrol needed her help because she was a medium, but she was also a threat to them because of that psychic ability. He had to let her in on things to get what he wanted, but that also made him vulnerable. That's why you need to be really careful about agreeing to help with stuff like this. It might make you more visible to them—to the killer or killers. Then *you* could become a target or endanger Anson's program."

Simon recoiled at the thought. "A target?"

Claire let out an exaggerated breath before glaring at me. "Great. Thanks, Richard."

"I'm just trying to see Dr. Anson's side of it," I said.

Simon looked worried. "So helping might be dangerous. That's not good."

I turned away from them. Flashes of glowing light from one of the televisions caught my eyes. An alcohol commercial with fast cars and explosions was on. It showed studly men hanging around with women that looked way too young for them. It was actually sort of disturbing. Then I was distracted by a man stumbling out of the bathroom. His zipper was down. "What if we find a way to convince Anson to *let* us help with the case? Instead of doing it behind his back?"

"*We?*" Simon smirked. "What about it being too dangerous to help?"

I shook my head. "I don't know. I was just trying to figure out why he wouldn't want you to help on something like this. You'd think he'd want some answers, too."

"Yes!" Claire yelped. "Please ask him!"

Simon looked skeptical.

"Maybe if we both talk to him," I suggested.

He rolled his eyes back and slacked his jaw sarcastically. "Fine. Let's just talk to him. I'm sure he'll love all this shit. The worst thing he can do is kick me out of the program."

I explained, "We need to emphasize that the case you were working on is too important to ignore. Maybe he'll change his mind and—"

"He already knows!" Simon snapped.

"And what exactly did he say when you told him it had to do with Marisol? I mean, he knew her a little, didn't he?"

Simon's eyes shifted downward. He glanced at Claire for a moment with a heaviness in his brow and then took a drink. "He thought she was crazy."

"What do you mean?" I asked.

Simon wiped his mouth and set his elbows on the table. "Think about it. Some chick … sorry—*lady*—shows up at your office and starts telling you that some guy is forcing her to help him contact dead people … uh, then she mentions channeling some guy from the 1950s."

"Carrol wanted her to communicate with a man from the 1950s?" Claire asked.

"Don't go tellin' your detective guy this stuff," he turned to warn her before continuing. "I'm not sure if I remember everything right, anyway." He then turned back to me. "I think Anson said that Carrol—now remember, Marisol was scared out of her mind when she was sayin' all this—wanted Marisol to help him contact that guy from the 1950s … what did De Luca say his name was? Winston? She said Carrol told her this guy was obsessed with trying to raise the dead. Dr. Carrol showed her some old papers that made it look like Carrol was trying to do some legitimate research—probably those transcripts De Luca was talkin' about—but still, it all sounded crazy to Dr. Anson. I mean, this girl was known for doing kooky psychic readings and stuff, mostly about peoples' love lives, you know? You see why Anson kinda blew her off now? He thought she was messed up. He asked her a few questions, but that was it. He said he was only tryin' to make her feel better. She was cryin' and stuff. Anson was tryin' to comfort her. I think he felt bad when he found out she was dead."

Claire asked, "Who's De Luca?"

"Just some dude from Italy that Anson's workin' with on some stuff," Simon answered. "Don't worry about him."

"How'd Anson find out about Marisol's death?" Claire asked.

"He saw it online. Like, a headline on one of the local news websites."

"Why didn't you tell us about Dr. Anson's connection to her?" Claire pressed on.

"I didn't want Anson to find out that I was helping you guys find her killer. What's the first thing your detectives would do if I told you that she talked to Anson? They'd go interview him." He looked at Claire. "Look, I would've told you if I needed to."

I held my hands out over the table. "Okay, okay. Listen … if Anson feels any guilt over this, you know, for not taking Marisol seriously, then maybe he'll let you help. Maybe if he feels involved in it somehow, like, if he knows exactly how you're helping … maybe he'll change his mind and see that it's not a big deal."

"If he'd wanted me to help, he would've just let me finish workin' on the damn case after he found out what I was doin'."

Claire looked at me, waiting for me to think of another suggestion that might help her save face back at the station. So I said, "Let's try to make him feel like he has more control over things. Maybe we can give him some more information on the case." I looked at Claire, hoping that she would step in and agree with me. "He'll see how important it is to finish the work you started, Simon."

Her eyes looked eager. "I can talk to Detective Trevino, too. Maybe I can get you some more info about the case. Whatever helps," she offered.

Simon's face hung dark and low. "I think if we can convince Anson to let us do the viewing at the lab, in a controlled environment, maybe he won't feel like we're risking anything. You know? Plus, he'll be there to watch. That room we use for viewings is shielded."

"Yeah," I agreed. "We should also tell him that if we're able to find out what happened to her, it might help us find out more about what Dr. Carrol is up to—even if he's not involved in her death. Anson seems really into finding out what Dr. Carrol's doing."

"That's a good idea. You think he'll go for it?" Simon asked.

"He might," I answered. "You never know. And if you help solve the case, my dreams might change. They might begin to make sense to me. Then maybe we'll be able to see more about Dr. Carrol."

Claire focused on me, lost.

"He has visions," Simon told her. "Like Nostradamus."

"No, I don't."

"Yes, you do."

"It's not like that at all." I was embarrassed to talk about something I hardly understood. My own life was now mimicking fiction.

"How soon can you talk to Anson?" Claire wanted to know.

Simon and I frowned at each other.

"Tomorrow morning?" I asked him.

Simon looked nervous. "I guess. But you're doing most of the talking."

Claire let out a sigh of relief. "Perfect. I'll call Simon in the morning to let you know what Detective Trevino says."

"All right, thanks," I replied.

Claire's eyes were hopeful again when she asked, "You really think he'll agree to it?"

Simon raised his eyebrows and said in a stale, monotone voice, "If we tell him that she was found with every part of her insides burned to a fuckin' crisp, like it was done with lasers or something, then maybe he will. Then he'll know it's something right up his alley."

Claire slapped Simon's arm. "You weren't supposed to talk about that!"

I was stunned. "But I thought she'd been …" my throat tightened just thinking about it, "ripped apart."

"That was a cover story," Claire said with a hardened look on her face. "We have to do that sometimes."

Simon glanced around before speaking again. "Yeah. Because nobody's gonna believe, or want to believe, that there's somethin' out there that can char your insides without leavin' a trace of damage to your bones. Or your skin. It's not that spontaneous human combustion stuff, either. In fact, it was like she was a porcelain doll afterward … just translucent and hollow on the inside."

And Simon said this with the most intense look in his eyes—a look that I can still remember, like a photograph. I dreaded meeting with Dr. Anson in the morning more than I feared going to sleep that night—which, of course, I did very little of.

17

The meeting.

Even without seeing it for myself—a person's body burned and emptied like that—I could still imagine it. Simon didn't have to say very much to make it stick inside my head, either. His eyes and the lack of emotion in his voice had said it all. I tried not to look at Claire as he spoke, but my eyes went to her magnetically. I could see that she was reliving it—the photo, or the video … the autopsy report … something. Something awful. Something her job had forced her to see.

The meeting with Anson wasn't going to go well. I didn't have any psychic intuition on that or anything. I knew it because Simon had a hangover and was forty minutes late. He'd already sent me ten sloppy text messages layered with excuses. I checked the messages as I sat in Dr. Anson's office with Raul De Luca, my stomach rumbling, and wishing I could just walk the halls or something until Anson showed up. He, too, was late.

De Luca stared at me while chewing on a pastry and finally decided to speak. "You ever thought about writing a comedy?"

It looked like a blueberry scone, and I wanted one. "No." I smiled politely. De Luca was just making small talk, so I decided to do the same. "You flew out from Italy?"

"Yes," he answered. "I live in Spain most of the time. But I teach and investigate in Italy. I work independently

… raise my own funding. I love it."

"That's nice," I said. "What kind of investigating do you do?"

"Ah, yes." De Luca tilted his head back. "Interesting question, but very loaded, as they say." He placed his scone on top of a paper towel and reached for his steaming coffee. "Demonic possession, hauntings, poltergeists, witchcraft … black magic."

It was hard not to look discomforted by his list of research interests. I swallowed back the next question I'd had and diverted my attention to a plaque on the wall instead.

"Yes, it's not an average lot of things to devote one's life to." He chuckled. "But, there is a market for it, people do contact me for help, and it pays the bills."

That had been exactly what I was going to ask next—I wondered if people actually hired him to look into that sort of stuff. And if so, what kinds of people?

De Luca sipped his coffee from a plastic cup, somehow managing to make it look elegant, although not on purpose, I thought. I recognized the cup from the university cafeteria that I wished I'd visited. He was watching me watch him, his eye glasses getting foggy each time he took a sip. "What part of that bothers you the most?"

He must have seen the discomfort in my eyes, but I was still surprised and unprepared for the bluntness of the question. "I don't know. Maybe the witchcraft part."

"Not all witchcraft is for evil, Mr. Ravestone."

"Yes, I understand that," I replied with care. I had some knowledge on the subject. "There's good and bad in everything."

"Exactly, Mr. Ravestone. It's the balance of nature. And so fighting the bad can't always have the outcome that one would prefer."

"How so?" I asked.

"If we fight evil and always win, how will things balance out the way they should on their own?"

The office door creaked and Dr. Anson slowly entered. "Good morning," he said cautiously after looking at us for a few seconds.

"We were discussing my resume," De Luca joked.

"Try not to scare him off." Dr. Anson smiled at me. "Are we still waiting for Simon? I took my time in the cafeteria because I knew he'd be late."

"Uh, I think we can start without him," I said with a light shrug. I knew Claire had probably called Simon that morning with Detective Trevino's input. I needed Simon there because that information would have helped. Either way, I was ready to wing it, because it was obvious to me that Simon didn't care enough to show up anyway. Plus, I was seriously hungry and craving a cappuccino, and now a scone, from downstairs.

Anson set his coffee on the desk. "I think I know what this is about." He made his way around De Luca to take his seat.

De Luca raised an eyebrow at me.

"You do?" I asked. "Okay. So this shouldn't take too long then. It kind of looks like you already know what … well, actually … you look kind of angry."

Dr. Anson tilted his head and squinted at me. "Simon isn't here because he doesn't want to upset me. Again."

"He told me he had a headache."

"Hangover," Anson clarified.

"Yeah."

Anson smirked. "I see. Well, go ahead. Let me hear what it is that you have to say."

At that point, I felt that I stopped being Dr. Anson's

guest. Being put on the spot wasn't exactly the right phrase to describe the anxiety that flowed through me at that moment. I felt pressure on the sides of my head, my jaw tightened, and my hands were shaking. I didn't want to offend Dr. Anson by bringing up the case. I hadn't thought things through.

I should have waited for Simon. "All right. Well, I was talking with Simon and we were thinking that I might be able to make better progress in my dreams, you know, if I could get past what happens to Marisol. Because that's where the dream stops for me."

"Uh huh," was all he said in response.

I decided to keep going with my unplanned speech. "Yeah. So … okay. Um … the case that Simon was working on with the police, coincidentally, happened to be about Marisol."

"I'm aware."

"Yes, of course. But what I think—what Simon and I believe—is that if we learned more about the case, while working with the police, maybe I could dream *past* whatever happens to her. Like, it would unblock what I'm not able to see. Then Simon could view more of what Carrol is doing after that part of the dream. You know, because I would be able to dream past it or remember past it or whatever …" my voice trailed off. He wasn't saying anything in return, so I just stopped.

He looked down at his desk. "You can't get past that part of the dream due to *fear*."

I was concentrating, trying to look like I knew what I was talking about. "Yes, but I think that if I knew what happened to her, there wouldn't be as much fear there."

"Okay," Anson began shifting in his squeaky seat. "I understand that you're new to this sort of thing, Richard. And I appreciate your suggestion. But, do you realize how much danger Simon would be put in, and perhaps yourself as well, if he worked on this case outside the lab?"

"Yes. Simon and I talked about that."

"Did you?" He sounded more upset.

"Yes, and I was hoping that he could help them, the police, here. At the university."

"In the *lab?*"

"Yes, sir."

Anson looked sharply at me. "I don't want the police in my lab. It complicates things. I've got enough people watching what I do."

"I understand completely. What if Simon could do the viewing from inside the lab, pass the results on to me, and then I could give the police the information—"

"Richard," he interrupted with a smile. "Why would you want to get involved with things like this? Police cases? Wouldn't it affect your reputation as a writer?"

"I've worked with police before while researching for novels. It's no big deal. We wouldn't even have to go to the station to get the info to them anyway. We could do it over the phone."

He shook his head while thinking on it and leaned back in his chair. "I don't know."

"May I say something?" De Luca asked quietly, wiping the crumbs from his mouth.

Dr. Anson turned to face him. "Go ahead."

"In my experience with police cases, I can tell you that the energy surrounding something negative like this does appear to change after learning more about it. You know, digging through the mystery ... looking for clues. Like murders, for example." He took a swift glance at me. "Richard might be right. The dream may change. In fact, if we were to learn more about what happened to Marisol, the dream might become more intense, more vivid. It could help us."

Dr. Anson only responded to De Luca's input with a tight smile. Then, he focused back on me. "Okay. I guess I would feel more comfortable if Simon did his viewing here."

I said, "I'm sure he'd be fine with that."

"But do you think the police would be?" Anson asked.

I didn't know. "They'd have to be."

"And I don't know how I feel yet about helping him in this," Anson said. "Aren't you worried about your reputation, Richard?"

"As a writer? I've been connected with a lot of weirdness over the years. I'll be okay."

Anson still didn't look convinced. "I'm sure Simon told you how Marisol was found."

I reluctantly answered, "Yes."

"I don't know if you should be a part of that viewing," Anson warned me. "The trauma of death can be very intense. Simon's gift for seeing things that happened in the past isn't as strong or as controllable as his ability to see the present, but it can still be frightening. And if he doesn't see anything, I don't want you, or the police, to be disappointed."

"I understand."

"With that said, I guess I'm agreeing to it."

"Thank you, sir." I couldn't wait to tell Simon. Admittedly, I was excited for the both of us. And I thought I'd get a good night's sleep out of all of this, too. I felt one step closer to freedom, to erasing the nightmares.

Anson smiled a warm smile. "Thank you for believing in him, Richard."

"No problem."

"Perhaps we should start tomorrow morning, if that's all right with you," Anson suggested. "And don't worry about any extra days at the hotel. I'll be sure to take care of everything. Tomorrow morning, 8 a.m., and be sure to get a good night's sleep. The last time Simon described a murder, I believe he fainted or passed out afterward. It wasn't easy on him. And in this case, the killing part might be extremely difficult for him to endure. Especially because we had met Marisol. She seemed like a nice girl." He paused and looked into the air above him. "We didn't know the other women they found with her, though."

The other women? Anson and Simon both met Marisol??

I decided to hold it back, putting on the most neutral expression I possibly could. "Would it be all right if we started tonight?"

18

Italian food.

I didn't know what to do first. Call Simon and demand to know why he didn't tell me about the other women found with Marisol, or go straight to Claire to see if I could get more information out of her. I was sure they had a good reason for keeping those details from me. I'd seen enough movies and worked with enough law enforcement agencies to know that it must have had something to do with confidentiality. It's not that I was taking it personally or anything. But then I wondered why I wasn't seeing the other women in my dream.

"If you wanted me to help you see more of the dream, then why didn't you tell me about the other victims?" I asked Simon over the phone. I kept my voice calm. Kind of like we were having a conversation about something more natural, like, about the weather or what I'd seen while on an early morning jog that day. I didn't want to chance setting him off.

"We can't talk about this on the phone," he replied. "Where are you?"

"I got hungry. I'm at some Italian place down the street from the hotel."

I had taken a nap after the short meeting with Anson and De Luca. It was about two in the afternoon before I realized how hungry I was and made my way down to a little Italian place I'd seen down the street. It was the kind of place with tables and chairs set up outside. The weather was perfect—cooler than I was used to, and crisp when inhaled through the nose. It was a great excuse to sit outside and order a cappuccino and a plate of creamy Fettuccini Alfredo.

"All right, listen," I said to him. "I'm not trying to get you to tell me anything I don't need to know. You've got your reasons ... it's okay. I just want to help. Really."

"I know," Simon said with a sigh. "This stuff isn't always done logically. There's an out of order sequence to things like this. Only certain information that can be released, you know? I'm sorry."

He meant it. I could tell.

"Maybe if I talk to Claire, she can work a little harder on tryin' to find out how much I can tell you and Anson. I think the cops are spooked since you're in the media and stuff."

"So Claire didn't call you this morning with more information for us?"

"Yeah, but like I said, I think they don't like the fact that you're involved now," he replied. "She didn't have much to tell me."

Someone familiar was quickly approaching along the sidewalk. "I'm a novelist, not a reporter or ... an investigative journalist."

"I know, I know, but they're nervous about it. You know? I can tell. I've worked with these guys long enough to know how they operate."

"Yeah," I replied as the person I recognized started waving at me. "De Luca's here."

"*What?*"

I didn't know why, but I felt a little panicked. "I didn't tell him I was coming here."

"I don't know about that guy. I get a weird feeling around him."

I returned the wave to De Luca and put on a smile. "I think he's harmless."

"Watch what you say to him," Simon warned. "And don't tell him I'm talkin' to the PD about tryin' to get you more info. That's why I didn't show up this morning."

"I thought it was a headache."

"Yeah. That, too."

"You still should've been there," I added quickly. "I did everything by myself, and he already knows we're trying to get help from the PD. That was the whole point of the meeting this morning! To get people to work together on this. And I can't hide things from De Luca—he's always hanging around Anson."

"You know what I'm gonna do?" Simon asked with determination in his voice. "I'm gonna start lookin' De Luca up on the Internet. I should've done that days ago. I'll get back to you if I find somethin' on him."

De Luca hurried his pace and squeezed past the hostess while pointing at my table for permission to pass through. "Uh … okay. He's almost at my table."

"I mean it. Be careful!"

"Okay. Bye." I ended the call while remembering that De Luca's eyes were on me, so I continued to smile as I set the phone down.

He grabbed the back of the seat across from me with a timid look on his face. "May I?"

"Yes. Please do."

He seemed to be either in a state of controlled panic or in a hurry to get someplace else. He looked all around and fidgeted with a button on his vest. Vests were a style I happened to like, actually. With his rounded eye glasses and his bowtie, he was very much like a man of the late

1800s. He was kind of artsy-cool without even trying to be.

"How well do you know Simon?" De Luca leaned over the table to ask.

"Hmmm. I only met him a few days ago, but since then, we've been thrown out of a restaurant and held at gunpoint together. I'd say … it feels like I've known him a little longer than that. Why?"

De Luca nervously ran his fingers across the white linen table cloth and frowned. "Are you friends?"

"Uh … I'm still sort of undecided on that part of things," I answered half-jokingly. "Is something wrong?"

"Yes, but it's difficult to explain."

I nodded. "Because you're worried I might tell him?"

"Perhaps."

We paused as the hostess set a glass of ice water on the table for De Luca and kindly informed him that our server would return to take his order. De Luca's eyes were distant and he only nodded in agreement as she left.

I then said to him, "If it's important—whatever you know about Simon—you should probably tell Dr. Anson."

De Luca's expression went blank.

This concerned me. "You don't want Dr. Anson to know?"

"No. I don't." His voice was grave.

"And you're sure you want to tell *me?*"

"Richard, I have worked with people like Simon for many years," he began in his not-so-strong Italian accent, "and I know when I see strange behavior in these types of people. He is blocking me from knowing something."

"Knowing what? Wait. Like, blocking you from reading him?"

"Yes." His face then showed excitement. "I'm not

psychic. I used to be able to do that sort of thing, but … sometimes we lose a talent like that. Or it weakens. But I still know how to read people. I'm *very* good at that."

"Oh," I replied.

"And what I do know, from years of working with people like Simon, all over the world, is that he is hiding something very important. It has to do with the project. And I think it has something to do with your dreams."

"I don't understand."

"As he saw into your dream, something about him changed."

Out of nervousness, and not knowing how to react, I took a sip of my water before speaking. My hand was shaking. "You think he saw something more than what he was saying?"

"Yes."

"But why wouldn't he tell us? I mean, look how he acts. He loves showing off his abilities. Anson treats him like a celebrity at the lab."

"Yes. I understand this. But I'm telling you this because I know what I saw, Richard. He was acting very different," De Luca said with heavy and confident emphasis on the word very. "I've learned to pick up on these things in people. Researchers in this field are constantly being deceived by phonies. There are many people out there who want attention. They claim to bend metal and read minds … they see into the future and can speak to your dead grandparents. I'm fifty years old. I've been doing this a long time. I am dedicated to it and to the truths behind it. Simon is hiding something."

None of this was a shock to me. I was sure that it had to do with the police case he'd been secretly working on with Claire. Or so I thought at the time.

"Do you know what he's hiding?" De Luca asked,

hardly able to keep eye contact with me when he did.

I shook my head. "No. Simon was hiding that whole police case thing, but—"

"It's not that," he answered sternly. "It's something else."

"Well, I'm sorry. I just don't know what it is."

De Luca locked his eyes on me. "Have you had any other dreams related to Dr. Carrol?"

"Yes. I've had a few different ones about him. They're all pretty similar, though."

"Does Simon know this?"

I shook my head in frustration. "I tried to tell him, but he blew it off. All he and Dr. Anson care about is the main one—the one with all the details they want. The one with the ritual."

He lowered his voice. "Would you mind telling me about the other ones?"

"I don't know. Does Anson know you're asking me all this? What would be the point of keeping things from him? You think Simon is purposely trying to withhold information about Carrol?"

"No," he began, "I haven't told Dr. Anson my suspicions about Simon. But," he leaned forward again to say, "I do think that I can trust you to help me figure out what's going on here. You looked surprised when Anson told you that there were other women found dead with Marisol's body ... all of them had ties to Dr. Carrol. And I happen to know that it wasn't just a few women, but several men, as well. I think it totaled in the hundreds. I also know that they were all in a different state of decomposition."

He had to be wrong. *Hundreds?* There was no way. I looked around at the other tables, hoping no one had overheard what De Luca was telling me.

"If Simon knows more than he's saying, whether it is out of respect for police confidentiality or not, he could be doing more harm than good." De Luca's eyes were so focused, so intense. "He's very loyal to the police."

I stared at De Luca, unintimidated by the seriousness in his delivery or the stern wrinkles on his forehead. Thanks to him, there were disgusting images in my head of decomposing bodies, and I wondered if it was too late to cancel my plate of fettuccini. I'd ordered it with grilled shrimp instead of chicken. That turned out to be a terrible decision as I sat there picturing it. "You want me to ask Simon some more questions? To help find things out for you?"

"Yes."

"Why?"

"I just told you why. I know he tells you things. I think he feels comfortable with you," he explained. "Maybe because you both have psychic abilities."

"But he's *not* telling me things," I reminded him. "He didn't tell me about the other women ... the other *people* that were found with Marisol."

"*Parts* of them were found with her. Well ... inside of her." He gazed into my eyes, looking for a reaction. It chilled me.

"Inside?"

"She had been hollowed out." De Luca swallowed hard. "Have you ever heard of apports?"

"It sounds familiar."

"Yes, well, the body parts of the others were somehow placed inside of Marisol after she had been burned empty from the inside. I think they were placed there through what I believe to be a form of transference."

I couldn't picture it, nor did I want to. "Dear God. Why?"

He grinned. "To scare investigators. To keep them away. To prove to them that they were crossing into something unnatural, something powerful. Something unholy."

It was unreal to me. "It didn't work. They brought Simon in to help with the investigation. They—"

I stopped speaking when our server appeared from inside the bistro with a plate of food and another loaf of complimentary bread.

De Luca took a cue from my eyes and was careful. He leaned forward and spoke quickly. "Richard, the police have turned to Simon out of pure desperation. I'm sure they sincerely want to solve the case—it's nothing any department would want on their hands. But this isn't anything that a police department or the FBI can handle. Will you help me?"

"Help you what? Help you keep secrets from Simon and Anson? They're the ones that brought me out here to help *them!*"

The server set my plate in front of me, but as I looked into the writhing, steaming noodles of butter, cream, and garlic, there was nothing appealing about it to me at all. De Luca nodded and smiled as the server set down the bread and an appetizer plate.

"Can I take your order, sir?" the server asked.

"No, grazie. I'm fine for now," De Luca replied.

As soon as the server turned to leave, De Luca continued. "I'm asking you to help me find the truth. Something horrible is happening, and I think it could be much worse than Dr. Anson realizes ... or wants to realize."

How could I think it over? I had dreamed about this woman Marisol, and now I was linked to Simon through this dream. I wanted it solved and put out of my life. I knew that if I went back home with this thing unresolved, still stuck in my head, it would eat away at me until it won. I was this dream's captive.

I gave in. "Okay. What can I do?"

"First, you have to trust me," De Luca said. "You can tell me what Simon knows—what he shares with you about the case. Or what this police woman knows about it. Has she kept in contact with you?"

"Yes," I admitted, and then thought of something. "How do you know so much about the case?"

De Luca stared at the plate of bread and twisted his lips. "Dr. Carrol's group—his cult—has members in Europe. This is much bigger than you know, Richard." His expression then grew cold and distant. "I was called onto a few investigations in which I had the opportunity to interview followers that had failed to defect. They mentioned his name."

I asked before thinking, "What do you mean 'failed to defect?'"

De Luca looked up at me, saying nothing.

"Never mind." I knew. They had attempted somehow … the details weren't important. They didn't make it. Half alive, half dead? I didn't want to know. "And you want me to keep all of this a secret between us?"

"Yes," he confirmed. "Only until I can piece a few things together. Ethics aside, it's only for a little while."

"So you eventually plan to tell Dr. Anson that you don't trust Simon?"

"To be honest, I don't trust Dr. Anson entirely, either. Neither of them is telling one another the entire truth, Richard. And they're lying to you as well." De Luca grinned an awful grin. It was cold and empty. It turned him into a different person.

He was right. They hadn't told me the truth. They'd

lied about Marisol's death, and they were keeping me in the dark. De Luca was just giving it to me straight. I felt nauseated. The fettuccini sat there, practically daring me to vomit all over it in front of everyone on the patio as Marisol appeared inside my head again, reaching out for me, begging me to save her … to save us. "I feel trapped."

He adjusted his delicate-looking glasses. "I'd like to help you with that, Richard. As I'm sure you know, it is the truth that shall set us free."

19

Simon's house.

Simon's house wasn't disgusting or gross like I'd expected it to be. It was absolutely beautiful. Locating it had been an issue, only because navigating the streets of San Antonio was completely foreign to me, but after about forty minutes, I found it. Simon directed me to a part of the city referred to as Olmos Park. The area was filled with trees, some still hanging onto their leaves even though it was winter. The homes I drove past were grand and historic, with massive lawns and long, beautiful walkways. I was surprised when I pulled up to the address he'd given me. I thought, at first, it had to be a mistake.

Simon's house was an intriguing Tudor style that reminded me of a trip I'd once taken to Great Britain. Its steep, pointy roof and elaborate brickwork immediately drew me in. With some guilt, I wondered how Simon could afford the place. But it was something I couldn't help thinking—the place was gorgeous, looked rich with history, well-preserved ... in other words, expensive-looking. Standing before it, I almost forgot why I'd made the drive out. I was kind of into architecture and historical homes since I had to research them for stories sometimes.

"You found it," Simon called out from the front steps. He appeared from a beautiful, dark wood doorway and waited patiently for me to make my way up the paved walkway.

"Yeah." I was still stunned. "It took me a while, though. But, wow! This place is great!"

Simon gave me a side-smile. "It was my mom's."

As that made more sense to me, guilt struck again. "She had great taste. I love the area."

"Thanks. It has a good energy, too. Come on in."

"So De Luca stole your lunch, huh?" Simon joked. He was in the kitchen getting a couple of glasses for wine— wine he had purchased just for me, surprisingly.

"Yeah. I offered it to him," I told Simon. He was now looking around for a wine opener. "I lost my appetite after we talked."

Simon froze in place. "Oh yeah?"

"Yeah."

He turned around slowly with two glass tumblers in his hands, setting them down on the granite countertop. "What did he say?"

I took in a cleansing breath and prepared myself to do what I hadn't expected to do. "He asked me to tell him everything you know about the case. To tell him what you're doing with the PD. Stuff you might be keeping from Anson."

Simon's eyes widened and his lips formed into the beginnings of several words that he didn't speak.

"Then he told me about how Marisol was found."

He shrugged. "Yeah, So?"

"How she was *really* found."

"What the fuck, man?!"

"Dr. Anson told me a little about it this morning, too. He said you both knew her. Which means you *both* lied to me. De Luca just clarified it, I guess." It still sickened me to think about it.

"I hardly knew her. Met her years ago," he said quietly. "Way before any of this and way before she went to Anson for help."

Simon reached across the counter to grab his phone. "I'm calling Anson. Fuck that De Luca guy! What's he tryin' to do? Make me look like an asshole?!"

"Simon, no! Put the phone down and listen," I asked. "De Luca thinks something really bad is going on. We can't do all of this secret stuff anymore. We need to find this Carrol guy, and we're not going to do that if we're all lying to each other. You understand?"

"No shit!" Simon said in return. "There *is* something really bad going on! That doesn't mean De Luca has a right to know any confidential shit about the case! He's a fucking paranormal researcher! Not a detective!"

I waited for him to calm down. I watched as his finger was ready to dial, but he stopped himself and stared at me instead.

"I think De Luca means well. I think he really wants to help. He thinks Anson isn't ..."

"Isn't what?"

"Isn't understanding everything that's going on. Like he doesn't know how serious this all is. I guess it stretches out to Europe or something. I don't know. He thinks you know something that you're not telling us. Something you're hiding from Anson."

"I *am* hiding stuff," Simon admitted dryly.

"Yeah, I know. The police case stuff. That's what I figured."

Simon turned his attention to the bottle of wine and scowled at it. "I can't believe I bought a fucking bottle of wine. I hope you like it. Caber-something."

I smiled. "Thanks." I knew he was trying to be a

friend. It was strange and difficult for him, which made it awkward for me as well, but he was trying—even if it meant that he had to drag himself through the process.

"I don't even know how to open this thing," he admitted.

"You can't tell De Luca I told you this stuff," I said.

"Obviously," Simon added while fumbling with an ancient-looking corkscrew that squeaked while he messed with it.

"We'll play along if you want. You can just tell me things to say to him. You know, to make him think he's in the loop. It'll keep him off our backs while you and Claire work on things."

Simon shook his head in defeat. "Sure. Whatever."

I turned to get a better look at him, and the leather seat cushion on the couch made an embarrassing sound against my jeans. "What's your idea then?"

"What did he tell you about Marisol?"

In discomfort, I had to look away from him, and I felt a little light-headed at the thought of repeating it. "He said she was found … with the parts of other people … inside her hollowed out body."

Simon's lips tightened, infuriated, but he said nothing as I watched him.

I wanted to tread lightly. "Lots of people. I guess he said something about apports."

"What are those?"

"Items that supposedly materialize from the other side," I said. "At some point during the spiritualist movement in the mid-1800s, early 1900s, some mediums would try to prove their communications with spirits by trying to materialize things in front of their audiences. During séances, objects would appear—like gifts for the living that were supposedly from the dead. Most often, they ended up being objects that the mediums hid on themselves before the séance began. When investigators looked into it though, it was hard to figure out how some of the apports actually appeared."

There was a glint in Simon's eye after I told him that.

"What?" I asked.

"Okay. Well, Marisol was known to try and do stuff like that sometimes. Dr. Anson told me. He thinks stuff like that is bad. Like showing off. He says it's wrong to try to prove things to the living. He called it parlor tricks."

"Yes, but I think what De Luca was trying to say was that the way the body parts were found *inside* Marisol's body, inside where her organs were supposed to have been, was similar to how apports are supposed to have worked ... because there was no other way they could have gotten in there."

"Because it was like they were there and no one could figure out how?"

"I think so."

"De Luca didn't get into any more details about her condition after he realized I'd lost my appetite. But I understood what he was getting at. It was like things were just inside her, placed there perfectly without any incisions ... or any other logical explanation."

Simon's stare was blank. "Claire described it to me. She wasn't supposed to know the details, but the detectives told her because she was passing things on to me. I prefer working with her. She's not all brainwashed yet by the system."

"Yeah. That makes sense," I agreed. "She seems cool."

"But how the fuck did De Luca know how Marisol was found? Man, I swear ... if there was ever a crime that they didn't want people to know about—this is the one."

"He didn't say."

"Maybe he has some connections somewhere on the inside," Simon guessed. "Either way, I don't trust him."

"He doesn't trust you either."

Simon raised an eyebrow. "*Or* his buddy Anson."

There didn't seem to be a way around this circle of distrust. I couldn't be certain that De Luca actually trusted me either. There were too many variables at play here and too many minds on their own agendas. My own plan was to remain focused on getting past that part of the dream with Marisol so I could help Simon, and that was all. Without that, I was nothing anymore. I wouldn't sleep right or be able to function normally, ever again, it seemed. I had to help her before escaping from San Antonio. Otherwise, I was a failure in all of this.

I watched Simon pour the wine, the foil pieces around the opening of the bottle sticking out in all directions like a sharpened, evil crown. The cork was on the counter, torn to bits. "So we stick to the plan?" I wanted to know.

"Yeah." He looked concerned. "Anson already called me. He's okay with us doing a reading for the PD at the lab tonight. He thinks it's a more controlled environment. He says it's safer than going to the locations of crimes and lettin' all my mental energy spill out everywhere. Does that make sense?"

"No. What do you mean *us* doing the reading?" I asked. "I thought you were doing it."

Simon smiled. "Yeah, well, like I said before … the PD isn't givin' me any more info to work with. So, I'm thinkin' maybe we can just help each other out here. You know?"

"How?"

"We'll lead each other through it—through your dream."

"Okay," I said, not sure it would help.

"I know how they found her. I know the after part," he explained. "And you know the before. Understand?"

Unfortunately, I did. "Yes."

"We'll link 'em up. You know? Guide each other inside and outside the dream."

It actually did make sense.

"So I need you at the lab," Simon continued. "You and your dream."

"Yeah. Of course."

"But when we do this tonight, I need you to understand somethin'," he said.

"Okay."

"I've seen parts of your dreams that you haven't. It's kind of like we're leadin' each other through somethin' that neither of us is really a part of. Because we weren't even there."

I nodded, sort of understanding what he meant, but also feeling like it was intrusive of him to know that strange feeling … seeing something inside my dream that I didn't or couldn't.

"So tonight, I'm going to lead you through some things that you've missed in your dreams, things you didn't see before, and you'll do the same for me. You'll have to be ready for it."

"Okay. I think I can do that."

"Yeah," Simon laughed. "You're going to have to do it. I need you to. And when we do this, I need you to stay calm. De Luca and Anson will be watchin' us."

"Okay."

"Don't let them see somethin' in your face that we don't want them seein'."

"Like what?"

"Just watch how you react when we do this, okay?"

All I was thinking was, yeah sure, whatever it takes. I just want this over with already. "Okay."

"I'm gonna sneak some vodka in so we can do this right."

I smiled in agreement. Simon returned his focus to the bottle of wine and began to nervously peel away the spikes of the evil crown around the rim. Something in the way he avoided my eyes told me that De Luca was right. Simon was hiding something from me—from all of us. Something serious.

20

That next session was different because I knew a little more about how the routine was supposed to go. I didn't get a lot of sleep, but I was good enough. I was awake and had eaten a decent breakfast at the hotel. I arrived at the lab when I was supposed to, greeted everyone, and took my seat across from Simon. He hardly even looked at me as Anson entered the room.

Simon made sure the lights were going to be dimmed. Anson struggled with him on it for a few minutes, reminding Simon that the rest of the team needed to be able to his face clearly on the monitoring system. But then Simon told Anson that he had a slight headache and didn't want it to get worse. Anson relented, and Simon got his way.

"Did the detective give you more information about the case?" Anson asked Simon.

"No, they called Richard."

What?

Dr. Anson looked at me in surprise, eager for a response.

I had to hide my anger. Simon hit me off-guard, and I had to quickly think of something to say. "Yes. One of their officers called me last night," I lied, not sure how to go about it. "They couldn't tell me much. I guess it's classified or something."

Anson wanted more than that. "So obviously the police know that you're helping. Well, what did they tell you?"

I felt cornered. I didn't dare look at Simon because that would give it all away. "Just that she had a red dress on … and some boots with tall heels. But I already knew about the dress from our last session." I did everything I could at that moment to try and feel something coming from Simon that would tell me to stop talking, that I was giving Anson and De Luca too much information … so I kept it simple. "And that she had makeup on like she was going out."

"Signs of an attacker?" Anson asked.

"No. Nothing. No struggle either."

"And they told you where her body was found?"

I risked it. "Yes. An abandoned warehouse? I don't know. They weren't too specific."

Nothing from Simon.

Anson cleared his throat. "Okay then. Well, I guess having you and Simon working on this together is a good idea."

"Yeah," Simon agreed, nonchalantly. "It'll probably help."

Before leaving the room, Anson reminded us that he and De Luca would be watching closely for any signs of distress. He reminded Simon that he didn't need to push himself through anything that might cause any serious discomfort. According to Anson, viewings had caused heart attacks before—possibly. Anson turned his attention to me and requested that I please call out for help if I began to notice anything out-of-the-ordinary going on, anything that Simon couldn't handle. I agreed.

As soon as Anson closed the door behind him, Simon looked up at me with serious eyes. His breaths were shallow. He studied my face and I felt, and knew, that he was searching my eyes for something that had nothing to do with words, so I was patient and asked nothing. He then moved his gaze to the corner of the room behind me, to a camera, before bringing his eyes back on me. He was reminding me to be careful, not to overreact, and to follow his lead.

The lights dimmed and Anson's soft voice came over the speaker system. "You may begin when ready. Take your time," followed by a single click.

I hesitated to speak. "How do you want me to start?"

Simon's head was tilted downward and his palms flat against the table. His fingers were spread wide, tense, with the tips of his fingers moving and twitching. "Start with her reaching out for you."

That was the most difficult part for me. That thought, my inability to help her. It brought back the helplessness all at once. "Okay."

Simon closed his eyes. "She sees you."

Now or then? In the dream or …? Horrible thoughts I couldn't ask because it seemed too real.

I forced myself into it. "Yes," I agreed. "She's calling out to me and I'm afraid because there is something there, behind all of them, in the back of the room."

"Look at it."

It was more real this time. Simon had described it perfectly when he said it was like something we could both see that we weren't really supposed to be a part of. And it was for that very reason that I didn't want to look at it. I wanted to back out.

"Richard."

"Okay, okay. It's gray, mostly. Transparent."

"Think. Look at it."

Marisol is crying out for me …

In bits and pieces, I remembered the dream. The gray ghost had a face this time, but it was faded and difficult to see. I thought it was pointless to try describing it. It was just a face to me, without any definite characteristics, and that was all. "I see its face."

"Male or female?"

"I can't ... I can't tell."

"Why not?!" Simon snapped, startling me.

"Because it's dark! It doesn't want to look at me! The room is dark, the face is dark ... it's shadowy and see-through!"

Simon opened his eyes to look at me. "Describe the face."

I took a breath and closed my eyes. "It's damaged. I can see something on it that shouldn't be there."

"Sores," he said.

My God. "Yes!"

"The clothes?" he asked.

"They're ragged. Ripped."

"Time period?"

I opened my eyes, realizing in disbelief, "Medieval maybe? Wait, its wearing a uniform ... like a soldier. No, it's changing. I don't know."

Simon nodded. "It's okay. Marisol?"

"She's stopped struggling. She's still. They're laying her down. Carrol is approaching, yelling at her, standing over her. She's not responding to him. The others are holding her down."

"What's next?"

I could see it, and didn't know why. "Carrol begins chanting. He closes his eyes. I don't understand the language. I think it's Latin."

Simon's breathing increased. "He leans over her."

"Yes. He's going to whisper into her ear. He says, 'You are the host. Let them in.'" I opened my eyes, surprised that I knew that, to see Simon's reaction.

He was calm and said, "He wants her to channel someone?"

"I don't know. She's just lying there."

Simon frowned. "Keep going. The dream has to keep moving."

Telling him what appeared next was difficult. And I didn't know how, but I was remembering things that I hadn't before. "Then the gray ghost gets closer and it hangs over her. I think only Dr. Carrol can see it, or knows it's there. Carrol moves aside and watches it … the thing is above her, hovering. But—" I stopped. I saw in my head something strange. "It's changing … into different people. Like flickering. It's a soldier, then a woman … a man, a Nazi officer … and then it fades away and Carrol and the others are silent."

I paused and waited, waiting for Simon to trigger something inside my memories. I couldn't believe what I could see now with his help.

"It wants in," he said. "That thing is hundreds of people … horrible people from different places."

Then, Marisol's eyes shot open. Her eyes widened, painfully wide, and went gray. She sat up, mechanically and unrealistically—straight up, quicker than my eyes could register. I gasped. She was face to face with Carrol as he stood over her. Her mouth open and her face filled with what looked like shock.

Like I was in a trance, I said, "*Speak*," just as Dr. Carrol had commanded. He pulled back the hood from his head and studied her face.

Simon's voice jolted me. "What happens next? You know what happens."

"Dr. Carrol removes his hood. Marisol is sitting up. Her eyes are different and he's waiting for her to speak."

"The voice she speaks with is not hers," Simon began,

knowing and seeing everything inside my head. "Now, you have to tell me the *exact* words the voice said."

"It said, 'Yes, my Lord.'" And as I repeated it, I was horrified. I could hear it speak in my head. It was a deep male voice with an English accent.

"Then Carrol laughs," Simon added.

"Yes. He is happy. It worked. He has summoned the dead. He is communicating with someone … or something … that he wanted to speak to. He feels powerful."

Simon inhaled deeply. "Focus. Don't be afraid. Look at them."

I realized suddenly that something about the dream was different. My head felt numb. "He knows I'm there."

Simon held his breath for a second and his eyes went wide. "No, Richard. You just think that in the dream. Keep going."

I wanted to believe him, but I didn't. "Simon, I can feel his awareness of me."

"Ignore it. Tell me what happens next."

"He leans into Marisol's body, into her face, and tells the thing inside her that it will do as he asks."

"'*Yes, my Lord*'" Simon replied in a voice so similar … it sent chills through me. He was making it too real. I was inside this dream again, but awake. Still, I didn't feel that I could completely escape it if I wanted to.

"Then he tells it—"

"Say it exactly like he did!"

I closed my eyes tight. I wanted out. "'*I will call on many of you. Those who have suffered … those who wish to return, and I will give you life again.*'"

"'*Yes, my Lord. We are many.*'"

"'*In return, you will wait patiently until I call upon thee, and when it is time, you will do as I ask.*'"

"'*Yes.*'"

"'*Take this woman back with you. And to all of those listening ... all of those who wish to return to this world ... send back in her place, pieces from your existence on Earth. Memories from your past. Send to me ... your flesh.*'"

I felt Simon grab a hold of me and pull at my arm.

"Oh my God," I sighed, exhausted. I leaned back into my seat. "She's burning. Something is happening to her ... on the inside. She's glowing!"

"Its energy is high, the thing inside her. It's burning her."

"She's lying back down now and ..." I had to stop for a moment.

Simon stood up and his mouth dropped open as he watched me, his eyes glazed over—he could see it, too.

"The parts ... body parts. They're filling *inside* her. I can see them. I can see it happening."

Simon leaned across the table to whisper forcefully, "Stop! Don't remember anymore!"

"I see the marks of fingers pushing against her skin from the inside ... there's too many. They don't fit. There's other things too ... like, spoons ... watches, rings—"

"Stop remembering!" Simon turned to the camera and yelled, "Anson! Get me out of here! He can see what I see! GET ME OUT!"

But they couldn't get through the door fast enough to separate me from Simon's influence on my mind. I was seeing things too quickly, things I wasn't meant to see. Things Simon didn't think I would be able to see. And even through the panic I was feeling, I could tell that Simon didn't expect it to happen that way.

They were banging on the door because it wouldn't open.

We were locked into each other's thoughts. Simon ran around the table and shook my shoulders. "Stop, please!" he begged, frantically.

But then he saw my eyes and knew—it was too late. I had seen Dr. Anson. Simon desperately shook his head and stepped away from me. He knew I had seen Anson, standing in the back of the room—inside my dream—cowering in silence, watching Dr. Carrol laugh with delight as Marisol's body was ravaged by these hellish things … these apports. He stood and watched Dr. Carrol in awe and amazement at the success of his demonic ritual.

The door flew open and Simon jumped.

And as Dr. Anson entered the room, followed closely by De Luca, my eyes were still locked onto Simon's face as I heard Dr. Carrol's voice speaking from inside the nightmare, "*You see, Miller! This is your gift to the world! We did this together!*"

21

"Get out of his face. He needs room to breathe," I could hear Simon say in frustration from behind De Luca.

"Are you all right, Richard?" De Luca asked me, his hands on my shoulders. "Do you need some water?"

I needed to focus. I wanted to know where Dr. Anson was. I knew I'd seen him burst into the room, but then he was gone.

"He needs you to back up and give him some space," Simon snapped in anger.

De Luca gently removed his hands from my shoulders and hesitantly backed away. "All right," he calmly replied.

Simon quickly moved in to take De Luca's place. "You just need some air. Let's get out of here and get some air. Come on."

"He needs medical attention first," Dr. Anson firmly commanded as he entered the room again. "And I'm not letting him leave the premises until he's been looked at."

For a moment, Simon's expression froze. He then turned to Anson and smiled. "He's just not used to it. That's all."

"What happened?" I asked them.

"Your eyes started goin' back in your head and stuff. That's all. No big deal," Simon replied with a come-on-let's-get-the-hell-out-of-here look on his face.

"You were chanting," De Luca added. "I have it recorded."

"Excuse me," Dr. Anson said as he moved in between

the two of them. "Come on, Richard. I'm going to take a look at you."

I stood abruptly. "No! I'm fine. Sorry. I just need some coffee—"

"It'll only take a moment, Richard."

I was light-headed. "No, really," I insisted, doing my best to remain steady and composed while Anson scrutinized me with piercing eyes. "Please, I'd really just like to go get a coffee."

Anson stared at me and stiffened his posture. "Sure. That's fine. But De Luca and I still need to interview you. We'll get someone to bring you a coffee."

I glanced at Simon and De Luca. Simon's eyes were panicked and in De Luca's face, desperation. "Can we just talk about this tomorrow?" I asked.

Dr. Anson frowned. "I think it would be best to discuss things now. While things are still fresh."

"I'm sorry," I told him. "I don't think I'd be very useful right now. I'm kind of embarrassed. I don't know what happened. I don't remember any chanting," I shook my head and laughed nervously, "or anything like that. I don't remember … very much at all. Maybe I will later. Or maybe not. I don't know." I added a smile, hoping my excuses sounded authentic.

Anson's stare went to the wall behind me as he thought about it. "Take a break and get out of here for a while. I'll call you in a few hours to see how you're doing."

"Sorry about all this." I made my way to the door, knowing Simon and De Luca would do their best to follow.

"It's all right, Richard," Anson replied. "De Luca and I will go over the video and have our interview with Simon."

"What?" Simon asked in surprise. "But this was for the cops. Why are we—?"

"Because it's still a part of a study in *my lab*, Simon," Anson replied sternly. "I'm not just handing everything over to them without going over it carefully first. All of this is too complex for them to understand. We'll discuss the information you will provide to them. We'll simplify things first."

Simon looked uneasy, but was trying to hide it. "Of course. I understand. But I'd like a short break, too."

"Simon, I strongly suggest that you adhere to the rules of my lab."

"I'm just going to walk Richard out," Simon said with a grin. "I'll come right back up."

De Luca had a concerned look on his face. "Do you think it's safe for Mr. Ravestone to be driving so soon?"

Simon turned to him and whispered through his teeth, "Shut up."

I grabbed the door handle and waved at Dr. Anson. "Thanks for understanding." I held the door open for Simon and shot a quick smile at De Luca.

Simon was right behind me. "I'll be back up in a few minutes, guys."

We walked quickly to the elevator, and after a silent ride to the first floor, Simon cleared his throat. "This is insane."

The doors opened and we headed for the exit that led to the parking lot.

Simon warned, "Just keep cool. Even when we're outside."

We pushed through the heavy front doors, the cold January wind thrashing our faces as we stepped out. We made our way down the stairs in somewhat of a controlled panic.

"Is it okay to freak out now?" I asked as we quickened our pace.

"No."

I stopped and looked back. "He can't see us. The lab is—"

"His office is on the fourth floor. I can see his window from here. I'm sure he's up there at the window by now. Keep moving."

"He knows we saw him in the viewing, doesn't he?"

Simon kept walking and waved for me to pick up my pace. "Let's talk by your car."

I watched Simon pull out a tiny bottle of caramel-colored liquor from his coat pocket. He looked back at me and pointed at my car. I nodded yes, and he made his way toward it while fidgeting with the cap of what appeared to be whiskey. He'd already swallowed the entire contents of the bottle by the time I caught up with him.

"Get your keys out like you're leaving," he instructed.

"You really think he's watching?"

"Fuck yeah."

I held out the car keys and shrugged my shoulders. "What do you want me to do now? Just lie to him when he asks?"

"Yeah. It's not a big deal."

I couldn't help scowling at him. "Really? Maybe it's not a big deal to you, but all of this is getting out of hand. This isn't normal stuff. Do I have to explain that to you? You *do* understand that nothing about this is normal, right?"

Simon's hand went into his coat again. I knew he was fishing for another bottle of liquor. "There's some things I haven't told you yet."

"Like what?"

"I already knew about Anson's connection to Carrol."

"You *did?!*"

"Yeah, but I didn't know he was a part of the rituals." Simon suddenly threw his hands into the air and stomped his foot on the ground. "Damn! I thought I had another bottle!"

"I'm going back to the hotel," I said calmly. "If Anson calls me, I'm going to tell him I don't feel well. You need to tell me what you're going to tell him, so I know how to keep our stories straight."

"I'm not tellin' him anything. Whatever he heard us say up there is what I'm stickin' to. I'm going to try to get him to let me watch the video of the session so I can see how he reacts to it."

"So do you think he knows we saw him there or not?" I asked impatiently. My phone started vibrating inside my jacket.

"He knows he was there. He's been listening to us describe a scene that he's been a part of, and he's probably been waitin' for us to figure it out. So yeah, I'm gonna guess he thinks we saw him or felt him there or whatever. But, I'm also guessing he hopes we didn't see him, you know? So we gotta stick to our story." Simon stopped and froze for a moment in realization. "And I gotta call Claire."

"Did you see more than I saw?"

He looked at me with a blank expression on his face. "No. Unless you're not telling me somethin'."

The circle of distrust continues. I opened the door to the car. "No. I told you everything."

"Go take a nap or get something to eat. Don't talk to Anson or De Luca until I get with you later."

"Fine." I just wanted to leave. "When are you going to be done with them? Are you going to call me as soon as you're done?"

"Yes. And don't talk to Claire or anyone else from the police department either."

I let out a big sigh. "Why?" I looked at him and shook my head. "You know what? Never mind. I don't care. I don't want to talk to anyone anyway."

I got into the car and pulled my phone out to check it. "De Luca texted me."

Simon leaned over the open car door to ask, "What's it say?"

"It says 'Anson left.'"

"Shit!" Simon slammed my door shut, hitting my elbow and knee when he did, and ran around to the passenger side of the car and jumped in. "Let's go!"

"What?!" My phone lit up and vibrated again.

"What's it say?" Simon asked quickly.

"It says, 'I'm coming out to talk to you. Something's wrong.'"

"De Luca sent that?"

"Yeah," I answered.

Simon slammed his door shut. "Let's go!"

"Go where?"

"To the station!"

"The police station? What for?!"

"Let's go before De Luca gets here!" Simon yelled into my face.

I turned back a little to see if De Luca was coming out of the building, afraid that I might see Dr. Anson as well.

"Come on! Start the car! Let's go!"

"Fine!" I yelled.

Someone then tapped on the back of the car, startling both of us.

"Shit. It's De Luca," Simon hissed.

I didn't know what to do. De Luca rushed over to my

window, leaned in close to it, and smiled. He was gasping for air.

I let my window down and put on a fake smile. "Hi," I said casually.

"Can I get in?" he asked in between breaths.

"Tell him to *fuck off*," Simon suggested loudly.

"Yes," I said to De Luca while nodding and unlocking the back doors.

"What is your problem?!" Simon snapped at me.

"I don't know what to do!"

De Luca practically threw himself into the back seat, then slammed the door. "I ran the whole way over here. We have to go."

I started the car and got us out of the crowded university parking lot as quickly and calmly as I could, trying not to draw too much attention.

"Where do you think we should go?" I asked De Luca. I glanced at him in the rearview mirror.

"To the police."

Simon turned in his seat to face De Luca. "What's goin' on? Where'd Anson go?"

"I don't know where he went," De Luca answered. "But before I flew in, I did a lot of research on Dr. Anson and his friendship with Dr. Carrol. It's bad. It's really really bad. I didn't want to believe any of it, but when you both left the building, Dr. Anson got upset. He panicked."

"What did he do?" Simon asked.

"He made a phone call. He told whoever it was that they had to finish. Then he said he was going up to his office. I went up there to check on him, but he wasn't there."

"Finish what?" I asked before I realized that I had no idea where I was driving to.

"Like I was saying before, I did some research on Dr. Anson and Dr. Carrol before I left Italy—"

"FINISH WHAT?!" Simon yelled impatiently.

De Luca thought on it. "I don't know. Something really bad. I think it's something to complete whatever it is they're trying to do. Another ritual, maybe? Something that will bring the dead over. All at once. Lots of them. Well, their spiritual energies. I think Anson's been a part of it the whole time."

Simon asked De Luca, "So you knew he was a part of the rituals?"

"I suspected it," he answered. "I used a mind technique from the transcripts to help you and Richard see more than you had before … hoping to find out. I hope you don't mind. I was just trying to help."

It made sense.

Simon pointed to a highway onramp. "The viewings we've done … I wonder how much he told Carrol about them."

De Luca sighed. "Well, I'm not exactly sure how close their friendship really is. Perhaps Dr. Anson isn't a willing participant."

Simon nodded. "Anonymous investors … what if Carrol was one of them?"

"What?" I asked, completely lost.

Simon explained, "Dr. Anson's research is being funded by investors, some of them anonymous. Now I'm starting to think Carrol was one of them. You know? So he could learn everything he needed to about our experiments?"

De Luca jumped in. "Did Dr. Anson ever tell you his theory on what happened to Marisol?"

Simon answered, "No. But I'm beginning to think that those body parts and things inside her were like …

placeholders or something."

"Yes. And I think Dr. Carrol is bringing the dead back to life—*with* those body parts," De Luca said.

"How?" I asked. "They were just left there, right? When the cops found her ... the parts were still inside?"

"Yes," De Luca answered. "The fact that he brought them into this world, cements some of their energy here. Like Simon said. Placeholders."

"Hmmm." Simon frowned sarcastically. "Either way, the parts and things ... I think Dr. Carrol is up to somethin' weird. But he's not bringin' back the dead. All I know is that he sacrificed Marisol in exchange for whatever he's plannin' to do—whatever he *thinks* he's plannin' to do."

De Luca scooted up in his seat and leaned in toward Simon. "At first, I thought you were helping him."

Simon laughed. "Well, I'm not. I thought *you* were helping him. You're the devil guy."

"Occult specialist. I think he was using me as a cover to make it look like he didn't know anything about the rituals," De Luca clarified. "Or about Satanic behavior."

"Why would he risk calling the both of us out here like this?" I asked. "We figured out what he's doing, didn't we?"

Simon laughed again. "Not really. I don't know what he's doin' or why. Do you, Raul?"

De Luca sighed. "Not entirely. Not yet."

"Where am I driving to?" I wondered.

"I have to report back to the station," Simon replied. "Plus, I think we're in danger now. So we should go there anyway, you know? To be safe, I guess."

To me, it was over—crime solved. The cops could take over from here. They had another suspect so they didn't need me anymore. "That's great. After that, I'm getting on a plane and heading home."

Simon looked over at me. "If you do that, you'll be dead. They're doing somethin' serious. Let's just figure a few things out first." He pulled out his cell phone and scrolled through his contacts.

"What's going on?" I asked. "Am I in the right lane?"

"A struggle for power," De Luca answered. "Science can only take us so far, and money can only buy us so many things. Real power exists in secrecy, and that's because humans aren't ready for it yet."

Simon placed the phone to his ear. "Detective Trevino please," he said. "Get into the right lane, Rich."

I changed lanes and then decided, again, to make my plans clear. It seemed more official that way. "After we file this report, I'm going home. We're filing a police report, right? You don't need my help anymore."

"I think Simon is right, Richard," De Luca said. "I don't think that would be a good idea. We're probably in a lot of danger right now."

"Yeah. Shut up, Richard. I'm trying to keep us alive. Dr. Anson and his buddy are probably sending demons after us right now or somethin'." Simon cleared his throat as someone on the other side of the phone answered. "Yes, sir, I meant to call earlier. Yes, sir. Yes ... yes ... I'm here with Mr. Ravestone and this Raul guy. We're heading over there right now. Dr. Anson might be planning something bigger now. Like, something more than what we'd expected. Possibly tonight. We're not sure about that, but ... no, sir. He's gone. We don't know where he is. Uh huh ... okay." Simon ended the call and slammed has hand on the dashboard.

"What's wrong?!" I asked, startled.

"He's pissed at me. That's what's wrong."

And that's when it hit me. "You're a *cop?*"

"I'm a detective."

I sort of half-smiled in disbelief while trying to keep my eyes on the road.

"Okay ... *was* a detective. I was fired a few years back, but ... I kinda told you about that already."

22

We sat in some guy's office at the police station for about ten minutes before the guy finally walked in. Until then, Simon spent most of the time rubbing his forehead and temples with his hands. He was completely stressed out and was mumbling something about how someone was probably going to kill him.

De Luca didn't seem too fazed by anything. He sat in a chair off to the side of a large desk, smiling to himself. Not in any sort of smug way—just content, maybe glad to be away from Dr. Anson. I wasn't really sure.

The man that walked into the office wore dark brown slacks, a white shirt, and a black tie. His hair was mostly gray and his skin weathered. I guessed that he was in his early 50s. He looked us over for a few seconds before slamming a coffee mug on the desk. "What happened?" he asked Simon.

"I guess he's gone."

"Gone?" the man asked. If a smile could be angry … well, that's what he had on his face.

"Yeah … I mean … ask this guy what happened." Simon pointed a finger at De Luca.

De Luca reacted by correcting his posture and looking slightly confused.

The angry man shook his head and ran his fingers through his thick hair. He glared at Simon. "Wallace, what the fuck did you tell the chief to get his approval on all this?"

Simon sat back in his seat with a serious look on his

face. "He *asked* me to help."

"No. No he didn't. Sandoval got you involved in this shit. That's what I get for listening to a rookie." The man then turned to me. "And who's this? *The book guy?*"

I reached across the cluttered desk with the offer of a handshake, but the man only looked annoyed by it. "Richard Ravestone. Nice to meet you, sir."

"I'm Detective Trevino. Is that your *real* name?"

"No," I answered. "My last name's Covetree. In real life, I guess."

"Mr. *Ravestone*, I don't know how you got dragged into it this far, but welcome aboard," he answered with heavy sarcasm. He didn't shake my hand either.

Simon let out a forceful breath of frustration and leaned back into his seat. "Anson contacted Richard. He's the one that got him involved."

"No, he didn't!" the detective yelled.

"Yes, he did! I watched him look the guy up on the fuckin' Internet!"

"No, Simon!" the detective argued. "You *told* Anson to contact him! I've been getting updates from Sandoval, remember?"

Simon crossed his arms and scowled at the detective.

"Or, you know what? Maybe one of your ghost friends contacted him. You still talking to ghosts, Simon?" The detective's sarcasm was heavy and his face was red with anger.

"I'm not putting up with this," Simon declared.

The detective leaned over his desk and smiled menacingly at Simon. "You had one of your stupid fucked up visions or whatever they are, and you told Anson to call Mr. Ravestone. Stop the bullshit!"

Simon leaned forward, his eyes wide. "He's a part of this case. Dr. Carrol is a fan of Richard's work and Anson started saying that he thought Carrol was getting some of his psychotic ideas from Richard's stories and stuff. And Richard was havin' weird dreams about the rituals that Carrol was kind of ... summoning Richard to."

Dr. Carrol was a fan of my books? More details that they hadn't let me in on. More lies. My face felt hot. I couldn't even bring myself to look at the detective, but I could feel him staring at me—judging me.

"So, Mr. Ravestone is a psychic, too?" the detective asked calmly.

Simon looked at me, giving me permission to answer.

I didn't have a lot of time to think about how to respond. "Um ... I'm new at this. I mean ... I'm a writer. I write about weird stuff, but ... um ... I wouldn't say that I'm psychic, but I guess what was happening in the dreams was pretty hard to explain. You know? Because I was having dreams about Dr. Carrol and things like that."

"Really?" Detective Trevino asked in a bitter tone.

"Well, yeah," I began. "I do dream about things sometimes—things that come true—but it doesn't happen very often. It did when I was a kid, but it sort of started up again recently." I didn't know why I was still talking. I knew he didn't care.

The detective rolled his eyes back and shook his head. He then pointed at De Luca. "And this guy? He flew out from Italy to be a part of this mess? Did you talk Anson into that shit, too, Simon?"

"No," Simon snapped back. "Anson contacted him on his own."

"Excuse me," De Luca said with a broad smile. "I contacted Dr. Anson myself. He returned my call after I emailed him for several weeks. It took a while for him to get back to me."

"*Why* did you contact him?" Detective Trevino asked.

"Because I wanted to warn him about some disturbing patterns I'd noticed. And I had translated some papers I wanted his opinion on," De Luca explained. "Students were going missing in Europe. Most of them were psychology students. The students that went missing had links to Dr. Carrol. Some of them, weak links, but the links were there."

The detective sat down in his chair and started to show some interest in what he was hearing. "Links to the cult-guy, huh?" he asked.

"The students either had Dr. Carrol's publications in their possession, which all seemed to be basic psychology articles or similar works authored by him, or had contacted him through email or through another student that had established regular contact with him. The emails exchanged were vague. Cryptic. They made no sense to investigators or to anyone else who read them."

"Why didn't I know about these emails?" the detective looked at Simon expectantly. "Did *you* know about them?"

"No," Simon answered defensively.

De Luca continued. "The emails were pointless anyway. I believe that after some initial contact between the students and Dr. Carrol, the students would continue their communications with him, or one of his associates, over the phone. I think they were interested in learning more about this 'scientific discovery' Dr. Carrol was going on about."

"How long after the students contacted him did they go missing?"

De Luca crinkled his mouth and forehead in thought. "Months later. Some of them … about a year."

"How many total?"

"It's difficult to say, sir," De Luca replied. "Some of

the students abandoned classes long before they actually went missing. They became reclusive and stopped attending school. It was like Dr. Carrol had control over them. His teachings were all that mattered to them. They had only limited contact with others. By the time they started disappearing, many of them had already stopped talking to their families. It wasn't easy to figure out what happened to them."

Detective Trevino frowned. "He lured students into his cult with some propaganda? I don't get it."

"They wanted to be a part of this so-called world-changing discovery that Dr. Carrol would hint to on some of his websites—he had a few that I was able to find. The websites were registered to him, well … to an alias that he used, and they hinted at ancient forms of enlightenment. Things like that. They were very philosophical."

The detective looked around the room before setting his eyes on the coffee mug on his desk. He tilted his head to the side. "Mr. Raul De Luca, right?"

"Yes, sir."

"Do you really believe that Dr. Anson and Dr. Carrol are part of a satanic cult?"

"No, sir," De Luca answered flatly.

"*What?!*" Simon lashed out at De Luca. "Are you serious?! Look at what's going on! Look at the shit Richard writes about! Dr. Carrol is Richard's biggest fan! In the dream, he has Richard's book … the one with the devil guy on the front cover … what's it called? Devil's Markers or Markers or—?"

Oh no, I thought. I covered my eyes with my hands and had to lower my head. Memories of staying up late into the night researching various cults and rituals flashed through my head. It was the worst book I had ever written and was certain that it had been forgotten. "Are you serious? You saw that book in my dream?"

Simon nodded. "Yeah."

"Why didn't you tell me?"

"I don't know," he answered. "What's the big deal?"

Detective Trevino held his hand up over his desk to quiet Simon. "Then what's with all the satanic clothing and candles and stuff, Mr. De Luca? If it's not a satanic cult, what is it?"

"Well, now, sir," De Luca leaned back in his seat, beaming with delight. "Don't the rituals in Richard's and Simon's walk-throughs—their viewings—seem a little forced? I don't exactly know how detailed of a report you were getting from Miss Sandoval or Mr. Wallace, but, no offence. The robes and candles … quite cliché. Right out of a book on Satanism that some misguided teenager might have access to at the public library."

My mouth dropped open in realization—De Luca was right. He knew all along that what Simon and I had seen was an elaborate act. Questions raced through my head, but all I could think to ask was, "It was *fake?*"

"No no no," De Luca said to all of us, shaking his head. "The energy of it was real! *Your* belief in it was real … and so was Marisol's! That's the point, you see? Dr. Carrol put on an act to create fear in all of us … *and* his followers. He's just copying Winston. And it was fear that made the ritual work. It was the fear that made all of those psychology students join him. Fear and power. He *is* a god to them."

Simon laughed. "That doesn't make any sense. If all of Dr. Carrol's associates in this are PhDs and university students—they're supposed to be brilliant, right? How come none of them figured any of this out? You're sayin' the whole thing is fake?! What's the point?"

"I'm only speculating, Simon. To me, Dr. Carrol

performing a satanic ritual seems preposterous. But, if he was able to convince others to believe that it was real, then the energy he created in that belief could give him access to the power he was seeking. That power is real. The fact that his followers are intelligent might even make that mind energy stronger and more useful to him."

There was a silence that followed.

I decided to ask a question. "What does he want to do with it? The energy."

De Luca gave me a sidelong glance and paused cautiously before answering. "Bring back the dead. He wants to trade lives from this world for those of another."

23

"Bringing back the dead sounds a little *cliché*, you know?" Simon said into my ear just loud enough for De Luca to hear.

De Luca turned to me with a large smile.

Detective Trevino left the room, to "discuss something with someone," and said he'd be right back. He'd been gone for at least fifteen minutes.

I looked around the office to be sure the detective had closed the door when he left before I dared to ask De Luca what I wanted to ask. "I thought Anson was looking into the whole 'defectors' thing. If they aren't dead, than what dead people is he trying to bring back?"

"Carrol's using his defectors to contact the dead for him," De Luca answered. "To travel into their world and bring them back—with a promise of eternal life."

Simon groaned. "How do you know all this stuff, De Luca? Are you listening to yourself? Bringing back the dead?"

"He's not talking about zombies, Simon." I hoped.

"No, I'm not," De Luca agreed. "Those are what you saw in your dreams, Richard. Those phantom-like beings. Those were defectors, existing in between worlds. They can exist where they want to, but under Carrol's command. They communicate with the dead for Carrol, trying to convince them to join him."

Something inside me clicked. "Do you remember, Simon? When I tried to tell you I had dreams about these gray creatures, phantoms that would show up and hunt people … people that lived near a castle and people in a battle during the Revolution—different people in different places. Maybe those were the defectors, traveling back and forth. Maybe Dr. Carrol wanted me to see it, to see what he was capable of. They were stealing innocent people's lives. Their energy. Like a food, maybe so they could keep existing like that … so they could go back and forth."

Simon shook his head. "You're going nuts, too."

It was all starting to fit together. The defectors, missing students, the rituals to drum up the energy he needed to make it all work. His selfishness. "He's been using these students to test out his cross over thing. Turning them into defectors," I said.

"Exactly, Richard." De Luca nodded. "Using them to recruit others from different worlds."

Simon stirred in his seat, annoyed. "Okay, we get it, Raul."

"Simon, come on," I said. "I've seen it. That's what those things were in my dreams."

Simon raised his eyebrows at De Luca. "So the defectors can pop in and out of our world and they're recruiting ghosts to help Carrol? Help him do what?"

"I'm not really sure what he's trying to do with the dead, actually," De Luca answered. "I just know that he is trying to bring them back."

"Well, that sounds legit." Simon rolled his eyes. "I'm convinced."

De Luca asked him, "With everything you've seen, is it really that difficult to believe? I've seen the transcripts. I've done my best to piece it together."

"I don't think this whole thing's as big as you say it is, De Luca, but I know these defectors are dangerous. The rest of it sounds kinda stupid. No offense."

"I understand, Simon," De Luca said. "The defectors *are* dangerous. They are like poltergeists, but a hundred times worse. And I really do believe that Carrol is using them to contact and bring back others that will serve him."

"Either way," Simon began, "Carrol's doing all of this stuff with satanic rituals. And if he's contacting ghosts from the past—or whatever he's doin'—it's evil. It's demonic stuff and he needs to be stopped."

"He's *not* a Satanist," De Luca tried again.

Simon's phone dinged. "Whatever. Who cares. Where's Detective Trevino?"

"I don't know," I answered. "He said he was going to be right—"

"It's Claire." Simon's eyes were huge, staring at the screen of his phone. "She wants to know where we are." He lifted his head into the air and let out a long breath. "Shit."

"Tell her where we are," I suggested.

"You don't understand." Simon looked extremely worried. "I didn't tell her about getting fired from the PD. I just started talking to her one night because she looked upset … and she was in uniform, so it felt like I knew her."

"I'm sure she'll understand."

"No, she won't," Simon insisted. "She'll never trust me again. She let me in on some really horrible things goin' on in her life. I wanted to help her, but she wouldn't let me. I can't go into it. I promised I would never say anything about what's happenin' to her. Then, she put her ass on the line to try and get these detectives to work with me. So I started workin' on the case, but only through her … and Trevino. I kept my identity secret from everyone else involved. I never came up here to the station with her. I just really wanted to help. I knew Marisol from when I was a detective. She'd helped me out a few times, you know? I owed it to her. What's the point of havin' a talent like this if you can't use it for somethin' good?"

"So that's how you knew Marisol?" I asked.

"Yeah."

"Wow," I sighed.

"So when Claire—"

The door suddenly swung open. Some papers and plastic cups blew across the desk, and we all turned to see Claire standing in the doorway.

"Hi," Simon squeaked.

"What the hell are you doing here?" she growled.

Simon's face went pale. "We did the viewing and then something went wrong."

"Dr. Anson's gone," I added for him, trying to help.

"Gone *where?*" she asked.

"We don't know," I replied.

Claire stepped in closer to Simon and glared at him. He turned away like a frightened puppy. "You used to be a *detective* here?" She was doing everything possible to maintain her composure.

"Yeah."

"Well? What happened? Why'd they fire you?"

Simon's breathing doubled. "Because some pricks in Oklahoma made me look like an idiot after I helped them. They called the station ... and I have a drinkin' problem. I think you know that."

Claire's shoulders sank. "That's *it?*"

"It's a pretty *big* drinkin' problem, I guess," he muttered in return.

"I'm in trouble because of you," she told him.

"I'm sorry. I'll talk to them for you—"

"They don't want to talk to you!" she yelled back. "Why didn't you just tell me?!"

Simon quickly turned to face her. "You were tellin' me about things. Personal things. I wanted you to trust me … I didn't want you to think I was gonna tell anyone here at the station what you told me. Don't you see that?" He looked away from her and lowered his voice. "And you were the one that dragged me into this case. I didn't want to do it. I mean, I wanted to help Marisol, but I did it mostly to help you because you asked me to. Then I got all connected to it … and now Richard's here …" Simon turned to De Luca but then frowned. "And *him*."

Claire's eyes dropped to the floor. She grabbed onto the back of Simon's chair like she was trying to keep herself from falling over. Her arms shook and her lips trembled. In uniform, she was a different Claire than the one I'd seen before.

"I'm sorry," Simon said.

"You'd better have something from that viewing," she said in return. Her voice was cracked and weak when she said it.

"I think we can piece some things together, right?" Simon turned toward me and De Luca.

I really didn't know how to respond. I didn't think we had a lot to go on and wondered if Simon was just trying to quell her with false hopes.

"Yes!" De Luca said excitedly. "We do!"

Claire's face lit up. "Really?"

De Luca had a huge grin on his face. "Yes. Don't worry. We'll get them before things can get worse."

"Worse?" Claire asked.

De Luca shook his head to dismiss the *worse* part. "Tell Detective Trevino that all we need to do is find Dr. Anson. He'll lead us to the next ritual. Hopefully we'll catch him before he starts bringing the dead back to life—"

"SHHHHHHHHH!" Simon hissed while frantically waving his hands around in front of him. "SHUT UP, DE LUCA! No, Claire, there's no dead people comin' back to life. This guy's a little confused about what's goin' on here."

"Yes there are." De Luca crossed his arms confidently. The smile had vanished from his face and a sinister stare had taken its place. "You have to trust me. I've dealt with this before. The last time I saw it was in Russia. They did a good job of hiding it, but by the time they called me in, hundreds of people had already been killed. Sacrificed in an attempt to revive people that a group of selfish intellectuals wanted brought back in the victims' places."

"Bullshit," Simon huffed. "You can't hide hundreds of deaths."

De Luca raised an eyebrow as the grin returned. "Yes, you can, Mr. Wallace. They did it to prevent panic." He turned his gaze to me. "Do you really want to risk it after all that you've seen? The apports you saw in Marisol were only the beginning. If this case is even remotely similar to the one in Russia, then every person they deem worthy of sacrifice will be exchanged for spirit entities that don't belong here. Those defectors aren't recruiting innocent souls—many will be people that have been dead for years, people that should remain on the other side. And it will set everything off-balance in ways I cannot explain to you."

De Luca's words swelled inside my head. I was horrified in a way that made my face numb. I remembered Marisol … her mouth forced open and her eyes painfully distorted. It sickened me. I wanted De Luca to stop talking about it, because I was too weak to take it.

"There were so many … pieces inside her body." It hurt to say it out loud.

De Luca's eyes shifted between mine and Claire's in desperation. "Those were only *some* of the placeholders—like a test. He could bring over many more of those things if he wanted to. He'll get better at it. Soon, he won't even need placeholders."

I looked at Simon. "We have to find them."

"This is crazy," Simon replied. "You're crazy, De Luca. I don't want any part of this."

I was pissed at him. "Are you serious, Simon?"

"Yeah. You go tell Trevino this whole thing's about raising the dead. Go ahead."

"Then stay out of it," I said firmly before turning to Claire. "Are *you* in?"

"Yes," she answered without hesitation.

We both turned to De Luca.

"We need this department's help," De Luca said. "I think we should keep the government out of it, though. Of course, it would be easier if Simon would try to do a visual on Dr. Carrol and Dr. Anson's location."

Claire asked, "Please, Simon. For Marisol."

Simon groaned. He closed his eyes and lifted his head toward the ceiling. "Okay, fine. You're not doing this without me. I can't let you. I want to find Carrol as much as you do."

Claire's face softened. "Thank you, Simon."

Detective Trevino then opened the door and stormed into his office. He lowered his head and looked over his glasses to study each one of us before curling his lip. "You're all in our custody. You, too, Sandoval."

"What?!" she protested.

"It's for your own safety. Well, except for you, De Luca," the detective explained without a shred of emotion in his voice. He glanced at a small television attached to the wall next to his desk. "The game's coming on in a bit. We'll hang around here and order some food. Everyone just … have a seat and relax. I promise you, if the dead start comin' back to life, we'll be fine right here in my office."

"Fuckin' hilarious," Simon said under his breath.

Detective Trevino shot him a warning glance before turning to De Luca. "Captain Perez contacted someone with the Italian Government."

De Luca looked as if he'd stopped breathing.

"Raul Cesar De Luca," Detective Trevino said in a sour tone. "The Italian government really hates you."

De Luca looked up at him like a nervous child. "Did they … tell your captain that?"

"Yes," the detective answered dryly. "They also listed several other countries that want nothing to do with you. I laughed for a while about it, but then I realized that it wasn't very funny because that means you're wasting my time. I'm doing what I can to send you back home—but it seems that there isn't a country I can find that really wants you."

"No. We have to find Dr. Anson," De Luca moaned. He sank back into his seat with a dazed look in his eyes. "This is an extremely serious situation. I beg you to listen to me!"

Detective Trevino sat in his chair and leaned back. He reached for the remote control that was next to a pile of papers and a stapler, and pointed it at the TV.

"If Signore De Luca has another outburst like that, Sandoval, I want you to cuff him."

Claire glanced at De Luca and frowned. "Yes, sir."

24

About an hour had passed before Detective Trevino's cell phone vibrated against the top of his desk. "Bullshit!" he yelled at the television without bothering to look at his phone. His team was losing, and his mood was foul. Whenever De Luca coughed or cleared his throat, the detective would give him a death-stare that was very similar to the one my mother used on me as a kid.

Simon didn't want us to notice that he was into the game—really into it. So his eyes shifted around the room a lot, trying to avoid the TV screen. It was Detective Trevino's game. And in Simon's eyes, Trevino was the enemy. It kind of looked like it had been that way between them for quite a while.

Claire had taken to staring blankly at the wall behind Trevino in absolute hatred. She'd worked up a pretty good snarl and occasionally tapped her shoes on the floor to create an irritating clicking sound. She looked at me a few times in disgust when she caught Simon reacting to plays in the game. She didn't utter a word the entire hour.

De Luca's behavior confused me. I watched him take a nap with his arms crossed into his chest and his mouth hanging open. He was able to do this while sitting perfectly upright in his chair. His head would bob and tip back at times, but he would catch himself. I found this interesting to see since, from what I understood, some people had been assigned to start working on getting De Luca sent back home as soon as possible for interfering with an investigation or something. Detective Trevino did a good job of making whatever it was sound like it was something fairly serious.

When Trevino's phone vibrated a second time, he jumped in his seat. "Dammit! I'm watchin' a game here!" There was also a knock at his office door. "What?!" he called out.

A younger man in a dark suit cautiously opened the door and leaned in. "There's a man on the phone for you, sir. Says it's a lead."

"On what?"

The young man scanned the room. "On this, sir."

"Oh. Okay. Put it through."

This grabbed everyone's attention and even jolted De Luca awake. Claire sat forward and studied me for a reaction. She couldn't wait to find out who was on the phone. Personally, I guessed it was Dr. Anson. And from the look on Simon's face, I assumed he was thinking the same thing.

Leaning against the door frame, the man in the dark suit opened his mouth to say something, but hesitated a moment too long. "I think you should take it in private."

I guess it was only natural that every one of us then looked at Detective Trevino for his reaction. "It's fine. Put it through."

The man at the door did a half-nod in agreement and closed the door as he left.

"You don't believe any of it, do you?" Simon asked Trevino.

The detective didn't answer. He only stared at Simon with darkened eyes and a smugness about him that spoke volumes—it screamed that he was tired of theories and philosophical complexities. This was nothing but science fiction to him. It wasn't a case anymore—it was a mythical beast that had gotten out of hand.

The phone rang and a tiny light flicked along with it.

"Hello?" Detective Trevino answered.

And then, surprisingly, with the press of a button, he put the call on speaker.

"*I have important information for you.*" The male voice coming through had an accent that sounded almost French—it had to be Swiss French. And it was nasally and broken.

"About what?" the detective asked. He grabbed the remote control and muted the TV.

"*Do you want the information or not?*"

"I work a lot of cases. You're going to have to be more specific about what you've got."

"*I have Dr. Miller Anson,*" the man stated simply.

The detective's face froze and he looked at each one of us with his mouth in a twist.

"*Simon, did you enjoy seeing into my world?*" the man asked. "*It's over now. Don't try it again. You'll get nothing.*"

The detective leaned over his desk. "Why do you have Dr. Anson? Let me talk to him."

"*I have him because he came to me. He cannot speak to you because I'm preparing to sacrifice him. It takes a great amount of planning.*"

Simon jumped out of his seat, outraged, and pointed a tense finger at the phone. "Don't touch him!"

The man on the other end of the phone let out a chuckle. "*Is Raul De Luca with you, Simon? I was disappointed that Miller didn't bring him to me, because that was the plan. More sacrifices means more defectors ... more contacts with the other side.*"

De Luca, wide-eyed and alert, scooted to the edge of his seat. He lightly repositioned his glasses with his thin fingers. "I am here, Dr. Carrol."

"*Oh wonderful,*" the man answered. "*I wish we could have met in person, Raul. Your theories are faulty and your research weak, but I do have some respect for you, regardless.*"

"What you are doing will off-set the balance of the dead," De Luca warned him. "How many more impressionable students will be brainwashed and lied to? How many do you have planning to kill themselves for you? How much longer will you feed into this madness?"

"*You do not understand divinity, Raul. And once again, you are wrong. My ideas have a world-wide reach. I have followers—believers—everywhere.*" He paused. "*Mr. Ravestone, I don't know why you want to waste your valuable time with people like Raul. I hope you have been able to enjoy yourself on your visit to Texas, anyway.*"

I didn't know how to respond. Everyone's eyes were on me and I felt pressured to answer him. "Uh … okay."

"*You obviously don't know Dr. Miller Anson. If any of you did, you certainly wouldn't be defending him. Besides, it's too late. He will finally provide an important contribution to the world by sacrificing himself. He will be making room for others more deserving than he is.*"

"More deserving?!" Simon yelled.

"*Detective Trevino,*" the man said sharply, "*you can explain to your psychic ex-detective that his mentor, Dr. Anson, lied to him and deceived him from the very beginning. Dr. Anson used him. What he learned about Simon's abilities, he passed on to me. Why Simon would feel any sympathy for him makes little sense to me. You should all be thanking me for getting rid of him.*"

"You funded everything at the lab, didn't you?" Simon asked.

There was a pause. "*I did.*"

The detective tensed up. "Are you Dr. Peter Carrol?"

"*Yes,*" he answered, and I could picture him smiling as he said it.

"Are you willing to tell us where you're located?"

"*Of course not,*" Dr. Carrol replied in a chipper tone. "*But, I can tell you that Dr. Anson's death will provide something meaningful to this world.*"

Simon gritted his teeth. "That's your own insane opinion."

Dr. Carrol waited a few seconds before speaking again. "*The same fire that extinguished so many through the ages, will be the same fire that brings them back. It will burn within Dr. Anson and give a re-birth to the lives of those who will sacrifice themselves to serve a greater purpose. And under my command, they will reach out to bring back those that were taken from this material plane before they were ready to leave it. And as was offered by the serpent, forbidden knowledge will be ours again.*"

Silence enveloped the room.

"*Goodbye,*" Dr. Carrol said. The line went dead with a click.

25

The tone in Dr. Carrol's voice had something in it that was undefinable. It wasn't that he was *trying* to sound evil or anything, but because we all knew what he was up to—the evil was there. He didn't have to try … it just existed. It was felt by all of us as he spoke, and then left us suddenly in an unbalanced silence. As soon as the call ended I looked around the room, waiting for the others to react.

Simon rubbed his hands together and forced out a hard sigh. "He's gonna kill Anson."

De Luca jumped out of his seat. His eyes darted about the room excitedly and then quickly settled onto mine. "It's worse than that. You heard what he said. *More* defectors *and* the souls of the dead. It's a ritual for both. You and Simon need to find him!"

"How?!" Simon blurted out.

"You know how! View him!" De Luca leaned in closer to Simon. "Use the sound of his voice, the memory of it in your head, to guide you. Focus on it."

"You think this is a fucking circus or something? It's not that easy! Especially under this much pressure."

I turned to Detective Trevino. On his face was a hardened stare. "Sir," I began, "you see what we're dealing with. Please help us find Dr. Carrol. Even if you think he's just some kooky nutcase … he's going to kill Dr. Anson. You heard him say that. He's psychotic. He believes what he's saying about all this … weirdness."

"All right," the detective agreed. "But we're going to keep this as quiet as possible. This whole thing. Got it?" Detective Trevino stood and grabbed the beige suit jacket hanging over the back of his chair. He then looked at each of us with intimidating eyes as he spoke. "We're all going to get up, walk out of my office, and exit this building as if nothing is going on. All right?"

We all agreed.

"Then, we're going to get into our vehicles and meet up somewhere to figure out our next move."

De Luca turned nervously to Simon. "We don't have time to—"

"Then what do you want to do?!" the detective snapped.

De Luca tensed up. "Simon, can you try to view Dr. Anson's location?"

"Where? *Here?*" Simon asked.

Detective Trevino was already shaking his head. "No! We're not doing any of that stuff in my office." He rubbed the side of his face in frustration.

I could see in De Luca's eyes another idea brewing. "Can you do it in a car?"

Simon smiled. "I can do lots of things in a car."

Claire sighed. "Come on, Simon."

Simon looked embarrassed. "I can view from anywhere. That's not the problem. I just … I do things better without pressure. I'm stressed out."

Claire stepped over to whisper something into Detective Trevino's ear.

"Yeah," the detective answered her. "He's always got a bottle hidden in his desk."

I guessed that it hadn't been a very busy day at the station. Everyone just sat and stared at us when we all started filing out of Detective Trevino's office and into the large open room. It was filled with desks and cubicle spaces, many of them occupied by men and women in plain clothes and some in dark navy blue police uniforms. Claire smiled at a few of the uniformed officers as we made our way toward an exit at the other side of the room. Detective Trevino stopped to make small talk with someone at the entrance to another office. When Simon and I looked back at him, he nodded and waved his hand toward the hallway.

Claire caught up with us. "Just keep going. He's getting Simon a drink."

"Oh," I answered, having already figured that part out.

Then, in some freakishly strange and poorly timed twist of fate, a man in a suit jumped up from his desk and called out, "Isn't that Richard Ravestone?"

Oh no, I thought.

I stopped and turned to see Claire cringing.

The man rushed toward me. "I have one of your books in my car! What a coincidence! I just finished it yesterday. Are you in town for a book signing?"

"No, I …"

"Let me get it real quick! I'll be right back!"

Over Claire's shoulders, I saw Detective Trevino slip smoothly into an opened office door. "Uh … actually, I'm kind of in a hurry," I said to the man. I put on one of those fake smiles.

The man in the suit kept on ahead of us toward the hallway. He had a thick bristly mustache and a dark head of hair. "My car's right outside! I'll be quick!"

Simon stopped and tugged at De Luca's jacket. "Richard is so much fun to hang out with," he complained. He looked past me and smiled. "Let's go."

I glanced back to see Detective Trevino exiting the

office he'd slipped into. He had his beige jacket on now and was hurrying toward us with his arm held across his chest.

"We have to keep going," Simon reminded us. "Let's go. Now!"

And just as he'd caught up to us, a woman called out, "Detective Trevino?"

The detective's face froze. He stopped and turned to acknowledge the nicely dressed woman approaching him. He tightened his arm around what had to be a bottle of liquor inside his jacket and tried to look natural. "Yes?"

"Sir," the woman began. She had to take a moment to catch her breath before continuing. "There's a man on the phone who says he needs to speak with you about something important." Her eyes turned to me.

"I'm on my way out," Trevino explained. "I have to escort Mr. Covetree … or, um, Ravestone, … to an event. Please get Detective Baker to take the call for me."

"But, sir. The man has to speak with you." The woman's eyes were sharp on him. She wasn't going to say anything else about the phone call in front of us.

Detective Trevino moved in closer to her, gripping his jacket a bit tighter. He lowered his voice. "Look, I really have to go. Mr. Ravestone's been threatened. I have to make sure he gets back to his hotel so he can get ready for this dinner-thing. I'm in charge of keeping him safe. Please, get someone else to take the call."

The woman lowered her eyes and inhaled a deep breath through her nose. "That's what the call's about, sir. It's a man threatening to hurt Mr. Ravestone."

Detective Trevino's jaw dropped. He looked at me, his eyes wide with panic. "Okay, yeah. I guess that's a call I need to take." Awkwardly, the detective scooted closer to me and pushed the bottle of liquor into my jacket. "I'll take the call and you guys go on ahead to the car. Claire, stay alert. I'll be there in a few minutes."

Claire placed a hand on my shoulder and leaned in to my ear. "It's okay. Keep going. We need to get Simon to the car."

I knew she was right.

Why would someone want to kill me?

There were more important matters to deal with. I knew that. Simon and De Luca pushed on sloppily ahead of us. They looked like they might be squabbling about something, but I didn't care. In between thoughts of my possible impending death, a bottle of something now sloshed around in the hand I had hidden inside my jacket.

All for Simon, of course.

Once we got outside, a voice called out, "Mr. Ravestone!" causing me to flinch and duck instinctively. It was the cop that wanted my autograph.

"See?!" he shouted, holding the book into the air above his head. "I have the book! It's your latest one! Just finished it yesterday! Do you have a special pen you use or—?"

"Oh," I said while attempting to catch my breath. "Yes, I do, but ... no, I don't have it on me."

Simon glanced back and rolled his eyes at us before continuing on with De Luca to the car.

The officer smiled. "That's okay, sir. I have one you can use. We always carry plenty of pens with us. Right, Sandoval?"

"Oh yeah. I usually carry, like, four or five on me," she laughed nervously. "It's just part of the job."

The man then pulled out a handgun and pushed it against my abdomen. The smile never left his face. "Walk with me, Mr. Ravestone."

26

With the gun jabbed into my side, the officer led us toward a black sedan. He was giving Claire orders, threatening her as he forced the gun into my ribs, but I had a hard time focusing on what he was saying. For some reason, all I could think about was Detective Trevino and wondered who he could possibly be talking to on the phone.

"Richard!" Simon's voice rang across the parking lot. "*What are you doing?!*"

The officer gave Claire some commands.

"Richard's going to sign his book," she yelled back. "We just need to get a pen!"

"We don't have time for this!" Simon shouted back, seriously pissed.

The officer pressed the gun harder into my ribs and shoved the book into my hand. He dug into his pants' pocket for his keys and barked more orders at Claire. As she got into the front passenger seat of the car, I was pushed into the back. The officer then carefully pointed his weapon at Claire through the front windshield as he made his way around to the driver's side door.

"You still have the bottle?" she asked quickly.

"Yes," I exhaled.

"Think about Simon."

"*What?*" I asked in confusion.

The officer opened his door and got in. He checked on me and then pointed the gun at Claire. "We're going to visit your biggest fan. He's very excited to meet you, Rich."

He started the car with the gun still on Claire. She was frozen in her seat. I looked out my window to see if I could get Simon's attention, but they were too far away from us.

"You're not going to kill us," Claire said to the man. There wasn't a lot of confidence in her statement, though. It sounded more like a question. "You'll lose everything."

He let out a dark laugh. "I'll *gain* everything. Give me your piece. Your radio, too."

I could hear Claire unsnapping her holster. She handed over her gun and, moments later, her radio.

He started driving out of the parking lot while Simon and De Luca watched in disbelief. They were standing next to my rental car.

"What do you mean, you'll gain everything?" Claire asked carefully.

"Dr. Carrol is the Chosen One. A god. We all have a lot to learn from him. You should feel honored that he wants to meet with you," the man replied.

"Hey!" I could hear a voice cry out from behind us. "HEY!!"

"Don't look back!" the man instructed.

"They're going to follow us," Claire warned him. "And Detective Trevino won't be far behind."

I suddenly realized something—I had the keys to the rental car.

"It won't matter," the man said. "We'll be with Dr. Carrol soon. Besides, they'll be getting a late start with that phone call Trevino took." He drove faster, navigating through city streets. "I wonder how long it'll take him to figure *that* out."

I could tell by the sound of Claire's breathing that she

was starting to panic. "And then what? You'll kill us?"

He paused before answering and steadied his grip on the gun in his hand. "You will witness the most important ceremony of your life." His voice was deep and monotone. "It is like nothing you could ever imagine—like a merging of two worlds." He let his window down and threw Claire's police radio out.

The fear I felt was overwhelming.

"Jesus Christ," I sighed. "Please, just let us go and we won't—"

"SHUT THE FUCK UP!" he screamed at the top of his lungs. He leaned over the center console to jab the gun into the side of Claire's head. The veins in his face and neck protruding, his skin turning purple and red. "You don't know what you're saying! Shut up! Damn you for having any doubt in our living God!"

The car swerved violently.

"He is here! In human form! He exists and walks among us! How dare you speak of such filth in my car! SHUT YOUR FUCKING MOUTH!"

The man was deranged.

Claire begged, "Look at the road, *please!*"

I went through it all again inside my head … what had I said? What set this man off … to that extreme? I whispered, "*Jesus?*"

"NO!" he screamed with greater force behind it. "Repent to our Lord! Repent to our Lord!"

The car swerved again.

Claire screamed, "Please! What do you want us to do?!"

"Pray to the gods of the underworld for forgiveness! You speak of filth!" He tried to hit Claire in the head with his gun, but she ducked and it slammed into her shoulder.

"Okay, okay!" she yelled in pain. She started crying.

"Please, Richard. Please, just … just ask for forgiveness. We'll both pray for forgiveness. Please … I'm sorry. I'm sorry," she sobbed.

The man relaxed his excessive grip on the steering wheel. "Yes," he answered. "Repent. Ask the dark lords for forgiveness and they will forgive."

He recklessly merged onto a highway.

Claire turned her head slowly to look me in the eyes, her back curved and her hands in front of her face. She trembled uncontrollably. "Just pray with me, Richard. Ask for forgiveness."

I was horrified. He'd hit her. She was in pain. "Of course," I replied robotically, pissed off beyond words. "Please forgive me, dark lords. I ask for forgiveness."

The man exhaled and I could see a smile on his face. "Very good, Mr. Ravestone. And now repeat my words."

I swallowed hard and waited, expecting the worst.

He lifted his chin into the air. "All forces of darkness will be with us," he said.

Claire and I repeated it, just as he had instructed us to. And as we did, his shoulders seemed to relax a bit, and his driving steadied.

"In your presence, Great Lord, we will synchronize and open our minds to your endless power."

Again, we repeated his words.

"Great Dark Lord, the lives we take tonight will be in celebration of your power."

Claire's mouth dropped open. She began to hyperventilate.

"REPEAT MY WORDS!"

We complied and he continued.

"And the lives we will replace them with will grace this earth again in your honor, as they will serve and worship your unequaled greatness for eternity."

27

Thirty minutes later.

I had no idea where we were, and besides, San Antonio wasn't my town. We were on the fourth level of a dark parking garage. A highway sign we'd passed along the way read 410 West and the exit mentioned a street named Broadway, but I wasn't too sure. I'd been thinking about Simon the entire time—well, not *about* him, but sort of trying to send thoughts his way—after our prayer to the satanic forces, that is. And I hoped desperately that my psychic emails to Simon would work.

"Take off your seat belts," our captor instructed. "We're getting in the elevator and going up to an office."

The parking garage was attached to an office building. I didn't see the name of the building itself, but it was gray and had a large vinyl sign hanging from it advertising space for rent.

Broadway and 410 ... I think ... right off the highway. Come on, Simon. Hurry.

As Claire removed her seatbelt, she looked back at me and at the bottle of liquor in my jacket with raised eyebrows. I glanced quickly at the man in the driver's seat, the handgun still firmly pointed at Claire, and contemplated her unspoken suggestion. There was no doubt that I wanted to hurt the guy ... I didn't know if it would backfire, if the blow wouldn't be hard enough, if he would pull the trigger in the process … I remembered that he had two guns. He messed with his tie and reached for his door handle.

I removed the bottle from my jacket, grasping the neck tightly with both hands, careful to make sure that my reflection couldn't be seen in the rearview mirror. I leaned back, pulling the neck of the bottle back with me and over my right shoulder. Claire leaned over to her door as if to open it.

"Wait for me," the man said to her. "I'll let you out. Both of you—"

The second he started turning to face me, I slammed the end of the bottle into the side of his face with one forceful push. His body slumped and his head slammed into the top of the steering wheel with a sickening thud. I closed my eyes as nausea took over.

Claire grabbed for the guns and then quickly patted him down. "Come on! We have to get out of here!" she said to me.

"What do we do with him? Do we push him out and go back to the station? We need to get back over there," I said. "Do we put him in the trunk?!"

"No. We have to go up there and stop them. They're going to kill people. You heard him. Dr. Carrol's up there!"

I sat frozen in silence, imagining the two of us running around aimlessly looking for some crazy satanic ritual-guy.

"There's only two of us, and who knows how many of them," I reminded her. "It sounds like a whole cult is up there somewhere."

She swiped the screen of her cell phone and tapped on it a few times. After putting it to her ear, she pointed one of the guns at the man slumped over next to her, his head now bleeding. "We have to get up there and … Hello? Yeah! It's Sandoval! Stevenson forced us into his car at gunpoint and—"

We both jumped as her passenger side window suddenly shattered into a million pieces.

Claire screamed.

"End the call," a man's voice instructed.

My focus was on the large gun that was pointed directly at the side of Claire's head. "Okay."

"Give me both guns." The man held out an open palm through the broken window.

"Yes. Yes, of course," she answered. She moved slowly to place each weapon into the man's hand.

"Get out," he instructed next. "Leave your cell phone in the car."

Claire did as she was told, reaching for the door handle with care. I watched and waited, not wanting to make any sudden movements. After Claire was out, the man stepped over to my door. He grabbed Claire's arm and pulled her in front of my window, pushing her face against the glass with his gun.

"Get out and do everything I say," he said to me. His voice was stern. "Take out your cell phone and leave it on the seat."

Claire's eyes were frenzied and her mouth was open, quivering uncontrollably. Her eyeliner was messy and smeared with tears. The gun was pressed hard against her temple, pushing into the skin near her eye. Seeing her like that, in that state, with a second man now holding a gun to her head, was appalling.

Please don't shoot her. Please, God, please don't let him.

I was careful with the door handle. I did my best to pull on it gently while watching the look on Claire's face. The man yanked her backward, the gun still against her head. I pushed the door open and stepped out, waiting for my next command.

The man's face was set into a heavy scowl. He looked at me with sharp green eyes, his wiry hair unevenly patched with gray. It was parted to the side. His face was thin and he had dark circles under his eyes. "Are you Richard Ravestone?"

"Yes," I answered, hating the way he'd said it.

"Here," the man said while handing a gun to Claire. "Take care of your friend—the other cop."

Claire gasped. "He's not our friend. He brought us here at gunpoint ... isn't he with *you*?"

"Do it," the man said through his teeth.

Claire took the gun into her shaky hand and stared at it.

The man pressed his gun into her head again and moved in close to her ear. "Fucking shoot him or I'll blow your head off in front of your boyfriend here. Is that what you want? Dr. Carrol doesn't give a *fuck* about you. Do you understand me?" the man hissed at her like a serpent.

I felt helpless.

Claire was trembling. "Okay."

She held the gun out in front of her, moving carefully toward the car, glass crunching beneath her shoes with each step. When she got to the broken passenger side window, her hands trembled uncontrollably as she positioned the gun through the open window and took aim at the man inside. Broken glass was scattered all over the ground and glittered in the dying sunlight that came through the cement walls surrounding us.

The man inside the car moved his arm and moaned.

"Hurry up!" the thin-faced man yelled.

Claire's body jolted at the sound of his voice and she

steadied her grip on the weapon.

I could see the pain in her eyes and had to look away. She pulled the trigger. I turned to face the man that had his gun pointed at Claire's head just in time to see him smile. His crooked teeth gleamed in the rays of sunlight. I wanted to hide. I wished I could be stronger than I was. Claire began to sob.

"Both of you, come with me. Now!"

The elevator was too slow. With three guns available to him, our captor had two of them pointed at us. Claire was hunched over with her back to the wall. Silent tears streamed down her face and a thick string of mucus hung from her nose. I wanted to reach out for her. She'd just killed a fellow officer …

"Dr. Carrol's been waiting."

I wanted to risk it all. I had the urge to lunge at him, and for a split second, envisioned myself doing so. "Why did you make her do that?!" I asked angrily.

The man stepped in close to me. I caught a whiff of something that smelled cheap and musky—a bad deodorant maybe. "Shut up," he growled in a way that didn't seem natural. It was like he was an actor in a bad film. Like he was forcing himself to be tough. I had a feeling this wasn't who he was or wanted to be.

Claire's arms hung low and she was still shaking.

The elevator stopped with a ding.

"Get out!" the man shouted. He steadied his aim on Claire and kicked the back of her leg. "You first."

She slowly stepped out, her eyes swollen with tears. She was in too much pain to object or to fight anything. There was nothing left but to do what he said.

He pointed one of the guns at me. "We are going to walk down this hallway. If either one of you tries anything, I'll kill you."

I looked at him with an empty expression. "Okay," I agreed for the both of us.

So we made our way down the hall, the man with the thin face pacing himself behind us, pointing his weapons at both of us along the way. When I attempted to place a hand on Claire's shoulder, just to let her know I was there, the man hissed at me to get away from her. He warned me not to touch her again.

I remember the cream-colored walls and how they captured parts of the sunset on them. There were hot pink and orange colors that would have normally seemed beautiful to me, but now they were hideous. I wondered if those colors had been appreciated by anyone else in that way, as they coated the walls of this building. And I didn't know why I was thinking about it at all, with a gun pointed to the back of my head.

"This is it," the man said. He knocked lightly on the door then backed away from it. "You're going inside," he said while he waved the guns at us. Claire and I moved into position in front of the door. "Now open it."

Claire and I looked at each other, not sure which one of us the man was speaking to.

"You," he said, pressing the tip of a gun into Claire's back. "Open it!"

Claire turned the knob and pushed the door open into the darkened room.

"Bow your heads and walk inside," he instructed. There was fear in his voice.

Claire lowered her head and walked in. I followed closely behind. Once inside, the door was shut behind us, and we were immersed in total darkness. I instantly reached out to feel for the back of Claire's shirt. When I looked down to the floor, I could only see a small amount of light coming in from underneath the door behind us. The backs of Claire's shoes were illuminated by it, but just barely. I tried looking around to see anything I could, but my eyes wouldn't adjust.

"You may come forward," a male voice called out with an echo that followed close behind it. The voice had an accent I recognized.

I grasped tightly onto Claire's shirt, pulling part of it out from the uniform pants it was tucked into. I didn't want to move. She remained still, but through the grip I had on her shirt, I could feel her body brace itself for the unexpected.

"You want light," the voice said. "You need assurance of your own safety. As if the dark could harm you."

I tugged gently on Claire's shirt to let her know that I wanted to answer.

"It's not the dark we are afraid of," I said.

There was a rustling sound and then the man cleared his throat. "You are afraid of what's inside the dark. With light, do you really feel any safer? If you see what threatens you, are you really more prepared to fight it?"

Claire shuddered.

I did my best to gather the strength to answer him. "If I say yes, will you turn on the lights?" I asked.

There was a silent pause before he spoke again. It unnerved me. "What is it that you are expecting to see, Richard?"

"I don't know."

"Do you expect to see Dr. Anson lying here, prepared for ritual? Do you expect to see an exit that you might be able to use as an escape?"

"I don't know," I answered honestly. "I just … I would feel better if I could see you. That's all."

"Mr. Ravestone," the man began, "what you see, is

what you want to see. Sight is in your mind. You should know that with the lights on, nothing in here will change. I will still overpower you. I will still harvest Miller Anson and use him to revive those who will better serve me. I will change science. I will re-seed this world with great knowledge ... knowledge once forbidden to man. I, Richard, will change this existence. I will merge dimensions." The man stopped speaking and I could hear him lean forward like he was seated in a chair. "In light or in darkness, I will win."

For a moment as he spoke those words, with power and surreal confidence, I forgot that we were standing in the darkness of an office on the fifth floor of a space-available-for-rent building alongside a busy city highway. Overhead, the sound of an airplane snapped me back into place. The man was insane. Delusional. He had christened himself with a power that he truly believed would change the world.

"Yes," I said, unsure of myself and what point I was about to make. "I understand that light will only ... um ... allow us to see things, but—"

"You are a prisoner, Richard. A prisoner of your own mind. You drag yourself along a path that is smeared with lies ... and when given the choice, you wish to see it more clearly?"

"Please," Claire asked with a weak voice. "What do you want from us?"

I could hear the man shift again in his seat. "And you, Officer Sandoval? You want the light, also? You want to see what you have done? You wish to relive it in the light? Can you not see it still inside your head?"

"Stop," Claire begged him as she began to shrivel down in front of me. "Stop!"

"How did it feel to kill yourself out there in the

parking garage?"

"NO!" she screeched.

The man laughed. "Because that's what it felt like, didn't it? Like you had pulled the trigger on yourself? It was like killing a brother. Were you not bound by a code of honor? Didn't you share an oath? A family?"

I lost my hold on her shirt as she collapsed to the floor.

"Stop!"

"Now answer me, why do you feel this way? Didn't he betray you?" the man asked. "He held a gun to you. But when you pulled the trigger, you felt as if you had killed yourself."

Claire wept.

"Stop this!" I demanded.

"And now you understand why I must take Miller Anson from this world. He was turning against me … having second thoughts. He betrayed me, too."

"It's not the same," I said through my teeth.

"You still want the lights on?" he asked again, his voice so low that it croaked. "So you can see what's next? To see what I'll do to you, also? Do you think that if you can see what's going on around you, that you'll have a better chance of getting away? Do you really want to see how badly you are outnumbered, Richard?"

I was overcome with fear. I felt like something might reach out for me.

"Go ahead," the man said. "Turn on the lights, Richard."

Without hesitation, I turned and reached out blindly for the wall next to the door, and slammed my hands against it. I searched desperately for a light switch.

Please, please, please.

"It's right in front of you," the man whispered to me,

his voice right next to my ear. And I felt it—the warmth of his breath was on me, against my skin.

I flipped the switch and spun around, my heart stinging with fear. I expected to see him standing right in front of my face … but he wasn't there.

He was in a chair at the opposite end of the room, smiling a most wicked smile. The room was large and empty. And there was no one else there besides Claire and me. The fluorescent lights above our heads flickered and bounced off the bare white walls surrounding us, painfully flooding our eyes.

The man in the chair was wearing a black suit. I knew he was Dr. Carrol. My mouth dropped open as I stared at him. "There's no one here," I said, my heart pounding mercilessly.

He bit his bottom lip in excitement and leaned forward. "*Everyone* is here."

28

There couldn't be anything sane about him. I stared at him, in that blank room, wondering what to do next. He had no weapons in his hands and no armed men at his sides. It was just him—a middle-aged man in a black suit, wearing shiny black shoes. His hair was thick and dark brown with pieces of it hanging down youthfully over his forehead. He wore a goatee, heavily and stylishly peppered with grays. His smile showed a bright set of perfect teeth.

I had never imagined madness to look this way. It wasn't supposed to look clean and well-dressed. It wasn't supposed to be suave or presented in a charming package—but then again, evil was deceptive.

"Dr. Carrol?" I asked after a long silence.

"Yes?" he answered proudly.

"We," I said, with my hands outstretched—I glanced down at Claire who was still crumpled over herself on the floor—"are the only ones here."

Dr. Carrol sat back and grasped onto the arms of his chair. "So even with the lights on, you do not see. Isn't that something?"

To be sure, I quickly scanned the room again, and still saw nothing. Dr. Carrol then reached over to a small table beside him and picked up a cell phone. He only glanced at the screen and then set it back down.

"It's almost time," he said and then turned to his right. There was a door there. "Bring in Dr. Anson."

The door immediately opened and Dr. Anson was forcefully pushed into the room. There was a cloth sack over his head, but I recognized the suit he was wearing. His hands were tied behind his back and he was hunched over in fear. Dr. Anson took small, unsteady steps after balancing himself in his uncertain environment. It was clear that he didn't know where to go or what to do.

The door then closed on its own.

Dr. Carrol stood and rushed toward Dr. Anson to grab ahold of his arm, violently pulling him over to the middle of the room. The heels of Carrol's shoes clicked loudly against the floor. He then forced Anson down to his knees. Dr. Carrol removed the sack from Anson's face, yanking it off in a showman-like manner to reveal his prize. Anson's mouth had been gagged with some cloth that was tied around his head. "Dr. Miller Anson!" Carrol announced. He spun around flamboyantly on the heel of his shoe with his palm in the air.

I closed my eyes to take in a breath. It was hard to look at Dr. Anson like this.

Dr. Carrol walked back to the table to pick up his cell phone. "In two minutes, Dr. Anson will make a very important contribution to science … finally."

Dr. Anson's eyes were filled with terror.

Dr. Carrol gazed at the screen of his phone, his eyes gleaming with excitement. "And I'm guessing that you would like for me to keep the lights on, Mr. Ravestone?"

I was horrified at the question.

Claire cried out, "Now you want us to watch you *kill him?!*"

"It won't matter either way," he answered plainly in return. "And since I can tell that you will be a problem, Officer Sandoval, it looks like I will have to restrain you during the ceremony."

Claire jumped up, ready to pounce. "Stay away from me!"

Dr. Carrol looked around as he crinkled his face at her. "What are you going to do, Ms. Claire?"

Without warning, she lunged at him, running toward him as quickly as possible. But then suddenly, she froze in place, as if hitting a wall, and winced in pain. Claire started thrashing about, trying in desperation to free herself from something that seemed to have her by the arms and legs. It was something invisible. I could see impressions around her arms, like fingers—fingers that couldn't possibly have been there.

"Oh my God," I gasped.

Claire continued to struggle with whatever had her, but as she fought it, her body was lifted and thrown against the wall behind us. An awful thud sound echoed throughout the room. And when I looked back, to make sure she was okay, I couldn't believe what I saw—she was pinned against the wall, her feet above the floor, some unseen force holding her in place. She tried to scream, and I could see the fingermarks pressing against her cheek as if there was a hand across her mouth.

"There are hundreds of us in this room, Richard," Dr. Carrol declared. "Now, tell her to be quiet so we can begin."

I looked back at Claire again. Her arms were outstretched and firmly pressed against the wall. Her lips were flattened and pushed into her teeth. Her eyes blinked wildly and she was fighting to move her head.

I returned my attention to Dr. Carrol. "What do you mean, there are hundreds of you?"

"Richard, you have studied the occult for years. You really are very informed. That's why I am such a big fan of your writing—it's very realistic. And that's why you, of all people on this earth, should appreciate what I'm trying to do here."

I resisted the impulse to yell at him or to show any anger. Inside, I was enraged. I didn't want this man's compliments or his admiration. I wanted out. I wanted Claire safe. Simon's face flashed through my mind … *I wonder if he's nearby.*

Cautiously, I asked, "What are you trying to do?"

"I'm going to rectify the sins of man," he answered. I noticed then how dark and powerful his eyes were.

I thought I understood where he was going with things at that point and wanted to let him think that he could drag me along with him … with his insanity. I needed to seem interested, maybe even like I wanted more involvement in it. I had to formulate my questions with enthusiasm. I had to mask my anger. "So when De Luca said you wanted to bring back the dead, he was right? You're trying to sacrifice people to bring others back in their place?"

"Not exactly. De Luca has spent a great amount of time guessing the details of my research. Does it look like I would waste my time with zombies?"

I couldn't get Claire out of my head. I knew she was suffering. "Well, I don't think he meant it literally. Bringing back the dead, I mean. He said something about their energy." I glanced at Dr. Anson after saying this, wondering what he was thinking. I was trying to buy us some time.

Dr. Carrol checked his phone again.

"It's time," he said softly. He rose from his chair and positioned himself behind Dr. Anson. "Richard, I have to begin. Others around the world are depending on me."

"Others where?"

Dr. Carrol held his hand out and over the top of Dr.

Anson's head. Then he held the phone to his ear, saying into it, "We shall begin."

"Begin what?" I needed more time.

"Brothers and sisters," Dr. Carrol said into his phone. "It is an honor to participate in this ceremony with you. I trust that each of you are fully prepared. And I trust that you understand how to join me again when I call for you. You have your instructions and should know exactly where you will be traveling to … and who you will bring back. We must do this quickly. There is no doubt that the authorities will find a way to track us down, but by then, we will have already accomplished our goal, and all of you will be rewarded with greatness and eternal life."

Dr. Carrol closed his eyes, keeping the palm of his hand on the top of Dr. Anson's head. "Take, from this earth, this individual in exchange for those whom you wish to see live again in greatness and without material restraint. We will accept, for the life of this human, any number of beings that you will provide to us—to our undeserving material world. Make this place your unholy playground. Know that by taking this man, we will harbor your children again on our planet, and I submit myself to be your representative. A guide, leader, and master, here in this realm and in your name."

"No!" I yelled. "What are you doing?!"

Unfazed, Dr. Carrol raised his voice to continue. "Harvest the body of this person. Use it as an entryway into this world. Take the energy within it in exchange for those who have called out to you. My students, my loyal followers—who will sacrifice everything for you on this night—will seek out your lost children, answer their desperate calls, and bring them back to this world in your name. And I ask that you embrace these lost souls of the past, those special few who have sent to me their gifts—

pieces of themselves—and have proven to me that they wish to exist again in this world to serve you, Dark Lord."

The lights in the room started to flicker and Dr. Anson's eyes began to illuminate from within.

"Burn him!" Dr. Carrol yelled. "Make way for the lost—those who need and deserve a purpose! Bring them here so that I may give their new lives meaning!"

I smelled something foul and unthinkable—something charred. Dr. Anson's body was burning from the inside. Smoke poured from his mouth and nose. His skin glowed a hot yellow and red.

"WHAT ARE YOU DOING?!" I screamed.

The lights went out.

Dr. Carrol's voice cried out in the darkness, "NOW! DO IT NOW!"

And then, like a nightmare that I am forced to live through to this day, I saw what no man or woman should ever see—I saw life replaced with death. Many deaths. Dr. Anson's arms flew out to his sides and his entire body swelled. I expected to see a replay of what had happened to Marisol, but it wasn't like that at all. It was different. Dr. Anson's body did not fill with apports, those terrible "gifts" from the other side—it filled with screams and howls. It swelled with black swirls that had arms and legs that reached out from within his body, trying to cross into existence. Fingers curled and poked out from his eyes and mouth. Things … bodies … swarmed and became something inside of him before leaking out into the room. They ripped and tore at his skin, seeking an escape.

"Yes!" Dr. Carrol yelled and threw his phone down in excitement.

The beings in the room—mist-like abominations of black and gray—swirled all around us. There was a strong charge of electricity, and a faint, soft glow enveloped the room.

"You can't do this!" I yelled.

Dr. Carrol laughed in return. "It's already done!"

There was nothing left of Dr. Anson's body that could be described by a writer such as myself. What remained was charred and twisted. His body had been violently torn apart, ravaged by the beings that were reborn from it.

Dr. Carrol held his arms out above his head. "We have done this for you, Dark Lord! Lives given for you! And lives of the past reborn for you! Now these lost beings will be under my command as I direct them to do your bidding!"

There was a loud thud against the door behind me.

Dr. Carrol looked at me with eyes that were almost entirely black. "You believe now." His voice was now a deep groan.

"What did you do?" was my response.

Outside, something was being slammed against the door behind me.

"Simon's here," Dr. Carrol said into the darkness.

29

I could feel the evil beings swirling around me that Dr. Carrol had brought back to life. They were rushing past my face, brushing against me. I would feel a part of one inside my head and then another pulling at the inside of my stomach. It was maddening. "GET THEM OFF OF ME!" I screamed and tried to use my hands to swat them away.

The door swung open behind me and light poured through. Claire screamed and I could hear her body fall to the floor. Simon's powerful voice then carried through the room, and I remembered something horrible—Dr. Anson.

"Don't come in!" I warned Simon. "Dr. Carrol's in here! Don't come in!"

A flashlight was turned on behind me and I watched as it scanned the room, flickering. There was no sign of Dr. Carrol, but what remained of Dr. Anson's body was still there. It was almost everywhere, smeared and strewn across the entire room—dripping from floor to ceiling.

"God." Simon's voice was shaky. He took a moment to look around the room before asking, "Where's Carrol? What happened?"

I covered my eyes with my hands and cringed, pointing toward the destruction. "It's Dr. Anson! That's his body! It's everywhere! Dr. Carrol did this to him!"

Simon grabbed my arm and pulled me toward the door. "Where'd he go? Dr. Carrol? We heard him through the door."

"I-I don't know," I stammered, hardly able to breathe. "He killed Anson. I watched him do it." I opened my eyes, averting them from the inside of the room. As I turned, I recognized the silhouettes of De Luca and Detective Trevino standing in the doorway.

The detective took only one cautious step into the room. "No one's touching anything in here," he instructed.

Simon crouched down to Claire, still lying on the floor.

I didn't feel the strange beings in the room anymore, picking and pulling at me … trying to drive me crazy. "It wasn't real. It was an illusion," I guessed out loud.

"No," Simon objected. "I heard him. He was here."

Detective Trevino stepped back out into the hallway, and I could hear him talking to himself in frustration. "I need to call a team up to this room. My phone's dead." He started hitting something in his hands. "And now my flashlight's out, too. Dammit."

Claire clutched onto Simon's shirt. "The car? Is it still in the garage?"

"Yes," Simon answered solemnly.

"Stevenson … is his body there?" she asked fearfully.

Detective Trevino entered the room again, his face covered with shadows. "Yes, he's there."

Claire looked down and slowly nodded.

De Luca walked up to me and placed a hand on my shoulder. "Richard, Detective Trevino received several calls since we started looking for you. A great number of people linked with Dr. Carrol had planned to *kill themselves* or *murder* people tonight. There have been some reports of a few students and researchers that have gone missing already and—"

"That's what Dr. Carrol was doing on the phone," I told them. "It sounded like he was talking to a lot of people at the same time. Instructing them to follow his commands."

"We have to find him," Simon interjected. "Now."

Something inside me snapped. "But he was right here! He was in this room! Claire saw him, too!"

Simon helped Claire to her feet and gently leaned her up against the wall. "Claire? Did you see where Dr. Carrol went?"

Claire's head sank. "Yes."

"Claire, you have to tell us. We don't have a lot of time to figure out what's happening."

Claire sniffled and then lifted her head to look at the ceiling. "They all flew into his body and then they were gone." She broke down and lost her footing. Simon caught her in his arms, and she sobbed uncontrollably. "I shot an officer. I killed Stevenson. There was a voice in my head telling me to. It was laughing ... I heard it."

"It's all right, Claire," Simon said softly into her ear. "It wasn't your fault."

De Luca turned to Detective Trevino. "Simon and Richard need to find Carrol. They can find him. I know what's happening. I know what he's trying to do. He'll try to make the world into what he wants it to be if we don't stop him."

"Yes! I get it!" the detective yelled back. "Simon, you and Richard do what you need to do. Right now! I have to get a team up here, so hurry it up!"

"I can help you," De Luca said to us.

"Where's that bottle of whiskey?" Simon asked me.

"It's gone."

"Fuck."

I couldn't stop shaking. "You don't need it. Let's just

start. Sit down."

We both sat on the floor, just inside the doorway, forcing ourselves to ignore what remained of Dr. Anson. The others waited outside, keeping watch in the hallway and reminding us that we didn't have a lot time. Those awful beings … I had felt their electric charge, the way their horrible energy vibrated within the room, and I knew it could help me find them. Simon thought so, too. He told me to focus on it, to try and feel it again. He didn't think they were very far from us—he just knew they couldn't be. But we were having trouble focusing. This energy was enveloping and dangerous. It wanted to draw you in, smother and consume you—to make it a drug that you couldn't resist.

I don't think Simon expected it to be like that—to be that strong. "Richard, it's the worst thing I've ever felt."

30

When Simon and I went out into the hallway to join the others, we felt defeated. They stared at us with expectation in their eyes.

"I don't know why I can't do this," Simon said to De Luca. "I don't feel right. I can't feel Dr. Carrol at all."

"He's different now," Claire reminded him. "Those things went into his body."

"She's right," De Luca agreed. Then he looked at me. "How many of them—entities—did he bring over?"

"I don't know," I answered. "It looked like … hundreds. It was dark in there. There was hardly any light. They glowed a little, but they moved fast."

I was glad to be out of that room because it was starting to emit a terrible odor. I couldn't concentrate. Even with that resilient energy still surrounding us in the room, I just couldn't latch onto any of it. It wouldn't let us.

De Luca let out a sigh. "Is your phone working yet, Detective?"

"No." Trevino was either seriously annoyed or extremely frightened. "Are they done? I need to do my job now."

De Luca pulled out his phone. "Here. You can borrow … oh. Mine's dead, too. The energy in that room is strong. The lights aren't even back on in there yet."

I said, "My cell phone's in the car. Claire's too."

"This is pointless. Let's just go," Simon said. "I can't

find him anyway and Richard's not feeling it either."

Claire added, "It probably doesn't help that there's a dead body in there, Simon. It's probably too distracting." She was sounding a little more like herself again.

De Luca leaned in close to my ear. "You still felt them in that room? Even though they've left?"

"Yes."

"That's good. Maybe you can try again later," he said to me. "I know you can do it."

When we got to the parking garage, there was a swarm of police officers and detectives surrounding Stevenson's car. An ambulance was also parked nearby. I watched Claire as she kept her distance from it all, standing near the elevator with Simon.

"I guess we can't get the cell phones from the car," De Luca commented.

As a police officer walked past us, Detective Trevino snatched a cell phone out of his hand. He barked some instructions to the officer about getting a team up to the fifth floor before shooing him off, and then immediately placed a call to the police station. "It's Trevino. Put me through to my office."

De Luca had a distant look on his face.

"What are you thinking?" I asked him.

"Well," he began with a crease in his brow. "I was wondering why Dr. Carrol chose the United States for these rituals, or more specifically, San Antonio."

"Oh."

"Have any ideas about that?" he asked me.

"No," I answered. "I guess I hadn't thought about it."

De Luca smiled and lowered his voice. "Did you know that San Antonio is considered one of the most haunted cities in the United States?"

"No, I didn't."

"Well, it is."

I nodded. "Interesting."

"There's a river that runs through the downtown area," he added. "Water is known to be a conductor of paranormal energy."

"There's water running through other cities, too."

De Luca smiled. "Yes, but it's a combination of things that … never mind. Listen, Richard. There's a reason Carrol chose to do this here. It may only be a starting point for him, but—"

Detective Trevino was raising his voice into the phone. "They gave you a name? Where? Germany, Spain, England. Yeah, more than one… okay, give me one name. Uh huh … and they checked it out? *No such guy?* What do you mean, *'that they know of?'* A famous researcher of … what was it? Quantum something … goes missing and they give us the name of the place he works, and no one can figure out if this guy is really missing or not? None of this sounds crazy to you? You got any names of anyone else we can check out?"

De Luca jumped in front of him. "Give me the name of one in Spain … or Italy."

"What's going on?" I asked.

The detective looked at him hesitantly, but then something seemed to click. "Yeah. Give me the name of the one missing in Spain. Or Italy. If you got one from Italy, give it to me," he said into the phone with excitement. "Right?" he asked De Luca.

"Right," De Luca nodded enthusiastically in return.

"Uh huh. Yeah … okay. Hold on." Detective Trevino pulled the phone away from his face and looked right into De Luca's eyes. "Trentino … "

"Italy?" De Luca asked.

"Italy?" Trevino repeated into the phone. "Yes."

De Luca didn't seem too sure. "Was he a teacher, a student ... ?"

Detective Trevino went back to his phone. "What did he do for a living? Okay ... yeah. I don't care if they're rumors. Interpol confirmation? No, I don't care ... just hold on." Trevino had a worried look on his face. "*She's* a paranormal researcher."

"Bullshit!" De Luca yelped. "There's no way! I know every paranormal researcher with any significant background in Europe! Is she supposed to have been one of Carrol's followers or someone who was abducted by them?"

Oh, the list of missing people, I realized.

"I don't know. None of the names have been confirmed yet, apparently," the detective reminded him. "What if they've mixed up the names on the list or—"

"Or what if the whole thing's been *faked?*" De Luca cocked his head to the side.

"What?"

"They know we don't have time to confirm anything, and all of this is happening too quickly," De Luca replied. "And all the names on the list ... they're international. Making them even harder for us to trace. Right?"

The detective nodded in agreement. "Okay, okay. Then you tell me what the point is of a fake list."

"Dr. Carrol did this to throw us off course. There may not be anyone missing. Or it could be that the suicides are real, but the abductions aren't. Or perhaps they are both real, but the names we've been given aren't." De Luca looked at us both while donning the smile of a madman. "Or this whole thing could be just a few people that Carrol's brainwashed into helping him so that it looks like something bigger than it really is."

Simon walked up to us with a smirk on his face. "That makes no sense. In our viewings and in Richard's dreams, there's other people there. There were rituals. There has to be an entire cult of people following him."

Behind Simon, Claire slowly made her way over to us.

"Well, yes," De Luca agreed. "Maybe there is. But I don't think he's stupid enough to risk getting caught up in some ... mass abduction. Especially the abductions and murders of well-known individuals. Suicides? Yes. Those are more controllable, but not abductions."

I thought on it as he spoke. "He could've taken people. He didn't seem too concerned about getting caught doing this stuff. He said that by the time he was caught, it would be too late anyway."

Detective Trevino seemed to agree with what I'd said. I could see it in his eyes. He turned to De Luca. "Then tell me what you think happened."

De Luca motioned for all of us to scoot in closer to one another, including Claire. "I think Dr. Carrol's got us all caught up in an illusion—a carefully crafted system of belief," he started with a spark in his eyes. "If you believe in something strongly enough—it really *does* happen. Science can't explain it yet, but it's true. And when you convince others that something's real, their belief in it can turn seemingly impossible events into a reality."

I could tell by the look on Trevino's face that De Luca's answer didn't feel like an answer to him.

It appeared to make sense to Simon, though. "The more people believe in something, the more likely it is to happen," he said. "Dr. Anson talked about that a lot. Belief in something is what makes things happen. That's how he got me to trust my instincts."

I asked, "So what's Dr. Carrol trying to make us believe?"

The smile faded from De Luca's face. "He's trying to make us believe that he's evil. He wants us to fear him. He wants *science* to fear him."

"It's working," Claire said in a tiny voice.

Simon asked, "Why would he do that? He's that crazy? He needs that much attention?"

De Luca answered, "Science doesn't believe in his theories. And if he can't get them to listen to him and he's already being made to look like a fool in journals and such, why not take a different avenue in his approach?" He paused so that we could take it all in. "This is all a show. I'm certain that, in all of his frustration with the scientific community, he really does wish to be powerful … to be in command of something. He needs to prove himself after years of being ignored and cast aside. But the only people who would listen to something like this— even if he is onto something scientifically important—are needy admirers with problems of their own. They're people who crave importance, or a role in something mystical or forbidden. So you see, he needs the power of belief to achieve this."

I looked at Simon to try to figure out what he was thinking. He looked at me and shrugged his shoulders in return.

"What do we do next?" I asked. "He *did* kill Dr. Anson. Claire and I both saw that. That wasn't an illusion. You saw the mess up there … that was real."

"And I was stuck up on the wall," Claire added. "Something was holding me up in the air."

"Yes," De Luca replied. "Dr. Anson is dead. Carrol has crossed the line. He's at the point where he believes his own lies. He's created something terrible. And his followers have fed into his power. *And* they have brought something over from the other side."

Simon sighed impatiently. "It's a cult, like I kept saying before."

De Luca gave in. "Well, yes."

"What do we do then?" I asked.

De Luca stared at the detective. "He needs more energy. So where do you think he might seek out that sort of thing here in your city, sir?"

The detective only stared blankly.

Simon jumped in. "Okay. Maybe Raul's right. Rich and I can't find him anyway. And I know how weird all of this probably sounds to you, Trevino. But the guy is still a killer. We gotta find him either way. Right?"

The detective's eyes were dazed. "Yeah."

"Raul's kind of weird," Simon continued, "but I think some of what he's sayin' makes sense." His hands were animated as he spoke. "Dr. Carrol's energy, the stuff I focus on to find him, is all different now. He's got, you know, according to Rich and Claire, an army of creatures or dead people in his body now ... so, since I'm not havin' any luck finding him, maybe we should just do what Raul says."

Detective Trevino nodded like a zombie. I felt sorry for him. The entire situation really was unfathomable.

De Luca covered his mouth with his hand to hide a smile. I was pretty sure that it was due to the fact that Simon had actually agreed with him on something, finally. He took a few steps back and turned away from where we all stood and gazed into the chaos of police officers and fire fighters working to secure the area. Detective Trevino and Simon began to contemplate our next move. It sounded more like an argument than a form of organized discussion, though, but at least they were trying to figure something out.

I walked over to De Luca and stood close behind him.

"What do you think we should do?"

"I'm hoping they'll listen to me. They're cops. They think differently. Simon's experience helps, though," De Luca replied.

"Yeah, I think Simon's a lot more like us than like these guys now."

De Luca grinned. "He still has a lot of that police training inside him, Richard."

I knew De Luca was right. Even if he did come up with a brilliant idea for our next move, it would probably sound too far-fetched for Detective Trevino to act on. So when De Luca walked away from them, he was doing so in hopes that they would figure it out for themselves and make the right choice, no matter how strange it felt to them.

But I was still worried that they wouldn't come up with an idea quickly enough. I really wanted to help, and leaving it to them felt like a gamble. "Okay, well, tell me your idea anyway. Maybe I can get them to listen. You're the expert. Remember that. What's Carrol's next move? Let's try to think like a Satanist … or something evil like that."

"He's no Satanist, Richard."

"Well, how do you explain all the rituals and … crazy 'Dark Lord' stuff he's been going on about then? I mean, I just heard him say all that stuff. And this time, it wasn't a dream."

De Luca sighed before turning to face me. "He's trying to convince people that he's something he's not. It's an act. He's simply grasped onto the most generic idea about what most people would idealize as evil. Don't you see that? Trust me on this. He's no Satanist. I would know."

"But—"

"Richard," De Luca smiled and got close to my ear. "*I* would know."

31

When I walked back toward Simon, I felt like I was in a dream. De Luca had briefed me on an idea, asked me to pitch it to Simon and Detective Trevino, and I agreed. But it took a lot of effort to concentrate on my legs as I moved. There was something strange in the way De Luca had spoken to me—when he'd told me his plan. I glanced back to see if he was watching, which he was, and so I smiled and continued on.

Simon and the detective were in a heated argument. I tugged on Simon's sleeve, trying to interrupt them, but it wasn't working.

"Hey," I tried.

"No no no," Simon continued. "This guy's known for being a pretentious jerk-off. We need to check the Internet. Carrol's probably bragging the whole thing out right now, and we're missing it!"

"Simon," I said quietly. "I need to talk to you. It's important." I felt De Luca's eyes on me.

Simon swung around and growled into my face, "We're busy trying to figure out where Dr. Carrol went."

"Okay, but, I want to talk to you about an idea De Luca has—"

Simon grabbed my arm. "Raul's crazy!" he whisper-yelled while looking over my shoulder to check on De Luca's whereabouts.

"Simon, you're not a cop anymore," I reminded him. "You said we should do whatever De Luca says.

Remember? De Luca's an expert and I think he's come up with a good idea."

"Really?!"

"Yeah."

"Okay then, tell me," he scoffed. "What is it?"

"No," Detective Trevino grunted. "Tell *me*."

"Okay, well, De Luca thinks that we should head for the most haunted place in the city."

They both looked at me with bulging eyes.

"Where the hell's that supposed to be? The Alamo?" Simon asked while crossing his arms.

"I don't know. I mean, it would have to be Dr. Carrol's idea of the most haunted place, I guess ..."

"That's stupid." Simon turned to Detective Trevino. "So now we have to guess where the most haunted place in town is? What for?"

Claire stepped in with a hypnotic look on her face. "It's the Alamo. Simon's right. I read it in a book once."

"We're packin' everyone up and going to the Alamo? *Yeehaw!*" Simon laughed. "Is this a joke?"

"Maybe it's not the *actual* Alamo itself," I suggested. "Maybe the area around it?"

De Luca snuck up and joined in. "The entire downtown area of San Antonio is highly active."

We all focused our attention on him.

Detective Trevino had a serious look on his face. "You really think Dr. Carrol would head downtown?"

"Yes."

"Then that's where we're going."

"This is so—"

"Shut up, Simon!" the detective snapped.

By the time we left the parking garage, it was completely dark out. It only took us about ten or fifteen minutes to get downtown. San Antonio was alive with colorful lights and people walking the streets. It was definitely a busy Saturday evening.

Detective Trevino drove us in an unmarked police unit. He'd managed to bring Claire with us by not giving investigators a chance to ask us any questions about Stevenson. I think Trevino realized that Carrol could have killed her if he'd wanted to. For some reason, he'd kept her alive. And since Trevino was ready to do whatever it took to find Carrol, he was ready to disobey protocol and told Claire she was coming with us.

He pulled into a parking lot that wanted ten dollars an hour … I checked my phone. It was 7:28.

"Okay," the detective said to us after turning off the engine. He looked back at me with fierce eyes. "Where's Dr. Carrol?"

I was squashed into the backseat next to the window. De Luca was in the middle with his arm practically in my ribs. Claire was on the other side of him removing her seatbelt. "I don't know," I answered.

"Isn't that your thing, too? Feeling for stuff? Vibes or something?"

"It's more Simon's thing," I explained. "I'm new at it."

"Great," he answered. He turned to Simon in the passenger seat next to him. "Okay, Wallace. Are you ready to try again?"

Simon looked around nervously. "Let's get out and head toward … over there." He pointed through the windshield.

Detective Trevino shook his head and sighed. "All right. Let's go."

As soon as we got out of the car, Detective Trevino, Claire, and Simon started running. They ran past the parking attendant, who didn't look too happy about having a badge flashed in his face, and headed down the middle of the street in the direction Simon pointed.

"Hey!" I yelled before turning to De Luca. "They left us!"

"Come on," he said as he began jogging toward them.

I certainly wasn't wearing the right shoes for a run, but it didn't look like I had much of a choice. I put my phone in my pants' pocket and worked to catch up to them. I shot a quick smile at the confused-looking parking attendant as I ran by. "We'll come back and pay you."

"Yeah right," the guy said in return.

We proceeded up a street with tall brick buildings on both sides of it. I saw a name on a street sign—Crockett.

I caught up to De Luca and then passed him as I watched Simon take a sharp right onto a brick walkway. He disappeared behind some bushes and trees. I kept running. I thought De Luca was going too slow, and I felt like I needed to catch up with Simon.

I made the sharp right that I'd seen Simon make, nearly tripping over a potted plant in the process. I ran into a woman that was holding a small child's hand. I apologized, glanced back to see De Luca close behind, and kept going.

There were crowds of people everywhere.

"Simon!" I called out as soon as I was close enough to him, but then something happened. The air around me changed—like it was too thick to breathe. And then a man reached out for me. He had a thick stream of blood dripping down his face and a rifle in his hands.

"You need your weapon," the man said in a hollow voice. "You can't fight without your weapon."

I felt sick. I could hardly breathe. I was having difficulty focusing because everything was suddenly different. I thought I was experiencing something like an asthma attack, but I wasn't sure.

Smoke lingered in the air and the sounds of gun shots, yells, and screams surrounded me. There were men in uniforms that I didn't recognize, running all around in panic, but they were faded and I couldn't focus in on them. Their faces blurred unnaturally as they moved.

The sound of a loud gunshot forced me to duck. I turned to see where it had come from and my jaw dropped. I was standing in front of the Alamo. Parts of it were grayed out and didn't seem to be there completely, but the rest of it was as solid as the groups of tourists in front of it. My body shook uncontrollably and I started to hyperventilate.

"Richard!" I could hear De Luca say. "What's wrong with you?"

It was like his voice was underwater. I couldn't turn to look at him. I was stunned, staring at the men in strange uniforms as they fired their weapons into crowds of tourists.

"Simon!" I heard De Luca call out.

A woman on her cell phone passed nearby, pushing a stroller. She stopped to look back for her husband but then noticed me—falling to my knees beside her. "Is he all right?" she asked De Luca with a concerned look on her face.

"You're in the way!" I yelled to her. "You're going to get hurt!"

"Richard!" Simon yelled. He grabbed a hold of my jacket and pulled me to my feet. "*What's wrong with you?!*"

I studied his face. I had to search deep into his eyes to see if he knew ... I didn't want to tell him. "Don't you see?" I asked, more afraid at that moment than I had ever been of anything.

Simon shook his head no. "See what?"

I looked around in disbelief. Over Simon's shoulder, a soldier was running toward us with a pistol.

"We're in the middle of a battle."

"Oh no." He moved in close to my face, suddenly realizing what was happening. "Don't look at it. You're not supposed to see it. It's just something that keeps happening here. Over and over, you know? You have to look through it. Don't look at it. We have to keep going, all right? Shake it off. Don't look at it."

"But ... it's ... it's right in front of me."

"I know, man." Simon nodded at De Luca. He wrapped my arm over his shoulder. We started walking. "We have to keep going. I'm sorry. I'm sure it's pretty fuckin' weird to see it happening, but ... we have to keep moving. We have to find Dr. Carrol. I think I have an idea what direction he took. I can kinda feel it. He's close."

I worked hard to compose myself as I walked through and stepped over the bodies of faded soldiers. Solid people—living people—stared at me. Simon and De Luca ignored them and continued to drag my limp body along with them.

"You got any whiskey?" one of the faded soldiers stopped to ask me.

"I'm sorry," I said to the translucent, bluish-gray face. He had a gaping wound in his chest. "I don't have any."

Simon yanked on my arm. "Focus through it. Think about Dr. Carrol's location instead," he said in a hushed voice.

I did what he said. I looked through the madness and recognized Claire's blonde hair and PD uniform up ahead. She waved for us to hurry.

"They're going down Houston Street," Simon told De Luca. "That's where I think he is. Up that street somewhere."

"What's happening to Richard isn't a bad thing," De Luca said.

"It is right now. He's probably going into shock or somethin'. There's a lot of energy in this place," Simon replied.

De Luca asked me, "Are you seeing the *actual* battle?"

I still struggled to breathe.

"He's definitely seeing somethin' that happened here." Simon patted me on the chest. "You doing any better?"

I was. I followed his advice and unfocused on all the people that looked out of place. They were easy to spot, most of them transparent in places and wearing clothing from a different time. But others, the ones that were more solid, those were the more difficult ones to ignore. I couldn't simply look through them as Simon had suggested. They were more opaque. And if it hadn't been for the grayness of their skin or peculiar mannerisms, I might have easily mistaken them for living people.

Simon quickened his pace to a light jog. "Richard, we have to get over there. Trevino and Claire can't find that asshole without us."

"Okay." I sped up. "It's okay. You guys can let go of me."

We crossed the busy street in front of the Alamo, dodging a few vehicles and a trolley. We continued on past a few tourist shops and rushed in between groups of people—more tourists. Simon took the lead and pointed ahead.

"We're turning here!"

It was Houston Street.

De Luca paced himself next to me. "Sure you're all right?"

I was still light-headed, but didn't want to admit it.

"Yes," I answered. A woman with sad eyes and a misty face looked at me as we passed her on the sidewalk. "I'm just trying to look through it."

Curious, De Luca asked, "Why do you think this happened? You couldn't see them like this before."

"I don't know," I said.

De Luca chuckled. "I would have never guessed that Simon could be such a good runner. Look at him! He's almost a block ahead of us!"

We ran past a drug store and some restaurants. I could see Claire and the detective speaking to a couple of police officers on bikes in front of an old theater. The old fashioned sign attached to it glowed beautifully onto the street below. Simon had caught up to them and nodded as we approached. De Luca and I picked up our pace so we could get in on what they were saying.

"Does he need medical attention?" I could hear Claire asking Simon.

"No, I think he's fine. I'll explain later." Simon looked back at me. "So do you feel it, too?"

"Feel what?" I asked.

"Come on. Don't you feel it?"

I stood there in the noisiness of the street and tried to focus. Expecting me to tune into Dr. Carrol's location in a hectic place like that was a lot to ask. Cars raced by and people walked up and down the sidewalks, talking and laughing. There was noise and movement everywhere. "I can't concentrate. Do *you* feel it?"

"Yeah!"

"Where?" I asked.

The two cops on their bikes looked at us in confusion.

"Somewhere nearby."

Detective Trevino grabbed Simon's arm and pulled him in close to his face. "You still want me to call in some backup? Where should I tell them to show up at? *Somewhere?* Is that where you want backup? *Somewhere?*"

Simon shook himself free and stepped in close to my ear. He had a desperate look in his eyes. "Richard, think! He's nearby. Help me out."

I turned to De Luca to say something, but the words just weren't there.

De Luca saw how much I needed his help. I knew he could sense how lost I was. "It's not a coincidence that you can see so many things going on around you, Richard. Something inside you has been awakened."

He was right. I felt different.

"Now, close your eyes and search for him," he said.

"But how will I know if it's him? There's a lot of *them* here. All kinds."

De Luca thought on it. "What did you feel earlier? In front of the Alamo?"

I hesitated to answer because the words to describe it would be difficult. "It was cold."

"What else?"

"I felt numb ... and scared. They could see me. Something in my brain was different."

De Luca smiled. "That different feeling in your brain, that's the feeling that you need to feel again. But these beings, the ones Dr. Carrol has with him, they will be more than just cold ... they will feel heavy and cause you some discomfort."

Simon joined us. "Yeah. He's right. That stuff I told you to ignore earlier, forget that. Tune into that again."

"Okay," I sighed.

I quickly scanned my surroundings, took a step back, and then closed my eyes. I can't explain what I was trying to do except to say that I was undoing myself—unraveling what I knew about things. Everything. I was trying to feel what didn't, or wasn't, supposed to be there. I was clutching onto a pattern or a vibration that I couldn't see or hear.

The voices on the street grew distant and my mind began to float.

Something inside me latched onto and connected with a hum that was being carried through the air. It didn't want me to become a part of it, but I didn't give it a choice. I reached out and forced it to carry me through everything. What was material didn't matter any longer, and that signal pulled me along like a radio wave.

I opened my eyes.

"He's in the lobby," I said to them.

"Where?" Simon gasped excitedly. "We're surrounded by hotels. Which one?"

I pointed up the street. I could see an outdoor patio area with tables and chairs. "That one. That's where he is."

Without hesitation, Simon and De Luca took off running toward the hotel. Detective Trevino got on his cell phone and motioned for Claire to stay where she was, but she didn't. Claire grabbed my arm and pulled me along with her as she, too, ran for the hotel I'd pointed at.

We caught up with Simon and De Luca in front of an entrance made of glass doors.

"This one?" Simon asked frantically.

"Yes," I confirmed. And surprisingly, the feeling I had was stronger.

"We should wait for backup," Claire suggested.

Simon rubbed his hands together. "We don't have time for that. What are they gonna do anyway?"

Detective Trevino strolled up to us with the two bike patrol officers in tow. "I'm in charge. You're not doing anything without my say so. You got that, Wallace?"

"Yes, sir," Simon said cooly. "You can go in first, sir. We'll follow you. That's fine with me."

Detective Trevino grimaced. "You're not going in at all. I'm taking *police* officers in with me."

"But what if he's in there?" De Luca jumped forward to ask. "He's dangerous. You can't just ask Carrol to go with you. You can't arrest him."

"Why not?" Trevino asked.

De Luca scrunched his lips together. "Because he's not really human any longer. And if he's inside this hotel, he's in it for a reason."

"And what reason is that?" the detective demanded to know.

"Detective Trevino, you didn't see what Richard went through back there," De Luca said, while pointing in the direction of the Alamo. "If this area is as haunted and full of activity as it's rumored to be, then Dr. Carrol knows what he's doing here. It's part of a plan."

"But you said yourself that he's a fraud!"

"Yes," De Luca agreed. "But right now, none of that matters. There is a powerful force inside him. Something inhuman."

Detective Trevino stared at the glass doors with a blank look on his face.

The bike patrol officers looked a little nervous.

De Luca lowered his voice. "It might be better if you let us go in with you. Just in case."

"In case of what?" the detective asked.

"In case he does something ... strange."

Detective Trevino put on a tight-lipped smile and nodded his head. "Because he might zap us with his devil powers and stuff? Okay. Yeah ... listen, De Luca," he said with a finger pointed in his face. "Dr. Carrol isn't going to get a chance to give us any problems. I don't give a shit if he thinks he can bring the dead back to life or if he can talk to ghosts or whatever the fuck. Okay?"

De Luca backed away from him slightly. "Okay. I was just offering—"

"I'll go with you, sir," Simon interrupted. "Me and Claire. Right, Claire?"

Claire nodded, but then glanced at De Luca with worry on her face.

"You're not going either, Wallace," Detective Trevino clarified.

"Why not?"

"Do I really need to explain this to you?" the detective asked with a smirk. "You're not with the department anymore. I don't know why the fuck I let you come along with us this far. You can wait out here with Mr. Ravestone and De Luca. *That's* what you can do to help us."

Simon was stunned. "How about this, Trevino?" He lifted his chin angrily. "How about I go home and you can let your little bike crew here watch Richard and De Luca? Does that sound good to you?"

The two officers didn't seem very pleased with the insult. And Detective Trevino looked even more upset.

"Fuck off," Simon groaned. He turned away from us and stormed down the sidewalk.

"Wait!" I called out to him. I turned to the detective. "You can't let him leave!"

Detective Trevino tilted at the hip. "Listen, Mr. Ravestone. No offense, but you don't know Simon the way I do. I've worked with the guy. If Dr. Carrol's in this hotel, we've got him, we book him, and it's done. I'll send Mr. Wallace a thank you card later. I don't have time for his ego right now."

I stared down the sidewalk as Simon was quickly

disappearing into the shadows of the night and into the crowds of people within it. I knew Detective Trevino needed him. I had a really bad feeling about going into the hotel without him. I didn't know why, but every part of it felt worse to me now.

"Just let him go," the detective said. "Stay here with De Luca. We're going in and asking the front desk if they've seen Carrol."

There was a glimmer in Claire's eyes. "Maybe they should come in with us? They could wait in the lobby. We can keep a better eye on them in there." She picked up on the detective's disapproval and quickly added, "You might need these officers for backup and then there won't be anyone out here to watch them anyway."

"Fine. They can come with us. But I want them to wait in the lobby. That's as far as they go." Detective Trevino turned to the two officers. "And you two, stand by on the radio. Watch the entrance … no, one of you go around back."

Detective Trevino pushed through one of the hotel's large glass doors and entered. Claire, De Luca, and I followed. I tried not to be too impressed with what I saw when we walked in—it really was a very nice hotel. That was apparent from the outside, but the inside was breathtaking. My eyes were immediately drawn to the ceiling. Its intricate, classic design meshed perfectly with the modern touches throughout.

"It's been recently renovated," Claire whispered back to me. She was a few steps ahead, doing her best to keep up with Detective Trevino and the pace of his determined stride.

"I love the pillars and lighting," I replied in awe. "The colors and the woodwork—"

The detective swung around with an ice cold stare.

"This isn't a tour, Ravestone."

"Sorry," I said.

"You and De Luca will stand right here," he instructed.

"Yes, of course."

"Sandoval, go to the front desk and ask about Dr. Carrol. Describe him or whatever … get some info and tell them that we might need to secure the place if he's in here. Got it?"

"Yes, sir," she responded. She straightened her posture and nodded obediently before making her way toward a large, beautifully crafted front desk area.

Detective Trevino studied De Luca carefully and then turned his attention to me. "You both need to stay right here. I'm going to look around. And if I find out that we've been wasting our time on this, I'll find a way to charge both of you with obstructing an investigation."

Something boiled inside me. "Uh … I was taken at gunpoint by one of your officers and forced to watch two people die. You want to charge me with something because you can't figure out what's going on? Should I call my lawyer now? He'll love this."

De Luca looked at me with a large smile.

The detective nervously scanned the room. "I knew the nice guy act would end at some point," he grumbled.

"It wasn't an act," I objected. "You're pushing my buttons. You're abusive and way out of line. We agreed to wait here like you said. We don't need your fucking threats."

"Whatever," he said before taking off in a huff.

I looked over to see Claire waiting to speak to a woman behind the desk, but there was a line of people in front of her, also waiting. There were quite a few people inside the lobby. A few children ran in circles near their parents, as others played on their gaming devices or cell phones.

De Luca and I watched Detective Trevino take his time surveying things as he strolled the perimeter of the lobby, his head and body turning in every direction. There were a lot of places to look; an elegant stairway led up to the second floor, ornate chandeliers hung from the high ceiling—everything about the place was eye-catching.

I noticed Trevino turn his attention to Claire. She was having a difficult time getting anyone's attention at the desk, and I could tell he wasn't very happy about her lack of progress. When she looked back at him, he waved his hand, indicating that she should move in closer. Claire frowned, and did what he asked. But the employees behind the desk still didn't notice her.

"Do you feel anything strange in here?" De Luca asked me.

"Sort of," I replied. "The whole place feels strange. I think I'll text Simon and try to get him back over here."

I checked my phone but it was off. "I guess my battery died."

De Luca pulled out his oversized phone and made a face at it. "Mine, too." He scanned the lobby with a sort of paralyzed look on his face. "Something's wrong."

Then, unexpectedly, De Luca ran toward the front desk.

In a panic, I looked over to see Detective Trevino's reaction to this, but his back was turned. He was concentrating on something, looking up one of the staircases.

I wondered what De Luca was doing, so I nervously watched, hoping the detective wouldn't notice. And when De Luca reached Claire, he halted very suddenly just feet away from her. He stuck his arms out, crouched down a little, and started to slowly back away. It didn't look good.

De Luca turned, his face filled with terror, looking for Trevino. "Detective?!" he screeched.

Instinctively, I started running toward De Luca. He called out for the detective again, this time his voice piercing the room. "DETECTIVE!"

In complete terror, I didn't know where to look, so I looked everywhere at once. It only took a side-glance to see that the detective wasn't responding to De Luca. In fact, he too, seemed to be stuck in place, petrified by something he'd seen—that is, until I saw him draw his weapon and aim it at the back of a man's head.

And that's when I realized how quiet it was. Everything in the lobby had gone still.

Unable to process what was happening, I grabbed onto the back of De Luca's shoulder and pulled him back, hoping to yank him away from whatever he was experiencing. He looked me in the eyes, his mouth gaping, and then pointed at the receptionist behind the desk.

Her eyes were dark gray—with something even darker swirling inside them—her face stuck in an awful smile.

The chandelier above us flickered.

Claire stood with her back to us.

I forced myself to look at the detective again. His gun was still drawn and his arms shaking. He was talking … giving instructions that I couldn't hear. Then he started raising his voice. "I said to put your hands on top of your head!"

Laughter came from somewhere—it sounded like everywhere.

"Claire, please. Turn around! Don't look at her anymore!" De Luca pleaded.

There are no words for the terror I felt. My eyes were

torn between watching what was happening with Trevino and my focus on De Luca as he tried to help Claire. I was trying to find the courage not to run from the thing that was standing behind the front desk—it stood there, unnaturally frozen, with its head tilted to the side, still smiling.

De Luca took a step backward and right into my chest. "Look at her hand," he said quietly while pointing at Claire.

I almost choked when I saw it. "God," was all I could say.

Her hand was rotten. It rested on the top of the counter, pale and bluish, the tint disgusting and almost fluorescent in the dim light that flickered and glowed around us. It was then that I noticed her neck. I could see through pieces of light blonde hair that there was something swirling, something decayed ... it was alive on her skin. Veins protruded in blues and purples—crawling beneath her skin. And I could swear that I saw it mocking her heartbeat.

"Claire," I tried in absolute fear. "Come here."

Her arm slid over and dropped like dead weight from the counter. She slowly turned her head to us and smiled, her eyes blank and cloudy white.

"Go help Trevino," De Luca said to me from the corner of his mouth.

"How?" I whispered, looking around, realizing that every single person in the lobby had become one of those things—blank and motionless. People on the stairway had ceased moving and their faces had changed. The families and business people who crowded the lobby were no longer walking or speaking. Everything was silent and still. The only sound I heard was the detective's frightened voice repeating the same sentence over and over. *Put your hands on your head.*

De Luca was still staring at Claire.

"What do we do?" I repeated.

"Carrol did this," De Luca said. And then he did something I wouldn't have thought of—he took a few steps closer to Claire, crouching down a bit, and unsnapped her holster. He wiggled the gun free and then rushed back over to where I stood. But I couldn't remember how she got the gun back, or why she had one at all after the whole situation with Stevenson ...

"What are you doing?" I asked.

"Here, take it."

"Why?"

Without answering, De Luca shoved the gun at me and then took off running toward Detective Trevino. I looked at the gun in my hand. I had never actually held one before, but wrote them into several stories. My characters automatically knew how to use them when it mattered, but not me. I looked up and realized that Claire was watching me with her colorless eyes.

"Give it back, Richard," she said in a voice that seemed to float inside my head. Her lips hardly moved as her words reached me. "It's Simon's. I took it from him. It's not yours. I need it. Don't you want me to like you?"

I didn't know how, or if, I should respond.

"Please be nice to me, Richard." I could feel her words drift through me. Her voice had a higher pitch to it, child-like and surreal. "Men are never nice to me." She frowned.

"Richard!" De Luca cried out. "Come here! Don't look at her!"

But I couldn't look away. I felt some horrible attraction to her—to *it*. She was doing something to my mind, caressing my thoughts, turning my fears of her into fantasies.

"Richard, my boyfriend beats me. Did Simon tell you?"

She's lying. She has to be. How could anyone hurt her?! I'd kill them!

"Richard, don't listen to her!" De Luca yelled. "Look at me!"

I couldn't turn my head. In Claire's eyes, I could feel more than I had ever felt for anyone.

I was enraged. "Who hits you? What's his name?!" I demanded.

"It's my boyfriend. I can't turn him in. He's a cop. No one will believe me … he said he would tell them I'm a liar." The tone in her voice was growing deeper. What started out as a surreal version of Claire's voice was getting louder and was losing its sadistic cheeriness. "He said he'd ruin me. He said he was sorry." Her voice was even deeper now. "He'll never do it again. He promises. He's sorry. He really is. He said so. *Claire. You bitch. Whore. I'll kill you if you say anything to anyone. And no one will believe you anyway. Women get hit all the time. We see it all the time … we respond to the calls every day. And do you believe all of them, bitch? Do you?!*"

"Richard! LOOK AT ME!" De Luca screamed.

Claire's laughter and promises of sexual passion filled my head, but she stood there only smiling. Her soulless eyes were locked onto mine. I breathed frantically and my heart pounded. De Luca was screaming something, but it was being drowned out by the vile groans of pleasure that Claire was forcing into my head.

Suddenly I was grabbed by the wrist and spun around—it was De Luca. He snatched the gun from my hand and gripped at the collar of my jacket.

"Don't listen to her!" I felt a sharp ache in my

temples. "Detective Trevino has Carrol! Come on, we're going to talk to him."

"Why?" I asked in a daze. De Luca was pulling me away from Claire. "Why doesn't he just arrest him?"

"He can't. Carrol isn't a man anymore."

I looked back at Claire—she wasn't moving, just frozen in place. So I backed away with De Luca.

The detective still had his gun aimed at Dr. Carrol's head. My eyes hurt and my head was foggy. Carrol sat in a chair facing the wall, and I didn't understand why his head was tilted down. He was so close to the wall that his knees were pushed against it. The only thing moving on him was a hand on the chair's wooden armrest, twitching.

De Luca nudged me to move in closer to Carrol and I hesitated.

"Hello, Richard," Dr. Carrol said. The voice was deeper than before, but the accent was there. It was distinct and clear.

I studied the way Detective Trevino held the gun to the back of Carrol's head ... his arms shaking.

I had to pull myself together. "Why did you come here? What do you want?" I asked.

He was silent.

"What's going on?" I tried again. "Don't you already have what you wanted?" I was starting to come out of my grogginess. I glanced at De Luca—he was sneaking over to Dr. Carrol's side, trying to see his face. De Luca nodded and waved for me to keep talking. "Are all of these people under your control now?"

Dr. Carrol's hand-twitch suddenly intensified. "Hello, Simon."

De Luca slowly turned to look behind me.

"Uh ... hello," Simon answered quietly. He moved in beside me and raised his eyebrows when I looked at him.

Dr. Carrol squirmed in his seat and the lights flickered above us more intensely. "I knew you were here, Simon. Hiding."

Simon scanned Detective Trevino from head to toe. He looked at Dr. Carrol and scowled. "Where's Dr. Anson?"

"He's dead," Carrol answered with a giggle. His voice was guttural, its tone falling deeper.

"No. Where's his soul … his energy?" Simon clarified. "I saw the fucking mess you made of him. You're sick."

Dr. Carrol tilted his head and laughed fiendishly.

De Luca pointed Claire's gun at Dr. Carrol. "Turn around."

Like a flash, Dr. Carrol jumped out of his seat and had a hold of De Luca's wrist, moving faster than my mind could register. De Luca screamed in agony as Dr. Carrol twisted his arm. De Luca's legs gave way and he fell to the floor.

"Why are you here?!" Dr. Carrol roared into De Luca's face. "Have you convinced these people that you're an expert at something? Did you convince them that they needed your help to find me?!"

"Let him go!" Simon yelled. He pushed me aside to grab the gun from Detective Trevino's hands. He quickly pointed it at Carrol.

Dr. Carrol turned to us, his face pale and lips cracked. "You can't kill me."

"Why not?" Simon asked.

"Because," Dr. Carrol began—and in what seemed like an instant, he was now face-to-face with Simon. "Hundreds of souls will have no place to go. They live inside me. I am their home. I let them out to play … in this hotel. If you shoot me, they'll be stuck here—inside all of these people."

Simon tried to control his breathing. "Is that why you came here? Because you needed hosts?"

"Lots of people from different places … all kinds … hundreds of them … like different flavors." Dr. Carrol put on a smile. "And the energy is so intense. You feel it, don't you? When you were a *real* cop … you knew. You could hardly come near this place because of its haunted history."

Simon cautiously lowered the gun. He didn't take his eyes off Carrol. "I'm not going to let you fuck with my head. You're still human, sort of. You're a murderer. I know you killed Marisol. You killed Dr. Anson. You're going to pay for what you've done."

De Luca got to his feet and pulled something from his jacket that made a click sound. It was a switchblade. A very large one.

Dr. Carrol's eyes rolled back and his smile intensified. "I'm going to do to you what I did to Dr. Anson." He spun around and laughed at the knife in De Luca's hand. "And I'm going to harvest you, Raul."

De Luca straightened his posture and pushed up the sleeve of his jacket. He turned the knife on his exposed arm. "No, Dr. Carrol. You won't be harvesting people anymore. You don't have the authority."

Dr. Carrol growled, "You can't tell me what to do! Go ahead! Kill yourself! You're a waste! I'm going to change everything with this! Don't you see that?!"

"No, I don't," De Luca responded dryly.

"You wouldn't understand what I'm doing! It's greater than all of this! The human mind is polluted and useless! Violence is everywhere!"

"And killing isn't violent? Do the ends justify the means?"

An echoing laugh filled the room. And from where I

stood, I never saw Dr. Carrol's lips move when it happened, but I knew the laughter was his. "So now you're a philosopher, Raul?"

"You have no idea what you're doing. I think we can fix this … if you're willing to listen to me," De Luca proposed.

Dr. Carrol smiled. "You're jealous."

De Luca shook his head in disbelief. "Jealous of what?"

"I'm going to take this technology and use it to change everything."

"You call this technology? Killing people to bring back the dead? Dead people that *don't belong here?*"

Dr. Carrol raised his hands into the air and lifted his head toward the ceiling. "Have you seen what I've done? Look around you! Look!"

"Yes," De Luca replied solemnly. "I see that you've found a way to possess humans. It's been done before, though. Not a very original idea, Carrol."

"It's much different than possession. They are all under my control. Now, some people would use this technology for evil. But I am going to use it for something good."

De Luca eyed him.

"I know it's difficult for you, Raul, to open your mind and go beyond what you've been taught. I envision things differently. I look for solutions."

"You're not making any sense." De Luca's eyes quickly shifted to me and Detective Trevino who was standing behind me, stunned.

"I can stop wars with this." Dr. Carrol took a step closer to De Luca. "Entire armies, under my control. The military would love this technology."

"You're not thinking things through," De Luca

answered.

"I'm sorry, Raul," Dr. Carrol began sarcastically. "What was your graduate thesis on again? You know so much more than I do about physics, don't you?"

"You're calling *this* physics?" De Luca scoffed. "It's witchcraft. You've cast an ancient spell that you know nothing about. That's all."

"Like I said before … jealousy."

De Luca stood in silence wearing a tight-lipped smile.

"That's right. So stay out of it, Mr. De Luca. Your job is hunting ghosts, isn't it? Or reading peoples' minds or something like that."

"I'm an occult specialist," De Luca answered. "In fact, you could say that I'm an apprentice of sorts. But I prefer not to talk about it usually."

I could see things moving along the walls and ceiling.

Dr. Carrol snarled. "That's very interesting, Raul. With so much going on in your life, I'm surprised you haven't tried to kill yourself sooner."

De Luca pressed the switchblade closer to his skin.

"Raul," I whispered. "Don't!"

Behind De Luca, a small child crawled across the wall—almost slithering, but with the quick movement of a spider. Simon gasped and latched onto my arm at the sight of it.

It was the hotel guests. I'd forgotten about the ones that were probably up in their rooms, maybe hiding. The few that were scattered around the lobby *had* definitely changed, but I hadn't thought about the rest of them. I let out a shallow breath and looked up to the ceiling—they were everywhere. Bodies writhing and crawling over and under each other, moving in ways that turned my stomach. I tugged on Simon's sleeve, unable to pull my stare from them.

"Look," Simon whispered and pointed to the top of the staircase, they were pouring out from the floors above, clinging to the wood molding on the walls.

I swung around and searched for Claire, but she was gone. When I looked back at De Luca, I noticed his eyes shifting around the room, scanning every corner. He saw them, the creatures that were hanging above us.

De Luca turned his attention back to Dr. Carrol. "My boss is very upset with you, Peter Carrol," he said.

Dr. Carrol held out his arms. "What are you going on about now, Raul?"

A thud and a muffled scream next to me—it was Detective Trevino. Claire was behind him, her hands wrapped around his eyes and mouth.

Simon grabbed at my arm to pull me away from them. "She dropped down from the fucking ceiling!"

"Stop what you're doing, Dr. Carrol," De Luca commanded. There was great strength in his voice. "Turn her back to normal! She's not one of them!"

"Or what?!" Dr. Carrol yelled. "Empty threats, Raul! You have nothing!" He smiled. "You and Simon will make a great sacrifice. Even if you kill yourself, Raul, I'll still find a way to use you."

De Luca pressed the blade hard into his wrist, through his skin, grimacing as he did. Blood ran down his forearm. He took an uneven step backwards and announced loudly, "You have angered him! You have taken what is rightfully his!"

God protect us, I thought.

"Taken what?!" Dr. Carrol demanded to know.

De Luca pulled down on the blade inside his wrist and forced it through the flesh of his entire forearm before pulling it out. The gash bled profusely, spilling his blood onto the floor. "They are his souls. You called upon the weakest, the most desperate. The souls of criminals, monsters of the past … the unwanted—"

"NO!" Carrol screamed in anger. His hands were in tight fists at his sides. "I called upon the fighters! Those who wanted a second chance! Those with the desire and strength to come back to this world! Those still hanging on to something! Those who were not finished with this world when they were taken from it!"

De Luca violently swung his arm around until blood was splattered everywhere. "Those transcripts were not for human eyes! Now he's coming to take back what's his! Those transcripts never belonged to you!"

De Luca's body trembled and his legs wobbled beneath him.

"He's losing too much blood," I said in horror.

De Luca was fighting to keep his balance. "Carrol," he struggled to speak. "You can't fake something like this and get away with it. You deceived so many people, and you called upon a power that cannot be controlled by humans."

De Luca collapsed and lost consciousness.

I started toward De Luca, but Simon held me back. All I could focus on was the blood pouring out of his arm. I needed to help him, I couldn't see another death … not in my dreams, not in real life, and not like this.

"You can't go over there," Simon warned. "He's doing something."

I stopped to figure out what Simon meant. I tuned in to the sounds coming from the bodies that hung above our heads. And behind me, Claire still had her hands wrapped around Trevino's face, but she was blank and motionless. He struggled and groaned, trying to break free. I couldn't look. I didn't want to see her like that. So I stared in disbelief at De Luca's body lying in a crumpled heap, in a pool of his own blood. Simon was frantic, his eyes going everywhere. Then Dr. Carrol slowly turned to us.

"My condolences," he smiled proudly and made his way toward us with his head held high. "Raul was just a bonus. I still have the both of you to work with, that detective ... and the police woman."

As he spoke, I could see something happening near De Luca's body. I noticed the blood, so much of it spilled everywhere, changing. It looked richer and thicker than it should have. The color was darkening ... I thought I was imagining it.

"De Luca did the right thing," Simon said to Dr. Carrol. "You think I'm gonna let you use my body to bring more of these things over?" Simon pointed to the ceiling and shook his head in disgust. "Fuck you, man."

Dr. Carrol moved in close to Simon's face. "Do you know how many people have given their lives to me tonight, killing themselves just to be a part of this? To be something greater than they were?"

"You promised them something impossible."

Dr. Carrol shook his head and held out his hands. "But you see it all around you. They've done what I asked! They've brought to me the souls of many centuries. And the ones who didn't survive the cross over completely, well ... at least they tried. More room for the souls of the past—the ones that fought to be here."

"You lied to them. I've seen your defectors—the ones that left your fucking cult after learning how to do it, how to cross over. They're disgusting. They have no control over their power and neither side wants them."

Carrol gritted his teeth. "You have no idea what you're talking about."

"Really?" Simon replied. "They aren't ghosts and they

aren't people. They flicker in and out of this world … lost. By the time they realize what they've become, how strong their emotions still are and how they can't stop feelin' things that they don't want to feel—they're trapped!"

"Don't you want world peace, Simon?" Carrol smiled. "I didn't teach them to cross over without a purpose. If they had stayed with me and completed their training, I would have given their new existence meaning—their new power a focus."

Simon gripped tightly at the gun in his hand. "You're crazy."

I peeked behind Dr. Carrol for only a second. De Luca's blood *was* doing something—it was boiling, coming to life. Parts of it rose and fell like it was breathing. I had to pull my eyes away from it because I didn't want Carrol to notice.

Dr. Carrol inhaled a breath in deep thought. "All revolutionary thinkers have been called 'crazy,' Simon. But nothing in this world changes without people like me. That is the undeniable truth. Just because you don't understand it, doesn't mean it isn't true."

Simon's eyes were on him like daggers.

Behind Carrol, the blood continued to boil intensely. A large part of it curved into a dome until the shape of an arm reached out from it. I couldn't hold it in any longer. All I could see was the bloody hand and the dripping fingers … fingers with claws.

"De Luca," was all I could say.

Dr. Carrol spun around. The blood was rising, coagulating into something.

Simon stuck his arm out across my chest and guided me backward. His eyes shifted between the grotesque figure that was forming in front of Carrol, and the festering ceiling packed with hotel guests that now seemed to be agitated by what was going on beneath them.

The loudest, darkest roar imaginable seemed to come from nowhere. It echoed throughout the lobby as every wall and every piece of furniture vibrated along with it.

A face appeared from within the dark mass of blood, sticking out of something that protruded from it—something that was shaped like a head. And the thing was still growing. It breathed at an impossible rate of speed and pushed out a second arm.

"WHAT IS THIS?!" Dr. Carrol screamed at it. "I didn't call you here! Identify yourself!"

But the thing continued to grow, dripping with the thick, dark blood—the blood that had once flowed through De Luca's veins—and it did not answer.

"I command you to identify yourself!" Dr. Carrol insisted.

Simon pulled me down and pushed against the floor with his feet, scooting us backward, until our backs were against the front desk. "Where did that thing come from?" he asked me.

"From De Luca ... from his blood," I answered. My eyes were fixated on the vile creature. It now looked to be over nine feet tall, its face only part human—but also resembling a bull. It was like a mythological minotaur. "It came from his blood."

Dr. Carrol gazed up at the creature in amazement. It looked down on him in return, its eyes bluer than any I had ever seen—like they were made of shining crystal. Its face was bloodied and red, its large nostrils flaring in anger.

The enormous creature, with its muscular frame and fierce eyes, stepped in close to Dr. Carrol. It snarled at him. After only seconds, it slammed down a large black hoof and splashed blood onto Dr. Carrol's crisp designer suit. "I want back what is mine."

The creature's voice was a profound, dark baritone. Grave and booming, it carried throughout the large room so strongly that I could feel it within my heart. It was almost soothing, and admittedly, I was entranced by it.

"I don't know what you mean," Dr. Carrol answered weakly.

"MY DOMINION!" the creature yelled. "Give them back to me!"

Dr. Carrol cowered down, quivering and shielding his face. "I didn't take anything of yours! I don't know who you are!"

The massive creature frowned and gazed down at Dr. Carrol with those bright eyes, explaining simply, "You took my name in vain."

Dr. Carrol's eyes widened and he trembled violently, falling back onto the floor. "I-I called upon those who w-wished to come back ... to help me. To bring peace—"

"You murdered. You killed." The creature moved in closer, not allowing him any space. "You stole from me. You took my name in vain."

Dr. Carrol rose to his knees. "I beg you. I beg for forgiveness. Please ... what I did, I did for a better world. I did it to advance the human race—to bring peace!"

"By slaying?" the creature leaned over him to ask. "Selfish man. You wish to take from man what is a part of his nature, a part of his progress—war."

Dr. Carrol's eyes flashed wildly. "You can have them back. I'm sorry."

The creature swooped down on Dr. Carrol and got in close to his face. Dr. Carrol was like a tiny child faced with his greatest, most terrible fear.

"I do not need your permission to reclaim what is mine."

"I'm s-sorry!" Tears streamed down Carrol's face.

The creature sniffed around the top of Dr. Carrol's head. "You are not one of mine ..." it pointed a dark-clawed finger into the air above, "... *or his.*"

Surprisingly—or at least to me—Simon crossed himself.

"I—" was all that Dr. Carrol had a chance to say before the creature placed its large hand on top of Carrol's head to silence him. The creature opened its other arm wide and tilted its head back, closing its eyes.

The gruesome hotel guests suddenly scattered in panic, frantically vacating the ceiling and walls, scurrying like rats, in every direction. They seemed to sense that the creature was about to regain control of them, or whatever was inside them. It opened the hand on its outstretched arm and called out, "Come to me, my children. You have been released from this mortal. You will return to where you belong."

Immediately, hotel guests turned to face the creature and made their way toward it, their movement more fluid now. They filled the stairways and climbed down from the walls. There was intent and purpose in the way they harmonized. A crowd formed and stood at attention, awaiting instructions.

I spotted Claire in the crowd and jumped to my feet.

Simon pulled on my pant leg. "What are you doing?!" he hissed.

"I'm getting Claire and Trevino." I shook him off and pushed through the bodies of people that moaned and swayed around me. They were easier to move through than I'd expected, sort of limp and docile. I pushed them gently aside with my arm, even though the thought of touching them sickened me. Some of them turned to look at me with those gray swirls in their eyes, but did nothing except stare. Then I saw her, only a few rows back from the front of the crowd.

I placed a hand on Claire's shoulder and hoped that she would turn to look at me, but she didn't. She was still under some hypnotic spell. Detective Trevino was on the floor at her feet, unconscious. I felt a heavy force nearby and I dared myself to look—the creature's glowing eyes were on me.

Without taking my eyes from its expressionless stare, I lowered myself to the floor and got ready to lift the top half of Trevino's body. "Claire," I said with caution. I looked up at her face, her eyes were still a cloudy white. She was different from the others—I knew she couldn't be one of them.

The creature removed its hand from Dr. Carrol's head, causing Carrol's body to fall to the floor.

"Claire, help me," I asked, hoping to snap her awake.

The creature stood, immense and powerful, watching as I trembled. Claire still remained stuck in place, staring straight ahead, as all the others did.

"Please," I begged the creature, at a loss for what to do. I didn't know why, but I thought I might have a chance, and I was desperate to try anything.

The creature furrowed its brow at me and tilted its head. I realized then that there were no horns, as I had expected to see. This didn't make the creature's presence any less difficult to withstand, though. Part animal, part man, it was still appalling to look at, and even more so up close. I had to fight myself not to run. It was enshrouding me with its darkness, whether on purpose or not, and I didn't know how I would be able to escape.

Its eyes went to Claire. "You are released."

Some transparent force instantly launched itself out of Claire's chest and jumped into the creature's readied hand. A mist, blue and white, swirled in the creature's palm. Claire immediately went limp and collapsed to the floor.

My heart slammed against my chest. "Thank you," I whispered, lifting my eyes.

The creature studied my face for a few seconds before turning to look down at Dr. Carrol's body. Carrol was struggling to pull himself up. I gripped both Claire's and Trevino's shirts and pulled them as hard as I could in an effort to drag them across the floor and back toward the front desk. "Dammit, Simon!" I complained to myself.

And I was surprised when I heard Simon reply, "I'm right here." He grasped the detective's arms and pulled him through the crowd as quickly as possible. I was right behind him with Claire. We were able to lay them behind the front desk and then peeked out to see what would happen next.

The creature stood tall, spread its great arms, and then lifted its head toward the ceiling. Its chest heaved with strong breaths. "Return to me."

The bodies standing before the creature convulsed and shook. The most terrible sound of chattering teeth filled the room until that sound was muted by something much worse. Hotel guests threw their heads back, and the noise of crackling spines permeated the room. The bodies vibrated and began to glow until there was a ripping sound that came from each one of them. It was something unfathomable. The bodies then lifted and hovered slightly over the floor. They hung there silently until brilliant blue and white mists were expelled from each body and collectively flew across the room and into the creature's chest. The creature withstood the overwhelming force, bracing itself against the impact with its strong hooves.

And as the last of the ghostly beings returned to the creature, Dr. Carrol squirmed to get away, pulling himself toward the stairway. He slid past De Luca's lifeless body while keeping his eyes on the creature.

The creature bowed its head and struggled to regain its strength. "Carrol," it sighed in exhaustion. "We are not finished."

Dr. Carrol looked back in terror to answer, "No! I'll do whatever you ask!"

The creature turned and gazed down upon Carrol. It reached out its hand. "You belong with me now," it said without sympathy in its voice.

Dr. Carrol scooted his body against the wall and frantically waved his hands in front of his face. "No no no! WAIT!"

But the creature turned its palm upward and spread its fingers wide. Carrol's body succumbed to violent fits, his body twisting and contorting, his head repeatedly slamming against the wall.

The creature inhaled deeply and thrust its palm forward. The spectral substance within Carrol's being escaped through his chest and traveled toward the creature. What escaped from Carrol's body was wispy and gray. Transparent and light, it danced and swayed, with slight resistance and hesitation, until it reached the creature's open hand and was pulled inside. The body left behind was depleted. What was once Peter Carrol's face then shriveled into itself and faded—the rest of his body followed soon after.

The creature walked over to De Luca and knelt down on one knee. It placed a hand on De Luca's head and caressed it.

Everything was silent.

"Holy shit," Simon whispered.

From where I stood, I could only see the creature's profile, and I could see that there was sadness in its face. It stared at De Luca's pale, lifeless form. Between us and them was a sea of motionless people who had fallen to the ground. But somehow, I knew, in the silence, that they were okay. I knew that when the creature had taken back from them what didn't belong, they would recover.

I will never forget what happened next. The creature looked up to the ceiling and said, "Has your angel repaid his debts?" Moments later he looked down and sighed. "Then he is still mine."

The creature touched one of its shiny black claws to De Luca's arm and ran it along his open wound. It was hard to see exactly what was happening from where Simon and I stood, safe behind the front desk, but I had a pretty good idea. The beast-like creature was repairing De Luca's gaping wound.

The creature rose and waited as De Luca gradually stirred and came back to life.

De Luca slowly sat up and scanned the room with weak eyes. "You got Carrol?"

"Yes," the creature answered.

De Luca inspected his arm, then looked deep into the creature's eyes. "Am I free?"

The creature furrowed its brow. "No."

De Luca saw us watching from behind the front desk and lowered his head. "As you wish."

"It is not my wish to keep you, but you have served me well."

De Luca, looking weak and deeply saddened, lifted his head.

"Your time on Earth will continue," the creature said

to him softly. "And when I need you, I will find you."

"I understand," De Luca answered.

The creature tilted its head. "I have back what is mine, but the others are trapped. I cannot take them."

"The defectors." De Luca nodded.

"You did well." The creature then looked back at the front desk—and into mine and Simon's stares—and sneered slightly. "I am tempted to allow them their memories," it said.

De Luca smiled. "One of them is a writer," De Luca warned. "Well, he's more than that, actually. You wouldn't worry that he might—?"

And as it stared intensely into my eyes, the creature faded and disappeared.

I had no time to reflect upon it.

Police officers in tactical gear burst into the lobby. Hotel guests and employees awakened and started coming to their senses. There was confusion all around us. Somehow I knew that they would remember nothing.

I looked down at Claire. She was struggling to stand. "My legs are sore," she complained.

I asked Simon to check on Trevino as I helped Claire to her feet and then leaned her up against the counter in front of us.

"Trevino's fine," Simon replied. "He's got a cut on his face. That's all."

Detective Trevino jumped to his feet and swayed a bit, lightheaded. He looked around the lobby in disbelief—people covered every inch of the floor. Paramedics and police officers struggled to step over and through them, trying to piece together what happened. "What's going on?" he asked angrily.

Simon looked at me with raised eyebrows before answering, "I don't know."

The detective waved over a police officer. "What's going on?"

"We couldn't see through the doors, sir. No one could see in and we couldn't break the glass," the officer replied. "We tried everything."

De Luca walked up and studied us carefully. "How's Claire?"

"I'm all right," she smiled.

"Richard," De Luca said. "Can I talk to you for a minute?"

Simon grabbed my arm. "Only if I can come, too. Right, Richard?"

I looked at De Luca for permission.

"Sure, that's fine," he answered.

The three of us walked over toward the back of the building and stood next to a glass door that led out to a parking garage.

De Luca took a deep breath. "Do you remember?"

"Yes!" Simon spat out.

De Luca smiled and I waited for him to digest Simon's answer before giving him mine. "Yes."

De Luca looked around the room, watching the rush of activity that went on behind us. And when he turned his attention back on me, his eyes seemed to illuminate just slightly—just enough to make me wonder for a moment what it was that he had become, or had always been.

Then he said, "Dr. Carrol chose you, Richard, in hopes that you would document what he had been doing. As a fan of your works, he was inspired by them. He thought you'd be flattered. So he called you into his rituals, through your dreams, hoping to impress you with his new-found power. He wanted to become a legend."

"I wouldn't have given him the pleasure." I didn't

bother to ask how he knew that part of Carrol's plan.

He shrugged his shoulders and smiled. "At least he tried."

"Do any of these people remember what happened to them?" I asked. Shaken and disoriented, many of the hotel's guests had been provided water and were being systematically checked for injuries. Some of the employees were being questioned, and I wondered what they were being asked.

"No," De Luca began, "they don't remember."

"Then why do *we* remember?"

De Luca opened his mouth, as if to answer, but I could tell that he struggled with what he was about to say. He looked over his shoulder and motioned for the three of us to step further away from any ears that might hear us. "It's difficult for me to understand his methods. I could ask myself why over and over ... I could guess, I could be wrong." He shook his head. "I don't know, Richard. The world is changing. Soon, it will merge with the spirit worlds. And there are people, like you and Simon, who are here to ... connect with those different worlds, to help make the transition easier for your people."

Your people.

He looked behind us, and all around the room, before returning his eyes to me. "You will see the phantoms of the past and not understand why entirely, but we don't always understand what is necessary. I only know that I was sent to help you, and I did what I was told. Now, I have to go back and serve out the rest of my sentence. I have to keep my promise, until he lets me return to where I belong."

Of all the questions I had, the only thing I thought to say was, "Why?"

De Luca looked away in shame. "Years ago, I failed to stop a terrible accident. A large number of people died because of me ... on my watch. This isn't the way it was supposed to be." De Luca then moved in closer to my ear. "Richard, don't ignore the gift you have been given. When asked for help, sacrifice everything you can to do it. Treat them as you do your fellow man. Don't think of them as ghosts—they're real. From where they speak is just a different part of this world. Everything is connected."

De Luca pulled back and nodded, waiting for my reply.

"Okay," I said, not sure what I was agreeing to. "But, I really don't know what you want me to do."

De Luca smiled. "I can't tell you what to do. Just look around you and see, that's all. Be their voice. Some take watch over the living, and some watch over the dead, but it's all the same."

In his eyes, I could see what he meant and knew the sacrifices I would make. "They'll think I'm crazy."

He answered, "Only the fools will think you're crazy. Until the fools die and learn the truth."

I looked at Simon, who for some reason was being uncharacteristically quiet, and appeared to be in deep thought—taking it all in.

"You're leaving, aren't you?" I asked De Luca.

"Yes, back to Italy. I don't know how much longer I'll be there. It's beautiful." He sighed. "You should visit."

Something caught my attention on the stairway. A grayish, transparent woman stopped halfway down the steps and looked at me. She knew I could see her. She wore a long, early 1900s dress and there was hope in her eyes.

"I'm probably going to stay here for a while and hang

out with Simon," I replied. *And Claire*, I thought to myself. I looked over to her and smiled. She had a serious look on her face as she spoke with another officer—and I thought she was beautiful.

De Luca nodded in agreement.

Simon tried not to take it as a compliment and forced a smile off his face. "Whatever, Rich."

De Luca pulled his phone from his jacket and checked the screen. "I have to get out of here before one of these police officers tries to interview me, or takes me into custody."

"We'll tell Trevino we didn't see you leave," I said, eyeing the door next to us.

"Perfect." De Luca reached out to shake Simon's hand before taking mine. "And Richard?"

"Yes?" I replied, his grip still strong on my hand.

"I'm sorry."

It didn't make any sense to me. "For what? You saved everyone here."

My hand started to burn. The burn shot up my arm and into my head. I could see everything, everyone … all of it. In that one room there were a million faces, a million times, and endlessness.

De Luca looked at me in sadness. His face was like a piece of art—smooth, radiant, and angelic. "Don't ignore them, Richard. They might scream out to you in the night, but don't ignore them. Listen to what they have to say. I'm sorry I did this to you, Richard, but I had to."

Ronnie Stich